WORLD QUAKE

-DRAGON'S-
GREEN

SCARLETT THOMAS

CANONGATE

This paperback edition published in 2017 by Canongate Books

First published in Great Britain in 2017 by Canongate Books Ltd,
14 High Street, Edinburgh EH1 1TE

canongate.co.uk

1

British Library Cataloguing-in-Publication Data
A catalogue record for this book is available on
request from the British Library

ISBN 978 1 78211 704 9

Typeset in Horley Old Style MT by Palimpsest Book Production Ltd,
Falkirk, Stirlingshire

Printed and bound in Great Britain by Clays Ltd, St Ives plc.

MIX
Paper from
responsible sources
FSC
www.fsc.org   FSC® C018072

This book is for Rod, who took me to Dragon's Green
when I most needed to go there, and for Roger,
who showed me the way out of the enchanted castle.
It is also for Molly, a wonderful first reader who
reminded me why I always wanted to become a writer.

'We are ourselves a term in the equation, a note of the chord, and make discord or harmony almost at will.'

Robert Louis Stevenson

'Fold your powers together, with the spirit of your mind . . .'

T.H. White

1

Mrs Beathag Hide was exactly the kind of teacher who gives children nightmares. She was tall and thin and her extraordinarily long fingers were like sharp twigs on a poisonous tree. She wore black polo necks that made her head look like a planet being slowly ejected from a hostile universe, and heavy tweed suits in strange, otherworldly pinks and reds that made her face look as pale as a cold moon. It was impossible to tell how long her hair was, because she wore it in a tight bun. But it was the colour of three – maybe even four – black holes mixed together. Her perfume smelled of the kind of flowers you never see in normal life, flowers that are very, very dark blue and only grow on the peaks of remote mountains, perhaps in the same bleak wilderness as the tree whose twigs her fingers so resembled.

Or, at least, that was how Maximilian Underwood saw her, on this pinkish, dead-leafy autumnal Monday towards the end of October.

Just her voice was enough to make some of the more fragile children cry, sometimes only from thinking about it, late at night or alone on a creaky school bus in the rain. Mrs Beathag Hide was so frightening that she was usually only allowed to teach in the Upper School. Everything she most enjoyed seemed to involve untimely and violent death. She particularly loved the story from Greek mythology about Cronus eating his own babies. Maximilian's class had done a project on the story just the week before last, with all the unfortunate infants made from papier-mâché.

Mrs Beathag Hide was actually filling in for Miss Dora Wright, the real teacher, who had disappeared after winning a short-story competition. Some people said Miss Wright had run away to the south to become a professional writer. Other people said she'd been kidnapped because of something to do with her story. This was unlikely to be true, as her story was set in a castle in a completely different world from this one. In any case, she was gone, and now her tall, frightening replacement was calling the register.

And Euphemia Truelove, known as Effie, was absent.

'Euphemia Truelove,' Mrs Beathag Hide said, for the third time. 'Away again?'

Most of this class, the top set for English in the first form of the Tusitala School for the Gifted, Troubled and Strange (the school, with its twisted grey spires, leaky roofs, and long, noble history, wasn't really called that, but, for various reasons, that was how it had come to be known), had realised that it was best not to say anything at all to Mrs Beathag Hide, because anything you said was likely to be wrong. The way to get through her classes was to sit very still and silent and sort of pray she didn't notice you. It was a bit like being a mouse in a room with a cat.

Even the more 'troubled' members of the first form, who had ended up in the top set through cheating, hidden genius or just by accident, knew to keep it buttoned in Mrs Beathag Hide's class. They just hit each other extra hard during break time to make up for it. The more 'strange' children found their own ways to cope. Raven Wilde, whose mother was a famous writer, was at that moment trying to cast the invisibility spell she had read about in a book she'd found in her attic. So far it had only worked on her pencil. Another girl, Alexa Bottle, known as Lexy, whose father was a yoga teacher, had simply put herself into a very deep meditation. Everyone was very still and everyone was very silent.

But Maximilian Underwood hadn't, as they say, got the memo.

'It's her grandfather, Miss,' he said. 'He's ill in hospital.'

'And?' said Mrs Beathag Hide, her eyes piercing into Maximilian like rays designed to kill small defenceless creatures, creatures rather like poor Maximilian, whose school life was a constant living hell because of his name, his glasses, his new (perfectly ironed) regulation uniform, and his deep, undying interest in theories about the worldquake that had happened five years before.

'We don't have sick grandparents in this class,' said Mrs Beathag Hide, witheringly. 'We don't have dying relatives, abusive parents, pets that eat homework, school uniforms that shrink in the wash, lost packed lunches, allergies, ADHD, depression, drugs, alcohol, bullies, broken-down technology of any sort . . . I do not care, in fact *could not care less,* how impoverished and pathetic are your unimportant childhoods.'

She raised her voice from what had become a dark whisper to a roar. 'WHATEVER OUR AFFLICTIONS WE DO OUR WORK QUIETLY AND DO NOT MAKE EXCUSES.'

The class – even Wolf Reed, who was a full-back and not afraid of anything – quivered.

'What do we do?' she demanded.

'We do our work quietly and do not make excuses,' the class said in unison, in a kind of chant.

'And how good is our work?'

'Our work is excellent.'

'And when do we arrive for our English lesson?'

'On time,' chanted the class, almost beginning to relax.

'NO! WHEN DO WE ARRIVE FOR OUR ENGLISH LESSON?'

'Five minutes early?' they chanted this time. And if you think it's not possible to chant a question mark, all I can say is that they did a very good job of trying.

'Good. And what happens if we falter?'

'We must be stronger.'

'And what happens to the weak?'

'They are punished.'

'How?'

'They go down to Set Two.'

'And what does it mean to go down to Set Two?'

'Failure.'

'And what is worse than failure?'

Here the class paused. For the last week they had been learning all about failure and going down a set and never complaining and never explaining and how to draw on deep, hidden reserves of inner strength – which was a bit frightening but actually quite useful for some of the more troubled children – and not just being on time but always five minutes early. This is, of course, impossible if you are let out of double maths five minutes late, or if you have just had double P.E. and Wolf and his friends from the Under 13 rugby team have hidden your pants in an old water pipe.

'Death?' someone ventured.

'WRONG ANSWER.'

Everyone fell silent. A fly buzzed around the room and landed on Lexy's desk, and then crawled onto her hand. In Mrs Beathag Hide's class you prayed for flies not to land on you, for shafts of sunlight not to temporarily brighten your desk, for – horrors – your new pager not to beep with a message from your mother about your packed lunch or your lift home. You prayed for it to be someone else's desk; someone else's pager. Anyone else. Just not you.

'You, girl,' said Mrs Beathag Hide. 'Well?'

Lexy, like most people who have just come out of a deep meditation, could only blink and stare. She realised she had been asked a question by this incredibly tall person and . . .

She had no idea of the answer, or even, really, the question. Had she been asked what she was doing, perhaps? She blinked again and said the first thing – the only thing – that came into her mind.

'Nothing, Miss.'

'EXCELLENT. That's right. NOTHING is worse than failure. Go to the top of the class.'

And so for the rest of the lesson, Lexy, who ideally just wanted to be left alone, had to wear a gold star pinned to her green school jumper to show she was Top of the Class, and poor Maximilian, who couldn't even remember exactly what he'd done wrong, had to sit in the corner wearing a dunce's hat that smelled of mould and dead mice because it was a real, antique dunce's hat from the days when teachers were allowed to make you sit in the corner wearing a dunce's hat.

Were teachers allowed to do this now? Probably not, but Mrs Beathag Hide's pupils were not exactly queuing up to be the one to report her. Maximilian, despite being one of the more 'gifted' children, was often Bottom of the Class, and now he was on the verge of being sent down to Set Two. The only person doing worse than Maximilian was Effie, and she wasn't even there.

2

Euphemia Truelove, whose full name was really Euphemia Sixten Bookend Truelove, but who was known as Effie, could hardly remember her mother. Aurelia Truelove had disappeared five years ago, when Effie was only six, on the night that everyone else remembered because of the worldquake.

In the country where Effie lived, most people had been asleep when the worldquake had struck, at three o'clock in the morning. But in other countries far away, schools had been evacuated and flights cancelled. The shaking had lasted for seven and a half minutes, which is quite a long time, given that normal earthquakes only last for a few seconds. Fish flew from the seas, trees were dislodged from the soil as easily as plants from little pots, and in several places it had rained frogs. Somehow, no one in the entire world had been killed.

Except for Effie's mother.

Maybe.

Had she been killed? Or had she simply run away for some

reason? No one knew. After the worldquake, most mobile phones stopped working and the internet broke down. For a few weeks everything was complete chaos. If Aurelia Truelove had wanted to send a message to her husband or daughter she would not have been able to. Or perhaps she had tried and the message had been lost. Technologically, the world seemed to have gone back to something like 1992. A whole online world was gone. It was soon replaced with flickering Bulletin Board Systems (accessed via dial-up modems from the olden days) while people tried to work out what to do. They thought that eventually things would go back to normal.

They never did.

After the worldquake, everything was different for Effie in other ways too. Because Effie now had no mother, and because of her father's latest promotion at the university – which meant he did even more work for even less money – there was no one to look after her, so she had started spending a lot of time with her grandfather Griffin Truelove.

Griffin Truelove was a very old man with a very long, white beard who lived in a jumble of rooms at the top of the Old Rectory in the most dark, grey and ancient part of the Old Town. Griffin had once been quite a cheerful soul who set fire to his beard so often he always kept a glass of water nearby to dip it in. But for the first few months she went there, he barely said anything to Effie. Well, that is, apart from 'Please don't touch anything,' and 'Be quiet, there's a good child.'

After school Effie would spend the long hours in his rooms examining – without touching – the contents of his strange old cabinets and cupboards while he smoked his pipe and wrote in a large black hardback book and more or less ignored her. He wasn't ever horrible to her. He just seemed very far away, and busy with his black book and the old manuscript he seemed to need to consult every few minutes, which was written in a language Effie had never seen before. Before the worldquake, Effie and Aurelia had occasionally come here together and Grandfather Griffin's eyes had twinkled when he had spoken of his travels, or shown Aurelia some new object or book he had found. Now he rarely left his rooms at all. Effie thought her grandfather was probably very sad because of what had happened to his daughter. Effie was sad too.

Griffin Truelove's cabinets were filled with strange objects made of silk, glass and precious metals. There were two silver candlesticks studded with jewels next to a pile of delicate embroidered cloths with images of flowers, fruits and people in flowing robes. There were ornate oil-lamps, and carved black wooden boxes with little brass locks on them but no visible keys. There were globes, large and small, depicting worlds known and unknown. There were animal skulls, delicate knives and several misshapen wooden bowls with small spoons alongside them. One cupboard contained folded maps, thin white candles, thick cream paper and bottles of blue ink. Another had bags of dried roses and other flowers. A corner cabinet held jar after jar of seed heads, charcoal, red earth, pressed leaves, sealing wax, pieces of sea-glass, gold leaf, dried black twigs, cinnamon sticks, small pieces of amber, owl feathers and homemade botanical oils.

'Do you know how to do magic, Grandfather?' Effie had asked one day, about a year after the worldquake. It seemed the only reasonable explanation for all the unusual things he kept around him. Effie knew all about magic because of Laurel Wilde's books, which were about a group of children at a magical school. All children – and even some adults – secretly wanted to go to this school and be taught how to do spells and become invisible.

'Everyone knows how to do magic,' had come her grandfather's mild reply.

Effie knew perfectly well (from reading her Laurel Wilde books) that only a few special people were born with the ability to do magic, so she suspected that her grandfather was making fun of her in some way. But on the other hand . . .

'Will you do some?' she had asked.

'No.'

'Will you teach me how to do it?'

'No.'

'Do you actually believe in magic?'

'It doesn't matter whether or not I believe in it.'

'What do you mean, Grandfather?'

'Do hush, child. I must get on with my manuscript.'

'Can I go and look at your library?'

'No.'

And so Effie had gone back to peering into a glass cabinet that contained many tiny stone bottles stoppered with black corks, and several pens made out of feathers. Sometimes she went up the narrow staircase to the attic library and tried the door handle, but it was always locked. Through the blue glass in the door she could see tall shelves of old-looking books. Why wouldn't he let her go and look at them? Other adults were always going on about children needing to read, after all.

But adults only wanted children to read books they approved of. Effie's father, Orwell Bookend (whose last name was different from Effie's because Aurelia had insisted on remaining a Truelove and passing the name to her daughter), had banned Effie from reading Laurel Wilde books just before the sixth book in the series had come out. It was because he didn't want her to have anything to do with magic, he had said, which had been odd, given that he didn't believe in magic. And then one day, after he had drunk too much wine, Orwell had told Effie to keep away from magic because it was 'dangerous'. How could something not exist, and yet be dangerous? Effie didn't know. But however much she kept asking her grandfather about magic, he never gave in, and so Effie started asking him other things.

'Grandfather?' she said, one Wednesday afternoon just before she turned eleven. 'What language is that you're reading? I know you're doing some kind of translation, but where did the manuscript come from?'

'You know I'm doing a translation, do you?' He nodded, and almost smiled. 'Very good.'

'But what language is it?'

'Rosian.'

'Who speaks Rosian?'

'People a very, very long way away.'

'In a place where they do magic?'

'Oh, child. I keep telling you. Everyone does magic.'

'But how?'

He sighed. 'Have you ever woken up in the morning and sort of prayed, or hoped very hard, that it would not rain?'

'Yes.'

'Did it work?'

Effie thought about this. 'I don't know.'

'Well, did it rain?'

'No. At least, I don't think so.'

'Well, then you did magic. Bravo!'

This was certainly not how magic worked in Laurel Wilde books. In Laurel Wilde books you had to say a particular spell if you wanted to stop it raining. You had to buy this spell in a shop, and then get someone to teach it to you. And . . .

'What if it wasn't going to rain anyway?'

He sighed again. 'Euphemia. I promised your father . . .'

'Promised him what?'

Griffin took off his glasses. The thin antique silver frames sparkled as they caught the light. He rubbed his eyes and then gazed at Effie as if he had just drawn aside a curtain to reveal a sunny garden that he had never seen before.

'I promised your father I wouldn't teach you any magic. Particularly after what happened with your mother. And I also promised some other people that I would not do any magic for five years, and indeed I have not done any magic for five years. Although . . .' He looked at his watch. 'The five years is due to run out next Tuesday. Things should get more interesting then.' He chuckled, and lit his pipe.

'Are you joking, Grandfather?'

'Good heavens, child. No. Why would I do that?'

'So will you teach me magic, then? Real magic? Next Tuesday?'

'No.'

12

'Why not?'

'Because I promised your father, and I do keep my promises. And besides that, there are some very influential people who frown on magic being taught to children – well, unless they do it themselves, that is. But I can teach you a language or two if you like. Some translation. You're probably old enough for that now. And perhaps it's time I showed you the library as well.'

Griffin Truelove's library was a square, high-ceilinged room with lots of polished dark wood. There was a small table with a green glass lamp that held a candle rather than a lightbulb. (Lots of people used candles to read by now that lightbulbs were so dim, and so expensive.) The room smelled faintly of leather, incense and candle-wax. The books were heavy, thick hardbacks bound in leather, velvet or a smooth cloth that came in different shades of red, purple and blue. Their pages were a creamy sort of colour, and when you opened them their printed letters were deep black and old-fashioned looking. The stories they told were of great adventures into unknown lands.

'There is only one rule, Euphemia, and I want you to promise me you will always follow it.'

Effie nodded.

'You must only read one book at a time, and you must always leave the book on the desk. It is very important that I know which book you are reading. Do you understand? And you must never remove any books from this library.'

'I promise,' said Effie. 'Are the books . . . Are they magic?'

Her grandfather had frowned.

'Child, all books are magic. Just think,' he said, 'about what

13

books make people do. People go to war on the basis of what they read in books. They believe in "facts" just because they are written down. They decide to adopt political systems, to travel to one place rather than another, to give up their job and go on a great adventure, to love or to hate. All books have tremendous power. And power is magic.'

'But are these books *really* magic . . .?'

'They are all last editions,' said Griffin. 'Lots of people collect first editions of books, because they are very rare. Last editions are even rarer. When you are older you will find out why.' And then he refused to say any more.

The next few months went by a lot more quickly than the previous five years. Effie's grandfather started going out again, on what he called his 'adventures'. Sometimes she would arrive at his rooms after school to find him taking off his sturdy brown boots and putting away his battered leather bag and cloth money pouch. Once she saw him putting a strange-looking brown stick into a secret drawer of his big wooden desk, but when she asked him about it he told her to shoo and get on with her translation.

She'd quickly mastered most of Rosian and was now working on a different language called Old Bastard English. She dreamed of adventures – like the ones she now read about in the books in her grandfather's library – where she might have to ask someone in Rosian how much it would cost to stable her horse for the weekend, or, in Old Bastard English, what dangerous creatures were in the woods tonight. ('What wylde bestes haunten the forest this nyght?')

She also kept dreaming of magic, but she had yet to see any.

The next time she saw her grandfather put something in his secret drawer – this time a clear crystal – she asked him again.

'Are the things in that drawer magic, Grandfather?'

'Magic,' he said thoughtfully. 'Hmm. Yes, you do keep asking about magic, don't you? Well, magic is overrated, in my opinion. You must understand that you can't always – or even often – rely on magic, especially not in this world. Magic costs, and it's difficult. Remember this, Effie, it's important. If you want a plant to grow in this world, you put a seed in the earth and you water it and give it warmth and let the shoot see sunlight. You do not use magic, because to use magic to accomplish such a complicated task – the creation of life, no less – is not just wasteful, but unnecessary. Later in life I imagine you'll see some strange and wondrous things, things you probably can't even imagine now. But always remember that many things that happen in our everyday world – when a seed turns into a plant, for example – are stranger, and more complex, than the most difficult magic. You will use magic very rarely, which is why you need other skills first.'

'What other skills?'

'Your languages. And . . .' He thought for a few moments and dipped his beard in the glass of water, even though it was not on fire. He then wrung it out slowly. 'Perhaps it is time to start you on Magical Thinking. You need Magical Thinking before you can do magic. How old did you say you were now?'

'Eleven.'

'Good. We'll begin tomorrow.'

15

Effie's first Magical Thinking task had been impossible. Griffin had taken her to the entrance hall of his apartment and shown her three electric light switches.

'Each of these,' he said, 'operates a different light in the apartment. One operates the main light in the library, one operates the lamp by my armchair and one is the light in my wine cupboard. These are the lights I use most often, and the ones I always forget when I go out. Electricity is so expensive now, and of course there are hefty fines if there happens to be a greyout, so I had these switches put in, right by the door. You'll notice that you can't see from here which light is operated by what switch. Your task is to work out which switch operates each light. But here's the difficult bit. You can do what you like with the light switches out here, but you are only allowed to go and look at the lights once, and you are only allowed to have one switch on when you do. And you can only do this when you're sure you have the answer. You won't get a second chance.'

'So I can't try a switch, go and see what light it operates, then come back and try another one and memorise them?'

'No. That would be easy. When you give your answer you need to say how you came about it. It's the "how" bit that's most interesting anyway.'

'So it isn't just luck either.'

'No. You have to use Magical Thinking.'

'But how could I . . .?'

'If you get it right, there's a prize,' said Griffin.

'What's the prize?'

'Now, that would be telling.'

16

From then on, every time Effie went to the Old Rectory she stood by the light switches and tried to work out the puzzle. The answer failed her. Effie hated giving up on anything. She would ask her grandfather for hints, but he would never give her any. Instead, in between her translations, he got her to practise on other Magical Thinking problems. Some of them were a bit like jokes or riddles. 'For example,' said Griffin, a couple of weeks before Effie started at the Tusitala School, 'imagine a man throws a ball a short distance, and then the ball reverses direction and travels back to the man. The ball does not bounce off any wall or other object, nor is it attached to any string or material. Without magic, how does this occur?'

It took Effie the whole day, and in the end she had to give up.

'What's the answer, Grandfather?' she begged, just before she went home for the night.

'He threw it in the air, child.'

Effie laughed at this. Of course he did! How funny.

But her grandfather did not laugh. 'You must grasp this process before you can even attempt the very basics of magic,' he said. 'You have to learn how to think. And it seems now that we may not have much longer.'

'What do you mean? Why won't we have much longer?'

But he didn't reply.

3

The reason Effie had not yet arrived at school that Monday morning in October was because of what had happened the previous Wednesday night. Her father, Orwell Bookend, had come to pick her up from her grandfather's as usual, but instead of waiting in the car he had come up the two flights of stairs to Griffin's rooms.

Effie had been sent to the library 'to study', but she had hung around in the corridor to try to hear what her father said. She knew something was going on. The week before, Griffin had unexpectedly gone away for three days and she'd had to go straight home after school to help her step-mother Cait with her baby sister Luna instead of studying with her grandfather.

Orwell Bookend had once worn gold silk bow ties and waltzed Effie's mother around their small kitchen, singing her songs in the lost languages he used to teach. But less than two years after Aurelia's disappearance, he had started seeing Cait. Then everything changed at the university and he got a promotion that meant he wore dark suits, often with a name badge, and had to go to conferences called things like 'Offline Learning Environments' and 'Back to Pen and Paper'.

'It's happened again,' he had said to Griffin on that Wednesday evening. 'Your stupid Swords and Sorcery group has written to me. They say you are teaching her "forbidden things". I don't know what that even means, but whatever it is, I want you to stop.'

Griffin was silent for a long time.

'They are wrong,' he said.

'I don't care,' said Orwell. 'I just want you to stop.'

'You've never believed in the Otherworld,' Griffin said. 'And you think the Guild just administers something like an elaborate game. Fine. I accept that. So why do you care what I teach her? Why do you care what they say?'

'It doesn't have to be real to be dangerous,' said Orwell.

'Fair enough,' said Griffin quietly. 'But all I ask is that you trust me. I have not gone against the ruling of the Guild. Effie is quite safe. Or at least as safe as anyone else is in the world now.'

There was a long pause.

'I never knew where Aurelia had really gone when she said she'd been to the "Otherworld",' said Orwell. 'But I'm sure it was all a lot more down-to-earth than she made out. In fact I'm certain it simply involved another man, probably from this ridiculous "Guild". Yes, I know you believe in magic. And maybe some of it does work, because of the placebo effect, or . . . Look, I'm not completely cynical. Obviously Aurelia wanted me to believe in it all, but I just never could. Not on the scale she was talking about.'

Effie could hear footsteps; probably her father pacing up and down. He continued speaking.

'I don't know where Aurelia is now. I've accepted that she's gone. I assume she is dead, or with this other man. I don't even know which I'd prefer, to be honest. But I am not having my daughter get involved with the people who corrupted her. It's a world full of flakes and lunatics and dropouts. I don't like it. Do you understand?'

Griffin sighed so loudly Effie could hear it from the corridor. 'Look,' he began. 'The Diberi . . . They . . .'

Orwell swore loudly. There was the sound of him hitting something, perhaps the wall. There were then some quiet words Effie could not pick out. Then more shouting.

'I don't want to hear about the Diberi! They DO NOT exist in real life! I've already said that I . . .'

'Well then, you won't find out what is happening now,' said Griffin, mildly.

Later that night Griffin Truelove was found bleeding, unconscious and close to death in an alleyway on the very western edge of the Old Town near the Funtime Arcade. No one knew what he'd been doing in that part of town, or had any idea what had happened to him. Cait suggested that he had wandered off and perhaps been hit by a car. 'That happens to elderly people with dementia,' she had said. But Griffin didn't have dementia.

He was taken to a small hospital not far away. The next day, and the one after that, Effie had visited him instead of going to

20

school. Each day he asked her to bring him something else from his rooms. One day it was the thin brown stick she had seen him putting in the secret drawer (which he now called a 'wonde', spelling it out so Effie realised it was a word she had never heard before); another day it was the clear crystal. She also had to bring him paper and ink, his spectacles and his letter opener with the bone handle.

On Saturday, Effie had found him sitting up and writing something, or at least trying to. Nurse Underwood, who was the mother of Maximilian, one of Effie's classmates, kept getting in the way, checking Griffin's pulse and blood pressure and writing numbers on a clipboard at the end of the bed. Griffin was so weak that he could only manage a word every few minutes. He kept coughing, wheezing and wincing with pain whenever he moved.

'This is an M-codicil,' he said weakly to Effie. 'It is for you. I need to finish it, and then . . . You must give it to Pelham Longfellow. He is my solicitor. You will find him, you will find him, in . . .' Poor Griffin was gasping for breath. 'It is very important . . .' He coughed quite a lot. 'I have lost my power, Euphemia. I have lost everything, because . . . Rescue the library, if you can. All my books are yours. All my things. The wonde. The crystal. Anything that remains after . . . It says so in my will. I didn't mean this to happen now. And find Dra . . .'

The door opened and Orwell came in and asked his father-in-law how he was.

'We'd better go,' Orwell said to his daughter, after a few minutes. 'The greyout's going to start soon.'

Every week there were a number of 'greyouts' when people were forbidden to use electricity. There were also whole weeks when the creaky old phone network was switched off entirely, to give it a chance to rest. This was why most people now had pagers, which worked with radio waves.

'OK, just . . .' began Effie. 'Hang on.'

Orwell walked over and patted Griffin awkwardly on the shoulder.

'Good luck with the op tomorrow,' he said. And then to his daughter, 'I'll wait for you outside. You have three minutes.'

Effie looked at her grandfather, knowing he had been trying to tell her something important. She willed him to try again.

'Ro . . . Rollo,' said Griffin, once Orwell had left. There was a long pause, during which he seemed to summon all his strength. He pulled Effie close to him, so only she could hear what he said next.

'Find Dragon's Green,' he said, in a low whisper. Then he said it again in Rosian. Well, sort of. *Parfen Druic* – the green of the dragon. What did this mean?

'Do not go without the ring,' said Griffin. He looked down at his trembling hands. On his little finger was a silver ring that Effie had never seen before. 'I got this for you, Euphemia,' said Griffin, 'when I realised that you were a true . . . a true . . .' He coughed so much the word was lost. 'I would give it to you now, but I am going to use it and all the other boons I have to try to . . . to try to . . .' More coughing. 'Oh dear. This is useless. The codicil . . . Pelham Longfellow will explain. Trust Longfellow. And get as many boons as you can.'

22

'I don't understand,' said Effie, starting to cry. 'Don't leave me.'

'Do not let the Diberi win, Euphemia, however hard it gets. You have the potential, more, even, than I ever did . . . I should have explained everything when I could, but I thought you were too young, and I'd made a promise, and the stupid Guild made sure that . . . Look after my books. I left them all to you. The rest of my things don't matter much. Save only the things you brought to me here, and the books. Find Dra . . . Oh dear. The magic is too strong. It's still preventing me from . . .'

'What magic? What do you mean?'

But all her grandfather could do for a whole minute was cough and groan.

'I'm not coming back, dear child, not this time. But I'm sure we will meet again. The last thing you have to remember . . .' said Griffin, finally, again dropping his voice to a whisper. 'The answer,' he said, after a long pause, 'is heat.'

When Effie woke up on Monday morning she had the feeling something terrible had happened. Her father had contacted the hospital late the night before and had then gone there in his car. Effie had begged to go with him, but he had told her to stay at home and wait for news there. No news had come. And to make a bad day even worse, Effie's step-mother Cait had got up at five o'clock in the morning and, before doing her exercise video, had thrown every edible piece of food in the house into the outside bin. Not even in the kitchen bin – 'We might be tempted,' Cait had said darkly, to Luna, the baby, who was not old enough to say anything back – but the actual outside bin.

Everything was gone. All the bread, oats and cereals. All the jam. The sausages. The eggs. All the cheese. The last of the marmalade that Miss Dora Wright (Effie's old teacher whom Effie had even been allowed to call Dora out of school, and who, before she disappeared, had lived in the apartment beneath Griffin's in the Old Rectory) had made for them at Christmas. There were no crisps or chocolate – not that you would eat crisps or chocolate for breakfast unless you were really desperate, of course. Nothing.

Cait Ransom-Bookend (she had kept some of her old name when she'd married Effie's father) read a lot of diet books. She read these books because she wanted to be as thin and beautiful as people on television, even though her actual job was researching a medieval manuscript that no one had ever heard of. The latest diet book was called *The Time Is NOW!* and told you how you could live on special milkshakes that had no milk in them. These were called 'Shake Your Stuff' and came through the post in huge fluorescent tubs. Each tub came with a free book sellotaped to it, usually a romance novel with a picture on the front of a woman tied to a tree or a chair or a railway line. Cait read a lot of these books lately too.

It seemed that something in *The Time Is NOW!* (which had a chapter called 'Don't Let Fat Kids Ruin Your New Look') had made Cait choose today of all days to throw out all the nice food – food that might make you feel better if you were

24

feeling a bit sad and worried – and present Effie, who usually made her own breakfast anyway, with a glass of greeny, browny gooey liquid that looked like mud with bits of grass stirred in it. Or, worse, something that might come out of you if you had gastric flu. This, apparently, was the 'Morning Shake'. It was vile. Not that Effie was that hungry anyway. She was too worried to be hungry.

Baby Luna had her own shake that was bright pink. She didn't look that enthusiastic about it either. A pink streak on the wall opposite her high chair suggested that she had already thrown it across the room at least once.

'Looks awesome, right?' said Cait.

'Uh . . .' began Effie. 'Thanks. Any news from Dad?'

Cait made a sad face that wasn't really sad. 'He's still at the hospital.'

'Can I go?'

Cait shook her head. 'The school rang. You missed two whole days last week, apparently. Your father and I talked about this yesterday. You're not going to help your grandfather by . . .'

'Has something happened?'

Cait paused just long enough that Effie knew that something had happened.

'Your father . . .' she began. 'He'll talk to you after school.'

'Please, Cait, can you drive me to the hospital now?'

'Sorry, Effie, I can't . . . Your father . . . Effie? Where are you going?'

But Effie had already left the kitchen. She walked along the thin, dusty hallway to the bedroom she shared with Luna.

'Effie?' Cait called after her, but Effie didn't respond. 'Effie? Come back and finish your shake!' But Effie did not go back and finish her shake. She put on her green and grey school uniform as quickly as possible, buttoned up her bottle-green felt cape, and left the house without even saying goodbye. She could go to school after she'd seen her grandfather.

Effie took the same bus as usual to the Writers' Monument and walked up the hill to the Old Town, just as if she were going to school, through the cobbled streets, past the Funtime Arcade, the Writers' Museum, Leonard Levar's Antiquarian Bookshop and Madame Valentin's Exotic Pet Emporium until, after cutting though the university gardens, she turned right instead of left and walked down the long road towards the hospital, hoping that no one would notice her uniform and ask where she thought she was going.

Effie had looked up the word 'codicil' in her dictionary the night before. It meant 'a supplement to a will'. She'd had to use her dictionary several more times to work out what this might mean – there was of course no internet to help any more. A lot of people still had out-of-date dictionaries on their old phones, but Effie had a proper dictionary that Griffin had given her for her last birthday. All dictionaries – except for the very new ones – had a lot of old-fashioned words in them, like 'blog' and 'wi-fi'. Things that only existed before the worldquake.

Eventually Effie had found that a codicil was something you could add to a will to change it in some way, and that a will was a legal document that said who got what after someone died. Then she remembered the play they'd read with Mrs Beathag

Hide a few weeks before, where an old king kept changing his will on the basis of who he thought loved him most.

But why would Griffin be changing his will now? Was he going to die? Effie couldn't stop thinking back to him lying there weak and alone in his hospital bed, his long beard looking so fragile and wrong resting on the crisp white sheets. Effie saw him trying desperately to write the codicil, dipping his fountain pen in the bottle of blue ink that made Nurse Underwood tut every time she saw it. On the hospital table was a pile of Griffin's special stationery that Effie had got from his desk: cream paper and envelopes that looked expensive, but ordinary, until you held them up to the light. If you did this, you would see a delicate watermark in the shape of a large house with a locked gate in front of it. This watermark was on all Griffin Truelove's stationery.

Effie had never been into her grandfather's rooms on her own before last week. She hadn't liked it at all. Everything sounded wrong, smelled wrong – and she kept jumping every time she heard an unfamiliar noise. The heating was switched off and so the place was deathly cold. Effie kept picturing her grandfather in that alleyway, wondering what had made him go there in the middle of the night. People at the hospital said he must have been beaten up by thugs, or just randomly attacked by 'kids'. But Effie was a kid and she didn't know anyone who would be likely to attack someone like her grandfather.

And what about his magic?

Because surely *that's* when you would use magic? However difficult or boring you pretended it was, and however many lectures you gave on using magic responsibly, or trying all other methods of achieving something first, surely, surely, if someone was attacking you, almost killing you, that's when you would . . .

What? Turn them into a frog? Shrink them? Make yourself invisible?

Effie realised miserably that after all this time studying with her grandfather, she didn't even know what magic did. All she knew were lots of things it didn't do. 'Don't expect magic to make you rich or famous,' for example. Or, 'Magic is not how you will get your true power, especially not in your case.' But whatever it could do, her grandfather had not done it when he was attacked. It didn't make any sense to her.

Of course, the obvious explanation was that magic didn't really exist. After all, that was what most people in the world seemed to think, despite all the Laurel Wilde books they seemed to read. Orwell Bookend had always said that magic didn't exist. But then last Wednesday he'd said it was dangerous, and implied that he almost believed in it. What had that meant? Effie wondered yet again how something that didn't exist could have taken away her mother. How could something imaginary be dangerous? And, furthermore, if magic *was* so dangerous, why had Griffin not used it on the night he was attacked?

4

The small hospital was tucked away in the northeastern corner of the Old Town. It had wrought iron railings outside and a huge blue door with a big brass knocker. Effie, tired from all her walking, and a bit weak from having no breakfast, went in. Usually there was a nurse on the desk, but on this Monday morning there was no one, so Effie went up the stairs by herself and along the gloomy corridor. She opened the door to her grandfather's room, wondering how he was, hoping he had come through the operation OK, despite what he had said on Saturday.

The room was empty. Well, there was a bed and a bedside cabinet and an empty vase. But her grandfather and all his things were gone. Effie felt tears come to her eyes. But no – she must have gone to the wrong room. Or maybe they had moved him. Or maybe, maybe . . . But it was the right room. She knew that, really. And she understood what it meant.

The next thing Effie knew she was being taken into the nurse's special kitchen where someone gave her a cup of hot chocolate, and she was trying not to cry in front of everyone, and one of the nurses was saying that her grandfather had gone peacefully, during the operation, and that he had looked happy, almost, as if he were just at the gates of heaven.

'Where's my dad?' asked Effie.

Another nurse said she thought that Effie's father had gone off to clear out Griffin's rooms in the Old Rectory. The nurse offered to page him, but the Old Rectory wasn't far, and Effie said she'd go and meet him there. And so, all of a sudden, that was it. It was a hollow, horrible feeling. Except . . .

'The codicil!' Effie gasped. 'What about the codicil?'

The nurse frowned. 'The what?'

'And his things. His silver ring and . . . There should be an envelope for me, and some other . . .'

The nurse shook her head. 'I'm sorry, dear. Your father said he didn't want to take anything, so it's all gone to charity.'

'What? But I don't understand.'

'A lot of people do that. You know, to give back to the hospital trust. Your grandfather had a ring, you say?'

'Yes. It was an antique, I think. He wanted me to have his . . . Some of his things, very important things, and . . .'

The nurse sighed. 'I can show you the room where we put everything if you like.' She looked at her watch. 'I don't think the charity man has been yet. But we'll have to hurry.'

Effie followed the nurse out of the main hospital building and down a passageway to a herb garden full of lavender and sage, just starting to die down now before the winter. There was a little cobbled courtyard and some old steps leading up to a one-storey stone building. The sign on the door simply said CHARITY. Inside, there were clothes and books and alarm clocks and all sorts of other sad-looking objects. Effie looked for her grandfather's things, not wanting them to spend a moment longer in this gloomy place than was necessary. But there was nothing.

'Well?' asked the nurse. 'Any sign of this envelope? Or the ring?'

Effie shook her head. 'I'll just check one more time.'

The nurse looked around her quickly, with a slightly frightened look in her eyes. 'Well, you'd better be quick, before the charity man gets here.'

Effie didn't like the sound of the charity man. But she had to find her grandfather's things. She searched and searched, but they were not there. Eventually, her eyes filling again with tears, she had to thank the nurse and leave.

Outside it was still cold, despite the mellow autumnal light. Effie drew her school cape around her and walked quickly towards the Old Rectory. Perhaps her father had taken the things after all. Effie had only been walking for a minute or so when she heard breathing behind her. Someone was following her. She increased her pace; her follower did the same. Then, suddenly, the follower hissed her name – 'Effie!' – and grabbed her arm and dragged her into a thin cobbled passageway.

It was one of the nurses from the hospital. Nurse Underwood – Maximilian's mother. She was breathing heavily and her face was very stern and serious. She put her finger to her lips and

31

then took Effie's hand, opened it, and placed in her palm a silver ring with a dark red stone held in place by a number of tiny silver dragons.

'My grandfather's ring!' said Effie. 'Thank you! I— '

'Shhh!' said Nurse Underwood urgently. 'Don't tell anyone,' she whispered. 'And you must hurry away from here. The charity man is coming. He doesn't like it when we give things away. Don't let him catch you.'

Effie thrust the ring in the pocket of her cape and was about to run, but . . .

'What about the other things?'

Nurse Underwood frowned.

'My grandfather was writing a codicil. You were there when he was doing it.'

'I think your father may have that,' Nurse Underwood said. 'As for the other things . . .' She looked at her watch.

At exactly that moment Effie heard the sound of more footsteps. These were heavier than Nurse Underwood's and made a sharper sound. Then a man appeared.

'Oh good,' said Nurse Underwood. 'Dr Black. Have you . . .?'

'Hello, Euphemia,' he said. 'I'm the surgeon who operated on your grandfather. I'm so sorry for your loss. I did everything I could to get him to the Otherworld, but I don't know if he made it.' Dr Black took a cotton drawstring pouch from the pocket of his large overcoat. 'These are the items that remained. He particularly wanted you to have them, for, well, obvious reasons. He was concerned that if your father got them first they might be destroyed. I tried to catch you before, but you rushed

32

off. Luckily Nurse Underwood beeped me when she saw you leaving. It is of course vital that as few people as possible know about this.' Dr Black looked up and down the deserted alleyway. Then he gave Effie the drawstring pouch.

'Good luck,' he said.

And then, before Effie could even say thank you or ask what Dr Black had meant about the 'Otherworld', he and Nurse Underwood both hurried away.

Effie didn't want to be caught by the charity man. She opened the drawstring pouch and saw inside the wonde, the crystal, the letter opener and her grandfather's spectacles. She closed the pouch carefully and put it right at the bottom of her schoolbag. Then she ran.

When Effie arrived at the Old Rectory, it seemed as if there was no one there, not even her father. Effie reached under the flower-pot for the spare key, but it was gone. She looked through the downstairs window and saw Miss Dora Wright's things just as the teacher had left them. How awful to have lost two people so dear to her, one after the other. But Miss Wright would come back, of course. Wouldn't she? Effie couldn't see into any of the upstairs windows. Were her grandfather's books still there?

Just then a latch clicked from inside the Old Rectory, and the door started to open. It was Effie's father, looking pale and tired. He was tucking a cream-coloured business card into the pocket of his suit trousers, and looking so distracted that he didn't seem

33

to notice his daughter at first. Then he saw her and his face changed, reddening slowly like an angry sunset.

'Effie,' said her father. 'Why aren't you at school?' After a pause he looked at the ground. 'Oh dear. You know about your grandfather.'

There was a time when Effie and her father had been a lot closer than they were now. There had been a time when this situation would have led to a jumble of feelings and they would have talked and talked – each interrupting the other – until sense finally came out. Once, Effie would have cried, and this would have made her father get out an old-fashioned cotton handkerchief to give her. That was in the days when he still carried handkerchiefs, before Cait made him throw out all his old things, including his gold bow-ties, and buy some plain suits more appropriate for his new role as Dean of the Linguistics Faculty of the Midzhar New University of Excellence.

Orwell Bookend used to be the kind of university lecturer who floated around absentmindedly trailing great wafts of chalk dust and eager students wanting to know more about whatever lost language or medieval manuscript he'd just lectured on. And once upon a time Cait had been just another one of his adoring students and Effie's mother had been alive and everything had been different. Before the worldquake Orwell had been a lot kinder, and back then he would have put his arms around his daughter – however cross he really was – and told her everything would be all right.

This is not what happened now. Instead, Orwell Bookend just sighed loudly.

'Dad?' said Effie.

He frowned. 'I just wish you would do what you are told sometimes, that's all. I'm very sorry for you – for us all. Everyone loved Griffin, of course. But we could have talked about this later, properly, not in the freezing cold on some doorstep. Rules are rules for a good reason, whatever has happened. And now . . .' He looked at his watch. 'I'm going to be late for my faculty meeting and you are already VERY late for school.'

All the time this was going on a rabbit was sitting under the front hedge wondering why exactly humans were so complicated. Could they not just share a lettuce together and move on? The older human had a very complex aura, the rabbit noted, but one that was not at all magical. The younger human had an extremely magical aura of a sort the rabbit had never seen before, including a faint colour that didn't usually exist in this world. It made the rabbit want to help her – even though it did not know how.

'Grandfather Griffin left me a codicil, but I couldn't find it at the hospital,' said Effie. 'Do you know where he put it?'

Orwell sighed again. 'Look, Effie. I'm sure you know that your grandfather lived partly in a fantasy world full of people who believe in magic and other dimensions and so on. It probably seemed real at times, but you do understand that it was not real, don't you? I've been worried about what he's been teaching you recently. What Griffin thought of as "magic" is at best a complete waste of time, and at worst . . .'

'He hardly said anything to me about magic. He just said it was really difficult and that there were always other ways of doing things.'

35

'Well, that's something, I suppose. But whatever stories he may have told you about travelling to other worlds and battling the Diberi, or whatever he called them, Cait and I want you to understand that they were just stories and you should not take them seriously.'

'What's Cait got to do with this? She's not even my real mother.'

'Effie, please. We've talked about you hurting Cait's feelings by saying that.'

'Cait isn't even here. Anyway, what about my codicil?'

'I may as well tell you. I've destroyed the codicil. It's for your own good. I didn't read it. I burned the wretched thing immediately. I want all this nonsense out of our lives for ever. You should be learning about how the world really is, not how it appears in the addled minds of a bunch of freaks and madmen. You probably don't understand now, but you'll thank me later.'

'But a codicil is a . . . It's a legal document. I have to take it to . . .' Suddenly Effie decided not to mention Pelham Longfellow. Her father would probably just write him off in the same way he'd done with everyone else Griffin had known. 'I have to take it to a solicitor.'

'Effie,' her father said, sighing. 'Do you even know what an M-codicil is?'

Effie realised that she did not know. But she remembered that was indeed what her grandfather had called it. An *M-codicil*. She shook her head.

'The M stands for magic. The idea of an M-codicil is that it adds something to an M-will. A magical will. So the stories go:

when normal people die they leave wills, and when magical people die they leave M-wills. They might leave particular spells or magical items behind that can't be covered in a normal will. And these wills can supposedly only be dealt with by magical solicitors. So that's who he wanted you to find, I expect. Some sort of ridiculous "magical" solicitor.'

'But . . .'

'But these are just stories. Fantasy. Like those stupid Laurel Wilde books you used to read. And recent events have shown just how dangerous some of these fantasists can be. I don't want you anywhere near the people or the world that your grandfather was so caught up in.'

Effie's eyes filled with tears, but she refused to let her father see her cry.

'How could you? That codicil was for me.'

'You are eleven years old. You are too young for all this. Do you even know where magical solicitors supposedly live? Do you?'

'No.'

'In the "Otherworld". Another dimension! It's all just another story.'

Effie looked up towards the top of the building. 'Well, what about the books that Grandfather Griffin left for me? I'm supposed to look after his library and . . .'

'That lot of old leather-bound junk?' Orwell Bookend snorted, forgetting how passionate he had once been about rare books and manuscripts. 'Your grandfather was being completely unrealistic, as usual. Where would we put a library, for heaven's sakes? We've barely got enough room for the four of us. It was completely unfair of him to give you the impression that you'd be allowed to keep all those books. You can choose one book to remember him by, Effie. That's reasonable.'

'What? One book! But they're rare last editions and—'

'Don't push me, Effie, or there won't be even one book. I don't know what's happened to you lately. You used to be such a normal, happy child. Now . . . It's probably my own fault. I should have found you proper after-school care rather than leaving you in the clutches of a deluded old man. Anyway, you must try to pull yourself together and go to school and put all this out of your mind. After school you can come back here – five o'clock on the dot – and you can choose one book before the charity man comes.'

The charity man again.

'And then we can all talk about our grief together. I think Cait might have a book on the subject . . .' As well as diet books, Cait had a number of self-help books that either told you things that everyone already knew, or told you things that no one in their right mind would think. In the last few months the house had been filling up with these books, all published by the Matchstick Press.

Effie knew better than to argue with her father when he was in this mood. She would have to go to school and try to think of some way to rescue her grandfather's library before five o'clock. She could cry in the toilets if she felt upset. And as for Pelham Longfellow . . . He was apparently in this Otherworld, where her grandfather may also have gone. She'd have to work out how

38

to get there. There was so much to think about. Wiping the tears from her eyes, Effie looked at her watch. It was still only ten past ten. If she hurried she could be at school in time for the end of double English. At least at school she would be warm.

When Effie had gone, the rabbit noticed that the child's father was putting a human metal object – the thing they called a key – under a flowerpot. This was the object the child with the strangely-coloured aura must have been looking for. Would she need it again? When the man had gone, the rabbit went and knocked over the flowerpot and took the key in its teeth. It then took the key deep into its burrow where it would remain until the child needed it. Satisfied, the rabbit emerged and went back to chewing on the wild strawberry leaves that grew down by the well at the end of the Old Rectory garden.

5

Mrs Beathag Hide disliked many things – disobedience, excuses, weakness, children – but the thing she loved more than anything else was literature. She loved poems and plays and novels and long epics. Her eyesight was not what it had once been, though, and so she took any chance to have people read things to her. Even if those people were children, and abominably bad at reading, it was better than nothing.

And so the only good thing that ever happened in Mrs Beathag Hide's classes – now that there was no more creative writing – were the play readings. Each pupil was given a part, and then the whole class would read through a play, which sometimes took several double periods and did not, somehow, feel like work.

The Bottom of the Class got no part, or the very smallest part in the play, which suited Maximilian. Whoever was Top of the Class got the main part and was allowed to choose who played the other parts. This did not suit Lexy. She did not like main parts. Whenever she read a book, she decided in advance which character she was going to identify with most (in her mind, the character she was going to *be*), but this was never the main character. Sometimes it was the main character's little sister or best friend. Often it was someone helpful, like a nurse. Sometimes she chose wrong and the character died or only made one appearance in the whole book. But even that was better than having to be the star.

Now Lexy was reading the main female part in *Antigone*, which was a Greek tragedy. The children all had to practise saying it before they could even start reading it. You couldn't say it the way it looked, for a start.

'AN-tee-gone-knee,' tried the children, after about ten minutes of tuition, almost getting it right.

'NO!' said Mrs Beathag Hide.

'An-TI-gun-knee,' they tried again.

'GOOD!'

And then the play reading began.

Antigone was exactly the kind of main character Lexy did not want to be. In the play, Antigone's brother dies in a battle against her other brother, and Antigone wants to bury him but isn't allowed to. Then she gets condemned to death. The play was very sad – tragic, according to Mrs Beathag Hide, which is something more important than just sad – with everyone being mean to one another and then dying. The play was also very embarrassing if you happened to be playing Antigone and you had accidentally chosen Wolf Reed to play the part of your beloved, Haemon, who kills himself when he finds you have been sentenced to be buried alive and then killed yourself. But as the children read on, Mrs Beathag Hide seemed happier than ever, listening to the long, impassioned speeches, in which Antigone begs for her brother's body to be given a proper burial, and then Haemon begs for Antigone to be spared . . .

Until the door started to open. It was Euphemia Truelove. She was over an hour late.

The door creaked loudly as Effie opened it. Like everything else in the Tusitala School for the Gifted, Troubled and Strange, it was old and needed repair – or at least a good glug of oil. The whole room went silent. Maximilian gulped. Raven sat on her hands, silently, wondering if she had yet become invisible, but suspecting not. Wolf glanced at his watch. If the fuss that was bound to follow lasted long enough he would be spared having to read much more of this depressing play and would be able to think instead about getting ready for P.E. and how he might practise his mental toughness today. Coach Bruce, who trained the Under 13 rugby squad, had recently had a lot to say about Wolf's mental toughness, not all of it that nice.

The silence was becoming unbearable, although objectively it had only been going on for a few seconds. Then it was broken by a big metallic PLOP, as a drop of water fell in the tin bucket next to Maximilian. Then there was another plop. Then another. Rain. Coming through the ceiling, as usual.

'Can we help you?' said Mrs Beathag Hide to Effie.

'I'm sorry I'm late,' Effie began. 'I've had a bit of . . .'

Suddenly she felt as if she were about to cry. Everyone was looking at her.

42

'A bit of . . .?' prompted Mrs Beathag Hide. 'Trouble getting out of bed, perhaps?'

'No, I . . .' started Effie. But she now realised she didn't want to say anything about her grandfather in front of the whole class. It felt too private. And there was all that stuff Mrs Beathag Hide was always saying about never complaining or explaining. And anyway, if something like this happened you were supposed to bring in a letter from a parent, and Effie had no letter. 'Well, actually . . . Yes. Sorry. I slept in.'

'Do you not have an ALARM CLOCK?'

'Yes, I do, but— '

'Perhaps it broke?'

'Yes, I think maybe it needs new batteries.'

'Interesting. But we heard a different story, didn't we, class?'

The class froze. Was it meant to speak back? But Mrs Beathag Hide carried on.

'We heard of a SICK grandparent.'

Maximilian gasped. Oh no! This was *his* fault.

'It's amazing how many grandparents some children go through. At my last school one wretched child had SEVENTEEN. Another one died every time there was home-work due. Think about it, class. SEVENTEEN.'

Everyone tried to think about this, except for Raven, who was attempting to cast her invisibility spell on Effie, and Wolf, who was wondering how anyone could stay mentally tough in this situation.

'Which,' Mrs Beathag Hide went on, 'I think you'll agree, adds up to at least THIRTEEN betrayals of the truth. Or, in other words, LIES.'

43

Effie was looking at the floor. Her eyes were filling with tears. What if she just broke down and sobbed in front of the whole class? Her life would essentially be over. She reached into her pocket and felt for her grandfather's silver ring. Touching it made her feel a bit better. Stronger. She slipped it on her left thumb. It gave her a warm feeling, like eating a big bowl of porridge on a winter's morning.

There was another big PLOP in the tin bucket.

'Well?' said Mrs Beathag Hide.

'Stop it,' Maximilian found himself saying, suddenly. It came out as a sort of loud whisper, but somehow saying the words made him feel better, so he said them again, this time more loudly. 'Stop it.'

The words echoed around the room. Someone had dared to speak. It was the pathetic boy. The dunce. The Bottom of the Class.

Mrs Beathag Hide turned slowly to face him. Effie quickly found her seat, and tried to make herself as small and inconspicuous as possible.

Poor Maximilian was trembling as Mrs Beathag Hide approached him.

'Well,' she said. 'Well, well. What do we have here? Haemon in a dunce's hat, begging me to spare his Antigone. Speaking up for your little friend. Maybe your *girlfriend*.' She frowned. 'Such loyalty. Such fearlessness. And in one so clearly challenged, so socially doomed. I do so admire your bravery. Yes, I do. Enough to give you detention for just ONE DAY rather than a week. And your frightened little love-interest can have the same. You will both report to my office at four o'clock. Maximilian and Euphemia. It sounds almost Shakespearian! *O Maximilian, Maximilian* . . . Well, I'll lock you in a broom cupboard together for a while, and we'll see how this tragic romance blossoms.'

Somewhere in a dark corridor the elderly headmaster weakly rang the bell that meant it was – at long last – the end of this period. Everyone, with the possible exception of Effie, left the room feeling they had learnt something, almost, but probably not in the way the government and other adults hoped you would learn things at school. Effie looked around for Maximilian to thank him, but he had gone off in an embarrassed daze towards the changing rooms to get ready for double P.E. He had never had a detention before. He was very faintly excited about it.

Wolf Reed loved playing rugby. The feel of the ball under his arm or in his hands. Running fast, kicking, swallow-diving. Rugby was the only thing he really enjoyed in his life. Well, he also quite enjoyed other sports, but Coach Bruce always said that all other sports are simply preparation for rugby.

The thing Wolf loved most of all was passing the ball hard, making it spin in the air as it rushed towards its target, before . . .

THWACK.

Maximilian fell over in the mud. Again.

Mr Peters, the Head of P.E., blew his whistle.

'REED!' he said, for the third time. 'I am warning you.'

'What, sir?'

45

Maximilian had been put on Wolf's team precisely because if he was on the other team, Wolf would come close to killing him with tackles that almost certainly weren't allowed at this level of junior rugby. To be fair, this wasn't in the least bit personal. It was bound to happen, given that Wolf was the best rugby player in the form and Maximilian was the worst. So Mr Peters had put them on the same team with the result that Wolf threw the ball so hard at his team-mate that he was knocked over.

'It's all right, sir,' said Maximilian, cleaning mud off his glasses. 'Really.'

But five minutes later the whole thing happened again.

'Right!' said Mr Peters. 'Both of you. Inside. You can play tennis. I've had enough of this.'

'But Sir!' pleaded Wolf. 'This is so unfair.' He mumbled a few choice words.

'Go. Now. And you . . .' He pointed at Wolf. 'Detention. We don't have swearing on the rugby pitch.'

Which was actually a complete lie, given that all sports pitches throughout the land were sworn on a great deal by everyone from children to their parents to professional sports teams. But still, rules were rules.

Something strange was happening in the indoor tennis centre, which wasn't exactly unusual – the indoor tennis centre was a peculiar place at the best of times – but this thing was strange enough that it had attracted the attention of Coach Bruce.

46

Coach Bruce was in the tennis centre for roughly the same reason that Wolf was (or almost was; at this point he and Maximilian were silently trudging through the rain across the back sports field, which was currently full of annoyed-looking alpaca from some city farm project). Both Coach Bruce and Wolf Reed took rugby Way Too Seriously for Mr Peters's liking. If they were allowed out there on the rugby field together, coach and star player, then Maximilian, and other small, slow-moving or otherwise vulnerable children, would almost certainly be maimed or killed. Official Under 13 practices were one thing. Mr Peters didn't care who got killed in official Under 13 rugby practices. It was his job to care only if someone got killed in a P.E. lesson.

The indoor tennis centre had been built with money sent from a boy who had been at the Tusitala School for the Gifted, Troubled and Strange a long time ago and then gone on to become a famous tennis player. His family sent enough money to build the centre, but not to maintain it, so it was now as rundown as the rest of the school. Its flickering orange lighting gave some of the children headaches, and Court Three was haunted. The store-room was full of old, dead tennis balls, and a broken ball machine covered with several layers of green fuzz. It had a large metallic garage-style door that functioned a bit like a guillotine, and could drop without warning at any time. If Coach Bruce had to go into the office for some reason, the children would dare each other to walk underneath the guillotine. If it came down while you were underneath it, you might die. And if it came down with you inside the cupboard, you might be left there for ever to rot. It was quite a stressful game, but also fun.

Anyway, there was a strange thing happening in the indoor tennis centre that had never happened before.

Euphemia Truelove, the dreamy girl who, despite being reserve Wing Attack in the Under 12 netball team, had never quite set the sporting world alight, was suddenly playing tennis like some sort of professional. She had beaten all the girls in the form and was now working her way through all the boys. She looked faintly surprised by this, but also as if she were quite enjoying it.

Coach Bruce suspected foul play – possibly doping, which he took very seriously – but why would an unprepossessing eleven-year-old girl take performance-enhancing drugs before a random P.E. lesson on a wet afternoon in October? It didn't make any sense. Coach Bruce put another boy on against her, but he ended up almost crying when Effie hit a forehand so hard the ball left a bruise on his shin.

'I'm not playing against her, Sir,' he said. 'She's gone mental.'

Which was when Maximilian and Wolf came in. Wet, and still a bit annoyed.

'Aha,' said Coach Bruce when he saw Wolf. 'Good.'

Maximilian was given a doubles partner and went off to play on Court One. Most of the other children were given a complex drill to complete on Court Two. And on Court Three . . .

'Right,' said Coach Bruce. 'Let's see what happens now.'

He put Wolf Reed on to play with Effie. Normally Wolf Reed wasn't allowed anywhere near girls, even quite tough girls, and even in sports where boys and girls could play together. He frightened all the boys, let alone the girls. But this girl needed to be beaten (or else she might get quite a big head) and Wolf Reed was the only person likely to do it. Wolf Reed wasn't as good at tennis as he was at rugby, but he was still the best boy in the first form, and probably in the whole Lower School.

What happened next was probably not helped by the fact that they were playing on the haunted court. Both Wolf and Effie developed a strange, ethereal green glow around them as they held up their rackets, which, from a distance, seemed like great ancient weapons.

To Maximilian, the whole thing looked oddly like some long-ago encounter between two soldiers, warriors or heroes. It was perplexing, and sort of beautiful. The ghostly aura around Court Three made it seem like a misty battlefield at dawn, with these two great fighters practising their moves. Effie's forehand had become like the great slap of a giantess, and Wolf's whole game looked like something from a cosmic boxing ring. Something very strange had happened, and no one knew exactly what it was. But everyone watched, awed and amazed, as a girl who wasn't usually that good at sports beat Wolf Reed at tennis.

Afterwards, Coach Bruce came up to Effie with a bottle.

'Pee in this,' he said. 'And don't get a friend to do it.'

Coach Bruce had a friend in the science department who was an amateur drugs tester and this was how he always made sure his junior athletes were 'clean'. He now had his eye on Effie for every girls team going, but not if she was on drugs.

This day was getting stranger and stranger.

49

6

At four o'clock, Maximilian Underwood, Effie Truelove and Wolf Reed reported to Mrs Beathag Hide's office for their detention. Maximilian was still mildly excited. After detention he thought he might ask his mother again about contact lenses, maybe try to do some weight-lifting and build some muscle, maybe not be the first one to put his hand up in class all the time. This detention, he felt, might well be his first step towards being – whisper it – *cool*. Or at least not totally uncool. Or however people expressed these things now.

Detention was supposed to last thirty-five minutes and take place in the dingy but serviceable classroom next door to the headmaster's office. Detention tasks were varied. Sometimes the elderly headmaster would shuffle in and read weakly to the children from his favourite Robert Louis Stevenson story, *The Bottle Imp*. When this happened, detention was almost pleasurable, although the headmaster would often shuffle back out again after a particularly exciting moment, saying he had to go for his medication, and then either would not return, or, having returned, would forget his place and have to start again. (The worst-behaved students in the school were the ones most likely to be able flawlessly to quote the beginning of *The Bottle Imp* from memory, but least likely to be able to tell you how it ends.)

But more often the teacher in charge of detention that day would simply give students an essay title – usually something like 'Why Rules Are Good' or 'Problems Misbehaviour Can Cause in Later Life'.

Mrs Beathag Hide approached detention in a different way. She preferred lines to essays, feeling that repeating an idea over and over again made a greater psychological impact on the children and was less risky – at least, when it came to basic discipline – than independent thought. In other contexts she championed independent thought. But detention was not the place for it.

She also really did like locking children in broom cupboards.

So at five past four on what had become really quite a wet Monday afternoon, Maximilian, Wolf and Effie found themselves in the school's basement, in the old, dusty cupboard of a long-dead caretaker, which smelled of dunce's hats (which, as we already know, smell of mould and dead mice), damp blotting paper, turpentine, congealed ink and ancient spiders. They faced rather a daunting task.

'Between you,' said Mrs Beathag Hide, almost smiling. 'Yes, *between you* . . . Ha! I like that. It may lead to cooperation and loyalty, or, more engagingly, to great betrayal and suffering. Between you, you will write the following, six hundred times: "I will always obey those in authority and . . ." Except . . . No.

51

Wait. We don't want to send you out of this school paying more attention to silly little traffic wardens and idiotic politicians than is necessary. Hmmm.' She thought for a while. 'You will write out the following, six hundred times: "I will always respect those with greater intelligence than my own." Yes. And you will spell "intelligence" correctly on every single line. When the six hundred lines are completed, you will pass the sheets of paper under the door to me, and then I will unlock it.'

The cupboard, which was really like a small room, had no windows and was very dimly lit with an ancient fluorescent light that must have had thousands of dead insects inside its cracked plastic casing. There were candles, too, in case of a greyout. Effie sat down on a rickety wooden chair at the old caretaker's table, and Maximilian sat opposite her on a paint-spattered stool. Wolf slumped down on the floor and leaned against the wall by a cracked porcelain sink. Mrs Beathag Hide turned the key in the heavy lock and went away to make a cup of Earl Grey tea and fetch today's newspaper, the one with the best cryptic crossword, from the staff room.

Effie got out some paper and a pen. She wondered whether you spelled 'intelligence' with an 'ance' or an 'ence' at the end. Maximilian would know. But Maximilian had taken out his calculator and was furiously tapping away on it.

'Shouldn't we get started?' Effie said. 'I've got to be somewhere by five o'clock. It's really quite impor— '

'Shhh,' said Maximilian.

'Can someone lend me a pen?' said Wolf. 'Oh, and actually, some paper?'

'Shhh,' said Maximilian again.

Wolf and Effie looked at one another. Why was this nerdy creature telling them to shhh? What on earth did he think he was doing anyway, messing around with his calculator when . . .

'I've seriously got to be out of here by quarter to five,' said Wolf. 'Can we just get on with it?'

'We'll do two hundred lines each,' said Effie. 'Right?'

'Only if someone can lend me a pen,' said Wolf.

'Maximilian will have a spare pen,' said Effie.

'And who's the fastest writer?' said Wolf. 'Maybe that person should do more.'

Maximilian was mumbling to himself. 'Six hundred lines. Let's say each one takes fifteen seconds if you're a fast writer and twenty seconds if you're a slow writer. So the total time it would take for a slow writer to complete the task on his or her own would be twenty seconds times six hundred, which is . . .' Here he gulped. 'Twelve thousand seconds, which is two hundred minutes, which is three hours and twenty minutes . . . But it's OK because there are three of us, and if we work fast we could do it in probably just under an hour each, as long as we take no breaks and . . .'

By now it was almost quarter past four.

'We're not getting out of here by five,' said Maximilian, looking up. 'It's not mathematically possible. Even if I do find a spare pen for Wolf, and even if we write as fast as we can, and even if I do more lines because I am probably the fastest writer, we won't be done until around five-thirty.'

Wolf swore. 'But I've got to work. With my uncle. At five.'

'Yeah,' said Effie. 'And I've got to meet my dad. We're clearing out my grandfather's place, and . . .'

She still hadn't worked out how to save her grandfather's books. Effie suddenly felt very tired indeed. Her head started to throb. All her muscles were aching from the tennis. For the whole hour she'd spent in the tennis centre she had felt invincible, and had forgotten about everything bad in her life, including the awful sad feeling about her grandfather. It had been incredible, but also quite mysterious. She had no idea where any of it had come from, but she had felt so strong, as if she could do anything. She had also felt lighter, faster, more agile. Every time Wolf had hit the ball she'd known exactly where his shot was going to land. And then where she should hit it back.

But what on earth did this mean? Why had she suddenly become so good at tennis just since this morning? Was it because she hadn't had any breakfast? Sometimes Cait said she felt stronger after fasting. But that didn't really make any scientific sense . . . Effie yawned. Twisted the silver ring on her thumb. She was actually so tired now that if she just put her head down on the desk she . . .

'Effie? Don't go to sleep!' Maximilian poked her shoulder.

She managed to lift her head. 'Sorry. I'm just so . . .' She put her head down again.

'Oh no,' said Maximilian, although secretly he didn't mind this situation being prolonged, and would have been happy to spend many hours in a cupboard with Effie and Wolf, who were two of his more interesting classmates. 'What are we going to do?'

'We are going to escape,' said Wolf, getting up.

Effie was now so tired that she could barely lift her head from the desk. Maximilian stood (because Wolf had taken his stool) watching in amazement as Wolf started looking around for a way out. He climbed onto the stool and checked different parts of the walls and the ceiling.

Of course there was no point trying to get through the door. Mrs Beathag Hide would be sitting there waiting, drinking her Earl Grey tea and doing her crossword. There were no other doors or windows in the cupboard. But before too long Wolf had found a panel in the ceiling that looked as if it might come out, only you'd need some kind of sharp device to poke into one of the corners. Wolf tried with a ruler, but the edge was too thick to fit in the gap. What would be ideal would be some kind of little knife, not that anyone was allowed to bring such things to school . . .

Effie was almost asleep again, but she could see what Wolf was doing, knew what he needed. What was that thing . . .? That thing . . .? Why wasn't her brain working properly? In her bag? Yes, she had something in her bag that would help, although she couldn't remember what it was. Oh yes, a letter opener. Her grandfather's letter opener. That was quite sharp. She gestured to Maximilian, who seemed to understand what she meant and reached for her bag.

'Letter opener,' she managed to say, before she fell into a deep, almost fairy-tale, sleep.

Maximilian found the letter opener – as well as several other very interesting-looking, and not entirely unfamiliar objects – in a pouch in Effie's bag. The letter opener was like a miniature dagger and felt heavy in his hands, even though it was quite small. He admired its fine bone handle, and the red jewels pressed into the sides of its sheath.

'Here,' he said to Wolf. 'Try this.'

Wolf climbed down from the stool and reached out to take the letter opener from Maximilian. It may have been Maximilian's imagination, but there was a sharp crack and sparkle in the air – a bit like lightning – as Wolf reached out for the small blade. Then something rather extraordinary happened. As soon as Wolf touched the letter opener there was another sharp cracking sound and a much brighter flash of light. Then more flashes of light, and more cracking, wrenching sounds as if a storm were happening inside. Then the whole room went dark for a few seconds.

When it was light again, Wolf was standing there looking terrified. He was holding a full-sized sword.

Effie was still asleep.

'You're . . . You're a . . .' said Maximilian, trembling.

Wolf looked down at the sword. 'What the . . .?' He didn't know what to say or do. He found himself unsheathing the sword. He couldn't really help himself. He looked even more like an ancient, like an ancient . . .

'Warrior,' said Maximilian. 'You're an actual true warrior! That's what sets off the magic. This is – I can't believe it – even though when it's enlarged it looks a bit like a Sword of Destiny, the way it works . . . I think it might be the Sword of Orphennyus . . .'

Wolf looked at the blade. He had never seen anything so

sharp, so sleek, so peculiarly beautiful. He was suddenly filled with a strange desire to protect the sleeping Effie, and even silly Maximilian too. With the tiny, sharp, trembling tip of this great weapon he casually flipped the ceiling panel and it fell open to reveal a long-abandoned hatch leading to an entrance to an old servants' corridor. Then, not knowing what to do next, Wolf cut into the air a few times with the blade. It made a pleasing swishing sound. He could do anything, go anywhere, become brave and true and . . . But this was insanity. He re-sheathed the sword and put it down on the table. Immediately, it shrank back to being a letter opener.

'Who has given me drugs?' he demanded. 'How have you done this?'

Everyone was a bit obsessed with drugs because of Coach Bruce. But Wolf couldn't see any other explanation for what was happening. And that business with the tennis earlier. That must have been drugs too. It was outrageous.

Maximilian wasn't listening. He was trying to get the ring off Effie's thumb.

'It's her, isn't it?' said Wolf. 'She's given us all drugs, somehow. She's . . .'

'Can you help me?' said Maximilian. 'Please?'

'What am I going to say to Coach Bruce? If he finds out that . . .'

'Please hurry,' said Maximilian.

'Why?'

'Because I think she might be dying.'

'What?' The feeling of wanting to protect Effie had not quite

57

left Wolf, even though he had now put down the sword. 'What should I do?'

'Do you have any sweets or chocolate?'

Wolf looked disgusted. 'Of course not. I'm an athlete.'

'What about a sports drink? Lucozade? Something like that?'

'What about one of these?' Wolf had a couple of bottles of the athlete's version of Shake Your Stuff that he'd bought with the wages he earned from his uncle. They weren't very nice, to be honest, and he'd be glad to give one away. Maximilian looked at the ingredients.

'No,' he said. 'This hasn't got any real nutrients in it. We need something with sugar or fruit or something.'

Wolf looked in his bag again. There was an old bottle of normal sports drink in there somewhere. As he pulled it out, Maximilian finally prised the ring off Effie's thumb. Immediately, she opened her eyes, but still looked very weak.

'Drink this,' Maximilian said, giving her the bottle that Wolf handed to him.

It was bright orange, fizzy and very sweet. Effie managed a bit and sat up.

'What's going on?' she said. 'What have you done with my ring?'

'Don't put it back on,' Maximilian said. 'Not for a while.'

'Why not? I like it. I want to put it back on.' Effie reached towards Maximilian to take back her ring. But he held on to it.

'Are you insane? It's a magical ring. Surely you must have realised that? You have to know what they actually do, and what that actually costs, before you mess around with them. For more information see any fantasy novel ever written.'

'Seriously? Are you sure?'

Maximilian paused for a moment. Chewed his lip. Put the ring down on the table. Effie picked it up, but did not put it on.

'Where did you get all those things?' Maximilian asked Effie. 'You've got the Sword of Orphennyus, the Ring of God Knows What and, I believe, the Spectacles of Knowledge, as well as . . . Anyway, there are more boons in your schoolbag than you'd find in most of the greatest collections, certainly in this world. Where on earth did they come from?'

7

'What are you talking about?' said Wolf and Effie together. 'Wolf,' said Maximilian. 'Show Effie the Sword of Orphennyus.'

Wolf picked up the letter opener again and unsheathed it. Effie watched as the small blade grew to almost twenty times its original size. Wolf then swished it around the room. It was huge, shiny and clearly very, very magical.

'I'm dreaming,' said Effie, shaking her head.

'I'm still pretty sure this is drugs,' said Wolf, putting the sword back in its holder and replacing it on the table, where it promptly shrunk again.

Effie reached across and took the letter opener. Nothing happened. She took off its silver sheath. Inside was a bluntish blade, ideal for opening letters, but impossible to hurt yourself with.

'You have to be a warrior,' Maximilian explained. 'The Sword of Orphennyus only shows itself to a true warrior. To anyone else it's just a letter opener. Completely harmless. But in the hands of a true warrior it's deadly. Orphennyus was a great warrior of the Otherworld who . . .'

Maximilian's voice faded as Wolf started thinking about what this meant. He rather liked the idea of being a true warrior, although he didn't believe it could be possible. All this had to be a trick – he just wasn't sure how. For a second, though, he did let himself imagine. Wolf Reed, standing on a hilltop in some kind of tunic – no, something less stupid – maybe just a really cool t-shirt and some combat trousers and some new trainers, perhaps, with his magical sword, protecting people and fighting on the side of an army that was good and noble and battled for peace rather than war. Where were all these thoughts coming from?

'How do you know all this?' said Effie to Maximilian. 'And what about my ring?'

'I confess I don't know that much about the ring. But magical rings are always complicated. Clearly, you were able to play tennis today like you did because the ring increased your strength, and maybe some other qualities too, but it looks as if it also drained you of energy. If you had carried on wearing it, I'm not sure you would ever have . . .' Maximilian gulped, 'ever have woken up at all.'

'How do you know all this?' asked Wolf, repeating Effie's question.

'I read things,' said Maximilian. 'While you others are busy playing sports and making friends and shopping and going on outings, I read things. It's what I do. I collect knowledge. Some of it was bound to come in handy one day.'

'But where do you read about things like this?' asked Effie. 'It's not what you'd find in most normal books.' Even Laurel Wilde's novels didn't cover such things. The children in her books simply waved their arms about and magical things happened. Sometimes they brewed things in cauldrons. They never had problems with magical rings.

Effie realised again how little she had really known about her grandfather and his life. Of course she had noticed him putting things in his secret drawer, but she'd had no idea that these were really magical items. And now . . . Effie's heart caught in her chest. She knew she was going to miss her grandfather so much, not just because she had loved him so dearly, but because he had left her with so many unanswered questions.

'You pick it up,' said Maximilian, vaguely. 'I have a small collection of fairly rare documents and pamphlets that I got from the dim web. I collect things to do with . . .'

'The *dim* web?' interrupted Effie.

'It's a closed web ring made up of connected bulletin boards. Like the old dark web, but mainly for scholars of magic, folklore and the disappearing arts. You have to dial in. With a modem. But it's quite good when you do, and . . .'

Effie looked at her watch. This was all very well, but what about her grandfather's books? She had almost lost these items, and look how special they had turned out to be. It now seemed even more important to save his library, but how?

Wolf had pulled a stepladder over to the place where he'd removed the panel in the ceiling. The three children climbed up – Wolf first, then Effie, then Maximilian – and wriggled through the hatch. The servants' corridor was thin and dark, but they were just about able to stand up in it. There was a little wooden shelf with some candles, matches and a taper. Each of the children lit a candle, and then they started making their way forward in the soft flickering light. Every so often there were little wooden hatches with tiny windows and old wooden ladders. This must have been how servants moved through the old house in the past, long before it became a school, going about their duties silently, invisibly. The children went past the vast dining hall with its polished floors and dark wooden tables; the laundry; the headmaster's study. And then, finally, they went down some steps to a wooden door that presumably led outside.

The door was locked.

Effie put her head in her hands. 'Oh no,' she said. It was now ten to five. She could just about get to her grandfather's place by five, but only if this door would open. And it did not look as if that were going to happen. Next to its large brass handle was a big keyhole – and no key. The children looked around every-where, but the key was nowhere to be found. The door must have been locked from the other side.

'The sword,' said Maximilian immediately. But he knew it would be no good. There was no space for Wolf to swing it at the door. Effie, now desperate, started trying to simply push her way out. It was ridiculous (especially as this was a door that opened inwards) but she remembered how strong she had felt before, playing tennis. If she could only get some of that strength back now. Maybe she could . . .

'Shall I try the ring?' she asked Maximilian.

He shrugged. 'Give it a try. But . . . I don't think the power will be enough.'

Effie slipped the ring back on. Again, that warm, lovely feeling. All the muscles in her body rippled with power and potential. She felt like she could pick up a bus, or run so fast she would start flying, or . . . But this time the good feeling didn't last long. Soon she felt tired and had to slip the ring off again.

'Maybe if I try?' Wolf said. Effie reluctantly gave him the ring. It fitted on his middle finger. But, as soon as it was on, Wolf turned a bit green and had to sit down because his legs went so weak. 'I feel sick,' he said. 'And – urgh – just horrible.' He took the ring off and went back to normal.

'These items,' began Maximilian, 'which are really called boons, by the way, they work with your true-born ability. They can't be used by just anyone. They only work if they sort of match you. They are very specifically designed to— '

'Be completely useless in helping us get out?' said Wolf.

Effie felt like crying. What were they going to do?

'Effie,' said Maximilian. 'Do you mind if I try something else from your bag?'

'Do what you like,' she said. It was now five to five and hope was running out for her to get to her grandfather's in time. 'But hurry.'

Maximilian reached inside the pouch and found what he was looking for. The soft red leather glasses case, velvety and smooth from centuries of handling. Maximilian opened the case and there they were.

The Spectacles of Knowledge. Who would have thought that

these things even existed outside of mythology and folklore? But of course Maximilian had learned that most mythology and folklore was real, and so he shouldn't have been surprised. But he was. He was surprised and awed and . . . The sword hadn't worked for him, of course, and the ring probably would do nothing either. But would these . . .? Would they . . .? Could they . . .?

He slipped the glasses out of the case. The lenses were very thin and old, and had been polished so much that they were almost clearer than air. The frames were antique silver. They were a bit tarnished, would need a bit of a scrub here and there with a silver cloth, but . . . Maximilian put them on. He looked around the cramped space and . . .

Yes. He was right. The whole scene was completely different. Maximilian could now see the original plans of the building overlaying the actual structure. The spectacles overlaid his normal vision with all the facts he could ever want about his surroundings, as well as a compass, a thermometer and layers and layers of historical knowledge about the place he was in.

He also had access to a dictionary, full translations of any language – including all the magical ones – and full subscription rights to the Digital Arcane Library, which cost hundreds of krubles to access via the dim web. He could also see vital statistics hovering around Effie and Wolf in the form of status bars. Her energy was still dangerously low, he could see . . .

'Wow,' he said aloud.

Wolf and Effie looked at one another. This nerdy creature was now totally blissing-out on having a new pair of glasses, which was actually quite sweet, but they really, really needed to get out of here, and . . .

'Give me the letter opener,' said Maximilian, with some authority. 'NOT you, Wolf. Don't you touch it. Thanks, Effie. Now. Let's see. Original brass mortice lock, manufactured in 1898. Aha. I see. If I press here and turn this and find that lever there, then . . .'

With a big, solid CLICK the mortice lock opened and Maximilian was able to turn the brass handle and pull the heavy door towards them.

Outside were the wet cobblestones of the road that ran down the side of the Tusitala School for the Gifted, Troubled and Strange. Somewhere a clock was striking five. They were free. But was Effie too late?

Wolf darted off with a simple 'Laters'. Effie took the spectacles back from Maximilian – they were hers, after all – and put them, and the letter opener, in her bag. She was tempted to try to use the ring again, to see if it would make her run fast, but she still felt too weak and tired to be able to use the extra strength properly. Instead, she hurried off into the early evening, drizzle falling all around her, wondering what she was going to find when she got to her grandfather's place. Maximilian offered to come with her, to help. But she just wanted to be alone.

'Effie . . .?' he began, jogging after her.

'What?'

'Wait . . .'

'I can't. I've got to . . .' Effie wished he would go away. But then she remembered that it had been Maximilian's mother who had hurried after her this morning with the ring. Nurse Underwood who had been so kind to her grandfather in the hospital. And if it hadn't been for Maximilian and his knowledge, she would never have escaped detention. And if he hadn't taken off the ring, then she might well even have been dead.

'It's my grandfather,' Effie said. 'He's . . . Well, he died, and left me his library. But my father says we don't have anywhere to put the books and so the charity man is coming and . . . My grandfather left me these things as well, these magical things, these *boons* that you seem to know all about, and . . . I can't explain now, but I have to save his library.'

'Probably full of magic books,' Maximilian mused, puffing. 'Definitely worth saving. Especially as your grandfather . . .'

But whatever he was going to say was lost to a loud clap of thunder.

'All right. Come with me. But hurry,' said Effie.

And on they went through the rain, a long-haired girl in a bottle-green cape followed by a puffing, slightly fat boy, neither of whom had any idea that their destinies were now linked for ever.

67

8

A t the Old Rectory there were several people standing
outside, none of them happy.

'I can get a locksmith in the morning,' Effie's father was saying
to a bald man in an electric-blue shell suit. Was he the charity
man? He must be. He looked extremely annoyed.

'My client doesn't like being kept waiting,' said the charity man.

'I do not like being kept waiting,' agreed a third man, in a
thin, cold voice.

Behind the charity man was a boy in school uniform. It was . . .
Wolf.

'Aha,' said Orwell Bookend, as Effie and Maximilian creaked
through the wrought iron gate and crunched up the wet gravel
driveway. 'Perhaps my errant daughter can shed some light on
the mystery of the missing key.'

Effie frowned. She didn't like it when her dad spoke to her
like this in front of other people, as if she were a character in a
book rather than a real-life person.

'What missing key?' she said.

'Did you, or did you not,' said Orwell, 'hide the key so that we could not get in and remove the books that now belong to this man here?'

'What man?'

The man with the thin, cold voice stepped out of the shadows and offered Effie a tiny pale withered hand.

'Leonard Levar,' he said, drawing out each L in his name. 'Antiquarian Bookseller. I believe that you are the official owner of one of the books in my new library. I had hoped to purchase a complete library, of course, as I have been explaining to your father, and so I wonder if we could come to some arrangement about the final book, and— '

'What are you talking about?' said Effie to her father, ignoring Leonard Levar. 'They're my books and I don't know anything about the key. You had it last.'

'I do apologise for my daughter . . .'

'And you said before that they were "leather-bound junk". Well, they obviously aren't junk. How much is he paying you for them? For my books?'

'Euphemia Truelove, please stop being so rude.'

'I have already said that I will pay the girl for the last book,' said Leonard Levar. 'How much do you want, child?'

'Don't do it,' whispered Maximilian, behind Effie. 'Keep the book.'

'All the books are mine,' said Effie. 'And you are not buying any of them.'

The charity man looked at his watch, and jangled a big bunch of keys. 'I can bust down this door at any time,' he said. 'With the help of my nephew here.'

Wolf looked very uncomfortable. Effie glared at him for a few seconds until his cheeks went pink and he turned away.

'That won't be necessary,' said Orwell Bookend. 'Effie?'

'I've already said I don't have your stupid key,' she said.

Her father's eyes flashed with anger and he strode over and grasped her firmly by the arm. He dragged her over to the hedge where in theory no one could hear what they were saying, but really everyone could. Maximilian moved a few paces closer just to make sure he didn't miss anything significant.

'You have to give me the key,' hissed Orwell. 'Look, I know I said the books didn't have any value, and that's what I genuinely believed, but when the charity man offered me money for them of course I agreed to take it. We are very lucky, Euphemia, that the charity man works for Leonard Levar, otherwise we probably would have had to throw the books away. It transpires that your grandfather was only renting these rooms, and we have to clear them out by next Thursday or pay another month's rent. He used to own the top floor of this building, and we should have inherited it, but it turns out that last year he sold it, no doubt to fund his ridiculous fantasies. We have nowhere to keep the books ourselves. Mr Levar's offer for the books is really very generous. We can put the money towards a new house, which means you can have your own bedroom. If you give me the key now I'm sure we can come to some arrangement with Mr Levar. Perhaps he'll let you keep five books. They're all the same really in the end and . . .'

Through gritted teeth Effie said again, 'I haven't got your key.' Her father's grip tightened around her arm, and then he pushed her away.

'I couldn't help overhearing,' said Leonard Levar. 'And if the child plans to break up the collection I will have to withdraw my offer. I thought I had made it entirely clear that the offer was for the whole collection only.'

'No, it's fine,' Orwell reassured him. 'As you know, I had promised my daughter one book, but I'm sure she won't mind you keeping the collection intact if that's the only way the books can be taken.'

Just then, the charity man's pager beeped.

'More good news, I presume?' said Leonard Levar.

'Yep,' said the charity man. 'Locksmith can do it after all. He'll be here in five minutes.'

'Wonderful,' breathed Leonard Levar.

After that, it all happened very quickly. The locksmith picked the lock and the big wooden door clicked open. Wolf and the charity man went inside with Orwell Bookend and before long they had put a dust cloth on the stairs and were going up and down carrying boxes filled with the books from Griffin Truelove's library. This was probably the worst thing Effie had ever had to watch. Wolf didn't catch her eye the whole time this was going on. She'd thought they were friends, almost, but obviously not.

Up and down they went, Wolf and his horrible uncle, and before long their van was filled with all Effie's grandfather's treasured books. Then there was a metallic sliding sound and the van was closed. The locksmith closed the door, the old lock clicking into place as he did so. Leonard Levar walked slowly over to Effie.

'Here's twenty pounds,' he said, offering her a damp banknote. 'For the final book. Of course, I already have the book, because I now have the complete collection, but I wanted you to see that I am a man of my word.'

'I don't want your money,' she said. 'I want my books.'

'Effie,' said Maximilian. 'Just take it.'

'Aha,' said Leonard Levar. 'Good. A sensible young man. You'll take the money, then, on behalf of your friend, and we can consider this transaction complete.'

Maximilian held out his hand and took the twenty-pound note.

'It'll come in useful,' he said, once Leonard Levar had got into his small black vintage car and driven away after the van. 'You'll see.'

'I can't believe they took my books,' said Effie, her eyes full of tears.

'We'll get them back,' said Maximilian.

'Yeah? How?'

The rain had now stopped but it was still cold. If only Miss Dora Wright hadn't gone down south or whatever had happened to her. Effie needed someone kind to talk to, but there was no one. Well, apart from Maximilian, but he was just a child like her.

Effie's father walked over. 'Right,' he said. 'I've got to go back to the university for a meeting, but Cait will be cooking dinner for you.' He looked at his watch. 'I can probably drop you home if we leave immediately, but . . .'

'I'm not going anywhere with you,' said Effie.

Orwell sighed. 'I don't know why you make everything so difficult,' he said. 'But suit yourself. We can talk about this later.' And he left.

Effie sat on the wall by the hedge. She felt like she might cry. Maximilian didn't know what to do. He couldn't put his arm around her or anything like that. It would be . . . Well, she was a girl, and it would just be wrong. He had never put his arm around a girl, or even thought about it. It would surely be years before he would even have to? He sat next to Effie and tried to think of something to say.

Just then, a rabbit hopped out from under the hedge. It looked this way and that way and then seemed to nibble some grass. It did this in a peculiar way, as if its mouth were already full and it were therefore only pretending to nibble the grass, and it kept throwing sideways glances at the children the whole time it was doing this.

Maximilian wondered what it was doing. He had never seen a rabbit acting more suspiciously than this one. In fact, he had never seen a rabbit acting suspiciously at all. A car went past in the street beyond, its headlights lighting up the wet cobblestones. Then, for a moment, all was quiet. Looking a little like something from a dream, the rabbit hopped over and dropped something at Effie's feet. Then it waited.

Maximilian nudged Effie. 'What's that?' he said.

'What?'

'The rabbit brought you something.'

Effie wiped her eyes and looked down. It was the key to

her grandfather's front door. She picked it up and wiped it on her school cape.

The rabbit looked up at her hopefully.

'Well, you came a bit late,' said Effie.

The rabbit immediately felt sad. It had not pleased the child with the special aura! Effie noticed the disappointed look start to creep over the rabbit's face, and understood that the way it twitched its whiskers meant it was about to cry. Of course rabbits don't cry in the same way humans do, but the main feeling is the same.

'Oh no!' said Effie. 'Oh . . . I'm so sorry, poor rabbit. I meant *thank you*. Thank you so much. Of course if you'd brought the key before, then my father would have been able to get in without a locksmith, and I would never have been able to get into my grandfather's rooms ever again. And even if the books have gone, I can still go in and see if there is anything else I can take to remember him by, and say goodbye properly to all my memories of visiting him there. You're a lovely kind rabbit. Thank you!'

Do rabbits really do things like this, in the real world?

Only if you have quite a lot of magic in you.

9

Maximilian walked into the Old Rectory with Effie and followed her up the stairs. The house had stopped being a rectory around fifty years before, when it had been converted into two large apartments. Downstairs, Miss Dora Wright's rooms sat quietly, waiting for her return. In the hallway a single coat hung limply from a hook, and an umbrella rested forlornly against an empty hat stand. Everything was a little dusty, and there were large cobwebs hanging across the ceiling. But thick oriental rugs spoke of a time of homeliness and comfort. There were several oil paintings on the walls, and glazed ceramic lamps on little tables.

Griffin Truelove's rooms began on the second floor. Here was his small kitchen and dining room and his large sitting room, all the glass-fronted cabinets still full of interesting artefacts from his travels and adventures. Although this room was familiar to Effie, who had been coming here regularly since the worldquake, Maximilian could not believe what he was seeing.

He walked around looking at all the strange objects in the cabinets with wonder, rather as Effie had done when she was younger. The walls were covered with framed maps and charts and paintings of mythical creatures and endless green landscapes. The furniture was old and sturdy, but none of it matched. There was an old red sofa, a yellow armchair, a turquoise chaise longue and a coffee table made from a very dark wood that Maximilian had never seen before.

'Wow,' he said. 'Your grandfather really lived here?'

'Yes,' said Effie. She sighed, and walked around, touching the chair her grandfather used to sit in. 'I suppose this is the last time I'll come here. I don't even know what to do.'

'And your grandfather was really Griffin Truelove?' he said. 'I mean, *the* Griffin Truelove?'

Effie shrugged, not knowing what Maximilian meant. 'I guess so.'

She was checking her grandfather's desk for any other secret drawers; any objects she might have failed to rescue before. She had the feeling that he had made sure she now had all the most important things but . . . She felt behind one of the large drawers on the left hand side of the desk and, indeed, there was a catch she hadn't noticed before. When she released it, a smaller drawer sprung out of the space between the large drawers.

Inside, there were three letters, two with the same gold stamp on them and one without. Each was addressed to Griffin Truelove. Effie scanned the first one. It was from something called the Guild of Craftspeople – it was their gold stamp, it seemed – and told him that he was suspended from performing magic for five years. It had been dated not long after the world-quake. So he hadn't been joking.

Another letter, also with the gold stamp but addressed more recently, told him that his application to become a wizard had been turned down. The third letter had no stamp, no address and no signature. It simply said, *You will pay*. It seemed like some sort of threat. Effie put all three letters in the pocket of her cape.

'Wow,' Maximilian said again, after sniffing a box full of incense. 'And where was the library?'

'Upstairs. I suppose it'll be empty now. I'm not sure I can even . . .'

'Come on,' said Maximilian. 'You can at least say goodbye.'

So they walked together up the wooden stairs, and through the black door with the blue glass window and the polished bone handle. And there it was. A room full of bookshelves with no books on them. One of the saddest things a book lover can see. Each shelf seemed to hold the memory of the books it had once housed. In some cases light had faded the wood around where the books had been; in other cases the shape was made by dust. The shelves seemed to be sighing to themselves, fretting and worrying about where their occupants had gone and when they were coming back.

The room echoed with the children's footsteps as they walked around looking at the places where the books used to be.

'It sounds weird in here,' said Effie. 'I don't like it.'

'Can I ask you something?' said Maximilian.

'What?' said Effie, touching one of the shelves.

'Do you think your grandfather knew that any of this was going to happen?'

'What do you mean?'

'Well, could he have known that your father was likely to sell the books? He made sure you got those magical items somehow. Did he leave you any instructions or anything to tell you what to do?'

Effie decided this was not the time to tell Maximilian that she had ended up with the items almost by accident – and that she would not have the ring at all if his mother hadn't come after her with it.

'He left a codicil. But my father took it and destroyed it. I . . .'

Maximilian looked uncomfortable for a moment.

'Do you think your grandfather might have hidden something for you? Something important?'

'Like what?'

'I don't know. Perhaps . . . Maybe if we used the spectacles . . .?'

Ever since Maximilian had taken the spectacles off, he had wanted to put them back on again. He felt it like an ache, a hunger. He'd read about these glasses, or ones like them, so many times, but he'd never dreamed he would get the chance to use them. He remembered reading that people had once tried to develop glasses like this that were purely digital, not magical, but they had never quite taken off. And they'd had nothing like the capabilities of these spectacles, of course.

Effie got her grandfather's old glasses case out of her schoolbag. She opened it and took out the spectacles. She could see her

78

grandfather wearing them and suddenly wanted to cry again, because she remembered that he was dead and she would never talk to him again. Effie put the glasses on herself for the first time, wondering what she would see, but the world simply blurred in that way it does when you try on someone else's glasses. It felt as if Effie's brain had tipped over to the side slightly.

'I can't see anything,' she said, talking them off. 'I thought you said that they were magic, that they gave you some kind of special power or something . . .'

'They do,' said Maximilian. 'But like I said before, you have to have the right ability – the innate potentiality – for them to work. Give them to me.'

Effie hesitated, then passed them over.

Maximilian put them on. Yes, there was the world, but clearer than ever before. He could see that Effie's energy level was almost half-full now, which was good. There were other stats that he didn't quite understand. He'd have to do a lot more research. He would never have told anyone this, but he was secretly pleased that Effie couldn't see anything through the glasses. He was also pleased that he could see things through them; it meant that he really was a true scholar.

Maximilian had often read about everyone having some innate magical ability, left over from a time when the world was a lot more magical, and he'd always hoped he'd find out he was a scholar, rather than a warrior or a mage or a healer. He felt special, probably for the first time in his life. Not only that; Effie needed him. She needed him to say what he saw through the glasses.

'Well?' she said now.

'It's the same as before. Your energy is looking a lot better, but you should get something to eat soon. Um . . . Right, well, these rooms are even more interesting with these on. I can see which books used to be shelved here – which will be useful when we have to try to get them back. And, well, I don't know where to begin.'

'Can you see if there's anything hidden?'

'Hang on.' Maximilian took off the glasses and gave them a polish with the little cloth from inside the case. 'That's better. You got fingerprints all over them when you touched them. Right. Let's see. There's nothing hidden behind the shelves or under the shelves or in the ceiling cavity or . . . But, *aha*. I see. Over there, under the table, there's a loose floorboard. I think there might be something underneath it.'

Effie got down on her knees and started pulling up the floorboard. And yes, there was something there. A brown package in the shape of a book. Was she going to get her one book after all? The package felt both soft and hard in her hands. She stood up, not bothering to brush the dust off her knees.

'You'd better unwrap it,' said Maximilian.

Again, Effie felt that she'd rather be alone. But she wouldn't have found the book at all if it hadn't been for Maximilian, so she started unwrapping it while he watched. There was a layer of bubble wrap, then brown paper, then another layer of bubble wrap, then another layer of brown paper, and then a layer of cloth, and then a layer of silk. It was a bit like a solitary game of pass the parcel.

Effie unwrapped the last layer very carefully. And there it was. A pale green hardback, with gold lettering on it. Its title was *Dragon's Green*. It was about three hundred pages long and looked very old and very new at the same time, like an antique book that no one has ever read. The cover was in perfect condition and the pages were still crisp and white. Effie opened the book and saw that there was an inscription inside, in her grandfather's handwriting, in his usual blue ink.

To Euphemia Sixten Truelove, the last reader of this book.

Something about the inscription made Effie tingle with fear and excitement. So her grandfather had meant her to have this book in particular. Of course he had – he'd told her to find *Dragon's Green*, after all. But how would he know she was to be its last reader? And what did that even mean? And why hadn't he made it a bit easier to find? Why hadn't he told her where it was? It was surely only luck that she happened to have been in detention with someone who could use the spectacles. This wasn't even a Magical Thinking problem – it was just completely random.

Suddenly there was a noise from downstairs. A scratching, metallic sound, which went on for a few seconds, and was then followed by some drilling. Clearly someone had come to change the locks. Effie and Maximilian crept down the stairs until they could hear what was going on.

'Yes, mate,' she could hear someone saying, in a familiar, gruff voice. 'House clearance tomorrow morning. Nine o'clock, mate. Locks today, clearance tomorrow.' It was the charity man again.

So this was it. This was her last chance to rescue any more of her grandfather's things. But what should she take? Griffin had already made sure she had the most important, magical and precious things. Apart from the books, of course, which Leonard Levar had taken. All except for this one, *Dragon's Green*, which she had almost not found at all.

While the men continued to drill downstairs, Effie walked around the sitting room, looking at the paintings and globes and charts for the last time. *The black book*, she suddenly remembered. The one Griffin used all the time when he was writing translations. The one that had seemed so important to him. Where was that?

It wasn't on his desk, or on the little table by his reading chair. Effie remembered the Magical Thinking problem she had never solved. The lights her grandfather used most were . . . The main light in the library, the lamp by his armchair and the light in the wine cupboard. But he didn't really drink *that* much wine. Maybe there was another reason for him using that light so often?

Effie went into the kitchen and found the cupboard. And there, resting behind a very dusty bottle of Pomerol, was the black book. If Griffin had hidden it, it must be important in some way. Effie put it in her bag.

Back in the main sitting room she scanned all the objects and artefacts, knowing she could only fit a couple more small things in her schoolbag. Maximilian was studying the maps and charts on the walls. She almost asked him what he thought she should take, as he seemed to know so much about these sorts of objects.

He still had the spectacles on. For a moment Effie felt cross that she could not use them to see whatever he saw.

Then something caught her eye. A candlestick set apart from the rest, which was silver and had the same pattern of dragons and the same red stone as on Effie's ring. She took it, and a few candles too. Then she went back to the kitchen and took the last two jars of her grandfather's homemade damson jam from the cupboard. He'd always given this to her on a spoon when she hurt herself, or when she was upset.

With a sad sigh, Effie prepared to leave the room for the last time. Maximilian gave her the spectacles and she put them in her bag. When the drilling was over, Effie and Maximilian hurried down the stairs. Effie was afraid that they would be locked in, but luckily the locksmith had only changed the Yale lock, not the mortice, and so, once they were sure no one was watching, they opened the door and made a run for it.

The children ran through the rain and back towards the Old Town. It was dark and cold and when they stopped running their breath steamed in the air.

'I'm late,' said Maximilian. 'I'd better go home. Will you be all right?'

'I'll be fine,' said Effie. She bit her lip. 'Did you mean what you said before?'

'What?'

'About getting the books back?'

Maximilian had said this when he had the glasses on. They had made him a bit braver somehow. But, yes, he had said it. He nodded.

'Because if you really meant it,' said Effie, 'and if you're really going to help me, then I think you'll need these.' She reached into her bag and pulled out the spectacles. 'Take them home. Do some research, if you can. Find out . . . I don't know. Find out about Leonard Levar and his bookshop. Maybe we can break in. And we need somewhere to keep the books once we have them.'

Maximilian's heart was bounding in his chest like a spring hare. Not just at the news that he could keep the wonderful, magnificent spectacles – well, at least, for now. But every time Effie used the word 'we' his heart soared again. He had a friend, a proper friend, for the first time, and he was determined not to let her down.

Well, that is, not again.

Maximilian blinked away his terrible secret and walked into the cold, dark, rainy evening, resolved to do everything he could to help his new friend.

10

Effie got off the bus in the usual place by the big triangle of grass that had once been a village green. In the depths of a nearby ditch lay a rotten stump of wood that had once been the village's maypole. And what had once been a cheerful pub called the Black Pig was now boarded up. Its windows and doors all drooped with the sad knowledge that their time had come and gone, and never again would they bring light, warmth and safety to the travellers and local people that used to come here to smoke their pipes, sup their ale and eat their rabbit pie.

This was now the bad side of town. Effie had promised her father and Cait that she would never take any shortcuts down any alleyways or speak to any strange people. She was to keep to the bright, well-lit paths, not that there were many of those. At least she wasn't entirely alone; down one alleyway she could see some older teenagers talking, and hear the beep-beep-beep of their pagers going off. Beyond them, some younger boys were practising football, using the lights of old phones to see by.

She was still four blocks from home when she saw something unusual. There, right in the middle of the pavement, was a wooden sandwich board with the words *Mrs Bottle's Bun Shop* on it and a crudely drawn black arrow pointing left down the next alleyway. It seemed to have come from nowhere. Effie was sure it hadn't been there this morning. And she'd never heard of the place. Mrs Bottle's Bun Shop? Round here all you got were cheap pizzas and kebabs. As Effie tried to imagine what such a place would be like, her stomach began to rumble. She'd hardly eaten anything today. She pictured herself walking in through the thin front door of the tiny family house and being presented with another of Cait's shakes. And then she imagined the taste of a bun. Her mouth started to water. Almost immediately she found herself doing the unthinkable and walking down the alley.

It seemed to go on for ever. As she went she could hear sounds coming from the backs of houses: crying babies, mewing cats, the thwacks and *ow*s of little brothers being beaten up by big brothers, sports or news on TVs turned up too loud. It was dark, wet and still cold. But at least there wasn't a greyout due, with the horrible spooky silence when everything is turned off.

At the end of the alley was another sign, just like the first. *Turn left for Mrs Bottle's Bun Shop*, it said. Effie turned left. She walked along for two or three minutes until she came to another sign. *Turn right for Mrs Bottle's Bun Shop*. More signs got her to turn left again, and again, and then right, until Effie was quite worried about how far from home she was. Then she came to a final sign that said, perplexingly and simply, *Turn around*.

And there it was, nestled in an old parade of boarded-up shops, between a long-defunct dry-cleaner and a derelict hair-dressing salon with shattered glass on the pavement in front of it. In a place like this, Mrs Bottle's Bun Shop was impossibly bright and cosy-looking. The façade was pink brick, like something from a fairytale. The windows had little yellow shutters, which were open, but all the glass was so steamed up it was impossible to see inside. Effie wondered what the remains of her lunch money – about seventy-five pence – would buy her in here. Lunch seemed a long time ago – although she'd hardly been able to eat anything. Then she remembered Leonard Levar's twenty-pound note. Not that she wanted to spend any of that. She wanted to give it back to him when she reclaimed her books. Oh – and Maximilian still had it anyway.

Perhaps this was a bad idea? But she was so hungry.

Just then the door opened and a woman poked her head out. She looked one way, then the other, then focused on Effie. The woman had blonde dreadlocks and was wearing bright red lipstick and a black apron.

'Well?' she said to Effie. 'Are you coming in?'

'Are you Mrs Bottle?' said Effie.

'Ha!' said the woman. 'The cheek! I love it. That'll be Miss Bottle to you. Mrs Bottle was my dear mother, now sadly departed. Well, are you coming in before we put the secrecy back on, or not?'

'The what?'

'Oh, do just come in, for the love of spoons,' said Miss Bottle. 'Have a bun. You look like you need one.'

87

'I haven't got much money.'

'Money?' Miss Bottle said this as if it were a completely alien word in this context, like 'owls' or 'muesli'.

'Er . . .'

'Oh lawks, oh bless, you're a newbie! A Neophyte! Have you recently epiphanised, love? Did it hurt? Was it . . . legal?'

'A Neophyte?' Effie said this the way Miss Bottle had. *Knee-o-fight*. It sounded weird, although not as weird as the other things she'd said. 'I don't understand . . .'

'You are a Neophyte, aren't you? Or higher? Otherwise you wouldn't be able to see us and I certainly wouldn't be able to let you in.'

'Yes,' Effie said, nodding. 'I must be. I mean, I am.' If it was true that only Neophytes – whatever they were – could see the shop, then Effie must have been one, since she could see it perfectly clearly. So it wasn't really a lie. Anyway, it seemed the best thing to say, especially as she was now very curious about what was beyond this oddly misty-looking door.

'Well, if you don't come in now, we're going to disappear, because I'm going to put the secrecy back on. Can't say it more plainly than that. You have three seconds. Three, two . . .'

Effie went in.

Inside, Mrs Bottle's Bun Shop was a café unlike any other Effie had ever seen. There were twelve small round tables, and no two were the same. Some were wooden, some were tiled, some had mirrors for tops. Each one had a silver napkin holder filled with pale blue paper napkins and silver salt and pepper pots that did not match. Each table was lit with a thin white candle stuck in an old green bottle. In one corner was a wood-burning stove in which some fragrant logs smouldered slowly. A black cat was asleep on its metal hood. A transistor radio was playing fast, complicated jazz and there was the faint murmur of conversation coming from the darkest corner.

On the wall to the left of the door were several blackboards on which were chalked the menus. BUNS said one of them, at the top, then: *All can be vegan (V), gluten-free (GF), or enchant-ment-free (EF)*. Then there was a list. *Sausage bun, Currant bun, Chelsea bun, Steamed bun, Honey bun, Cheese bun, Lotus seed bun, Cream bun, Cinnamon bun, Hot cross bun, Fried bun, Soup of the Day (with bun)*.

Beside this was a list of drinks, which included fourflower water (sparkling or non-sparkling), buttercup milk and four different types of hot chocolate. Then there was a whole other blackboard that had the word REMEDIES at the top. Under-neath this was a list of things that Effie had never heard of, including *Violet syrup ('for the easily startled traveller')* and *Threeweed tea ('for the hex')*.

In front of Effie was a counter behind which Miss Bottle now stood, drying teacups with a blue and white striped tea-towel. On the counter was an old-fashioned till with big round ivory buttons. The last transaction showing on the display at the top of the till was, rather improbably, 18,954.64. Someone had had rather an expensive afternoon tea. Or perhaps the cat had just walked on the keys.

'Well, sit down, sit down,' said Miss Bottle, waving her tea-towel.

Effie went and sat at the table closest to the wood-burner. Miss Bottle came over with a small blue pad and a thin black pencil.

'So, can I get you a bun?'

Effie's stomach rumbled so loudly that she was sure Miss Bottle could hear it.

'How much are they?' asked Effie. There were no prices on any of the boards.

'Oh yes, I forgot. A Neophyte.' Miss Bottle scratched her head. 'Is this the first time you've travelled, dearie? Apparently it can make you feel a bit sick the first time, but a bun will help. I think I'm not really supposed to let Neophytes through without a letter from the Guild, but if you've got your mark and your card I'm sure you'll be OK. Anyway, I haven't got time for all these questions! Let me scan you.'

Miss Bottle took out a device that looked like one of those old credit card readers they had in shops before the worldquake. She waved it around in front of Effie.

'Your M-currency stands at 34,578,' she said. 'Not bad for a Neophyte. That would buy you around four thousand buns or seven thousand cups of hot chocolate. The remedies are more, but not much more.'

'So I can afford a bun and a cup of hot chocolate?'

'You certainly can.'

'Well, I'll have a cinnamon bun and a hot chocolate with nutmeg. Thank you.' Effie had never had nutmeg before, but it sounded interesting, like something from one of her grandfather's books.

'And do you want those enchantment-free? If you're a newbie I would say a definite yes, although of course whatever you do is up to you. Mind you . . .' She looked at her watch. 'The girl who does the enchantments doesn't come in until later and I think we might be out of enchanted cinnamons anyway.'

'Oh. Well, thank you, yes – enchantment-free, please.'

There was a door just off the bar area, which seemed to lead to a kitchen. This door now swung open as a girl of about Effie's age appeared, with her hair in two plaits and a chef's hat on her small head. She was walking a bit too fast, carrying a bright white iced cake on a metallic cake stand with a glass dome. She put this on the counter and moved it backwards and forwards until she seemed satisfied it was in the perfect position before going back into the kitchen. She returned with two more cakes – one brown and one red – and arranged them in a similar way before taking a bag of what seemed to be dried daisy heads out of a cupboard and going back, too quickly, towards the kitchen.

'Oh, do be careful, Lexy,' said Miss Bottle. 'Slow down.'

Lexy? Effie looked properly and saw that the girl walking too fast between the kitchen and the shop was indeed her classmate Alexa Bottle. She must have been Miss Bottle's daughter or niece. Lexy saw Effie too, and couldn't have looked more taken aback if Effie had been a ghost or a dinosaur. She frowned, then half-smiled, then frowned again. She took off her hat and put it on the counter.

'Can I go on my break, Aunt Octavia?'

'Make it a quick one,' said Miss Bottle, winking at Effie.

Lexy came over. 'Hi,' she said, slightly shyly.

'Hello,' said Effie. 'I'm . . .' For some reason she wanted to say sorry, although she wasn't sure what for. But she did feel awkward now that she realised that she'd accidentally stumbled into a classmate's private life. This was an unspoken rule at the Tusitala School for the Gifted, Troubled and Strange (and probably at most other schools, too). Being invited round to your friend's house for tea was one thing. Going and gawping at them doing their after-school job was something else entirely.

And in any case, Lexy and Effie weren't friends. They sometimes shared a protractor during maths, but had hardly ever spoken. Effie couldn't have anyone round for tea for obvious reasons (imagine taking your friend home for a horrible milkshake with no milk in it). She'd been to Raven Wilde's house in the countryside once, but that was it.

But Lexy seemed not to mind at all. In fact, she seemed pleased to see Effie.

'Well,' said Lexy, sitting down. 'I mean, it's OK if I join you, right?'

'Yes, of course.'

'Well,' said Lexy again. 'Wow.'

'What?'

'I had no idea you were one of us. Well, one of them. Or one of us. When did you epiphanise?'

11

'Epiffa-what?' said Effie.

'Epiphanise. Like when you have your epiphany? Some people call it "the change". When you get your magic.'

'My magic?'

Just then, Effie's bun arrived. It was large, soft and fluffy, with sticky swirls of cinnamon running all the way through it. She ate it in about three mouthfuls and found she was so hungry she could have eaten another one immediately. But then came her hot chocolate – and Miss Bottle had brought one for Lexy too. The hot chocolate had whipped cream on the top, and marshmallows that tasted of cinnamon and cardamom and other spices that Effie couldn't possibly name. It was easily the most delicious thing she had ever tasted. Although not as delicious as what she had just heard. *Magic*. Her magic.

'You wouldn't have been able to see the signs for the shop unless you were at least a Neophyte,' said Lexy.

'What is a Neophyte exactly?'

'OMG – don't you know *anything*?' said Lexy, smiling. 'It's the first grade of magic. What you become after you epiphanise. The top grade is wizard, although no one ever gets there. Well, some people do but it takes for ever and . . .' She sipped her hot chocolate. 'TBH, not everyone notices when they have their epiphany, so it's not that weird. Sometimes people do some proper magic by accident and – bang! – their inner ability awakens. Or they touch something they didn't know was magical. Most people get secretly taught by a relative, although since the worldquake the Guild has made it totally illegal to teach anyone anything about magic. Anyway, only people who have epiphanised can see places like this. And only serious travellers really come here anyway. We're a one-way portal, after all. So I was a bit surprised to see you!'

'Travellers? Like . . .?'

Lexy grinned. 'You know, travellers to the Otherworld.'

The Otherworld. Where Pelham Longfellow supposedly was. Where Dr Black had tried to get Griffin. The place Effie's father had said didn't exist.

'Is the Otherworld actually real?'

'Oh yes. Of course.'

'Have you been there?'

Lexy shook her head. 'Nope. I'm not allowed, because I work in a portal. The Guild frowns on that. But I couldn't go anyway because I don't have my mark, or any papers. Anyway, I'm concentrating on my M-grades at the moment. If you get to be a wizard you can live in the Otherworld for ever, but it takes most people hundreds of years, and apparently the Otherworld is really weird anyway and . . .'

Effie sipped her hot chocolate, the nutmeg making it taste earthy and comforting. Her head was swirling with new information. So she had epiphanised, whatever that meant, and become magical. It was all real, despite what her father had said. All those years of asking her grandfather to teach her magic, and now it turned out that he couldn't anyway because this Guild wouldn't allow it. This was, presumably, the same Guild that had banned him from practising magic for five whole years. And stopped him from becoming a wizard.

'You can do your M-grades as well, now,' said Lexy, excitedly. 'Do you know what your ability is? I'm not sure about mine yet. I so wish I knew! If you can find someone to take you on, you can move up a grade from Neophyte to Apprentice. Aunt Octavia is a Proficient alchemist, which means she could take me on if I wanted to be an alchemist, but I really want to be a healer. I don't know any healers, let alone Proficient or Adept ones, so I'm stuck. But I can still train as a non-ability Neophyte. It's Monday nights in St George's Hall, if you're interested.'

'So can you actually do magic?' asked Effie.

'Sort of. Not very much, yet. I've got no boon, no familiar, no mentor and hardly any M-currency. Which is pretty rubbish, really. But everyone's the same since the Guild made it illegal to pass on boons or even talk about magic to anyone who hasn't epiphanised. Everyone starts from nowhere, really.'

Effie had heard that word recently. *Boon*. Wasn't that what Maximilian had called the Sword of Orphennyus, and the Spectacles of Knowledge, and her ring? The things her grandfather had left for her? Yes, that's right: and hadn't Griffin in fact called them 'boons' as well? 'Get as many boons as you can.' That was what he'd said, wasn't it? Effie wondered about showing Lexy the things in her bag, but she wasn't sure. She wasn't sure about anything, all of a sudden.

Effie remembered with a horrible pang the occasion when her grandfather had been angry with her for the first and only time. It had happened just over a year ago, on a stormy summer afternoon not long after she'd started using his library.

She'd been exploring all the books, flicking each one open to a random page to see roughly what it was about, and whether there were any interesting pictures. Some of the books did have pictures – of tall mountains, deep wells, mythical beasts and strange toadstools. She hadn't thought at all about the rule that she should leave out on the table the book she was reading, nor that she had promised to read one book at a time. She wasn't really reading them, anyway. She was just flicking.

Then Griffin had come in without Effie noticing and had shouted at her to put the book back on the shelf immediately. He'd used a horrible deep growly voice she had never heard before. 'Calm down, Grandfather,' Effie had said in reply. 'It's only a *book*.' The memory of it made her wince now. She'd made it sound so haughty.

'You silly, silly child,' he had said, sounding sad and disappointed. 'Some people think opening a book is a simple thing. It's not. Most people don't realise that you can get truly lost in a book. You can. Especially you. Do not open any of these books without my permission, Euphemia. If you can't promise me that I'll have to go back to locking the library door.'

On the way home that night, Effie had asked her father why

he was always so worried about magic. After all, if something didn't exist, surely it could not hurt you. But Orwell had just started going on and on about how lots of things that are untrue nevertheless become dangerous when people believe in them. In this category he had included all major world religions, all alternative medicines, all theories about what caused the worldquake, all forms of folklore, all Laurel Wilde books, any research produced by the Department of Subterranean Geography at the university and . . . Somewhere in the middle of his lecture he had paused.

'Your grandfather hasn't been filling your head with nonsense again, has he?' Orwell had said. 'I don't want you brainwashed with any of the rubbish that corrupted your mother.'

Effie sighed now in Mrs Bottle's Bun Shop as she realised how little she had in fact been 'brainwashed', and how much she did not know. Her father seemed to think that Griffin had been talking about magic all the time. She had no idea what Orwell had meant about 'the rubbish' that had 'corrupted' Aurelia Truelove. No one had ever really explained properly to Effie what had happened to her mother, or how magic might have been involved.

'What's it like?' Effie asked Lexy now. 'Doing magic, I mean.'

'What's it like?' said Lexy. 'It's really, really, really hard. It's different in here than it is out there,' Lexy nodded her head in the direction of the door to the street, 'and over there,' she nodded in the opposite direction, 'in the Otherworld. Magic is much, much stronger in the Otherworld, because that's the Otherworld's main driving force. It basically runs on magic. Electricity and other stuff like that does work there apparently, but it's all a lot weaker. Only the most powerful wizards have electric lights, for example; the rest of them still use candles. And magic does work in our world, the Realworld, just about, but you need a lot of M-currency to do it. And you have to really concentrate. It's like meditation but a lot more so. That's what Dr Green says, anyway. He's the teacher on a Monday night.'

'And do people actually go to the Otherworld?'

'Of course. And you're going, surely? I mean, I thought that's why you were here.'

'I don't really know why I'm here,' said Effie, sighing. 'I've had a very confusing day.'

She started to tell Lexy about everything that had happened, but when Lexy heard the name 'Griffin Truelove' she widened her eyes.

'OMG,' she said. 'I'd totally forgotten your surname was Truelove. Are you seriously related to *The* Griffin Truelove? I'm going to have to get Aunt Octavia out to hear this. She won't believe that you're Griffin Truelove's granddaughter.'

Octavia Bottle came out, wiping her hands on her apron.

'What's all this?' she said. And Lexy began to tell her.

'If you'd only said you were a Truelove,' she said to Effie, smiling. 'Well, your bun's on the house for a start. Poor old Griffin.' She sighed. 'You'd better start from the beginning again.' And she smiled encouragingly, as Effie started her story again and told all about her grandfather's death, and the things she'd inherited, and the charity man and how horrible it had been watching her grandfather's books being taken away by the horrible, shrivelled Leonard Levar.

'Diberi,' said Lexy. 'He must be.'

Octavia frowned. 'Probably best not to say that word, lovey.'

'But . . .'

'You know what the Guild thinks about the Diberi.'

'But . . .'

'What a lucky girl you are,' said Octavia to Effie, 'coming by all those boons, just like that. You be careful with the ones you've got. Especially that ring. That sounds rare. And how amazing to find a true warrior and a true scholar just like that! Although they do say that boons attract those with abilities that match them. If a boon doesn't match your ability it won't want to stay with you, so they say. Then again, it's much harder to pass on boons nowadays. You used to see them for sale in *The Liminal* for hundreds of thousands of krubles. But the Guild has cracked down on all that since the worldquake.'

'I don't understand,' Effie began. 'If Wolf is a true warrior and Maximilian is a true scholar, then what am I? What does my ring mean?'

Lexy shrugged and looked at her aunt. Octavia frowned again.

'I've no idea. You're not a healer, or a witch, I don't think. Pretty sure you're not a bard or an alchemist or a mage. Maybe a druid, but it doesn't fit, somehow. The ring's an unusual item for sure. Your grandfather must have kept it for you, or obtained it specially, probably when he realised that you weren't going to be a scholar like he was. You'll probably find someone to ask on the other side. They have big books there to help you, apparently. *The Repertory of Kharakter, Art & Shade* is the main one. Get someone with that to give you a consultation.'

'OK. Um . . . What "other side"?'

'The Otherworld. That's what you're here for, surely.'

At that moment, the whispering in the corner stopped and a man stood up. He was wearing black jeans, cowboy boots and a leather jacket. His hair was white-blond and stuck up in clumps all over his head.

'Excuse me,' said Octavia, and got up from the table.

She went over to the man and exchanged a few words with him, before scanning him with the same device she'd used on Effie. Then she walked with him to another door just beyond the bar. Effie hadn't noticed it before. Instead of having a sign saying something like EXIT or TOILETS it simply said OTHERWORLD. At least you couldn't get lost.

Octavia Bottle and the man in the leather jacket paused before the door. There was a little lectern there, Effie realised. It looked like the kind of counter you might go to if you were checking in for an international train journey or a flight. Octavia stood behind it and the man presented her with some documents and she scanned them before stamping something that looked like a passport. He then rolled up his sleeve and showed Octavia something on his arm. Only then did Octavia click the button that made the door open. Effie could see something like a blue mist beyond it. The man walked through.

When Octavia came back she didn't sit down.

'Well,' she said. 'I've got buns to make. Are you going through?'

'Sorry?' said Effie.

'Do you want me to let you through to the Otherworld before the rush starts?'

12

Effie suddenly felt afraid of the blue mist and the Otherworld beyond. But that was where she was supposed to go, surely? That was where she was supposed to find Pelham Longfellow, although of course she had no codicil to give him. But perhaps he could help her in some other way.

'All right,' said Effie slowly. 'What do I do?'

'Come with me,' said Octavia Bottle.

Effie gulped, stood up, and then followed Octavia over to the lectern.

'Papers?' said Octavia. But of course Effie didn't have any.

Octavia frowned. 'Sleeve?'

Effie rolled up her sleeve the same way she'd seen the blond man doing. There was nothing there. Of course there wasn't. She felt hot, suddenly, and very embarrassed. Did this mean she wasn't magical after all? Was she not a Neophyte? Not a true something? Of course Lexy had said that she couldn't go through this door either, so maybe it was just normal but . . .

Hadn't her grandfather told her to find Pelham Longfellow? And her father had said he would be in the Otherworld. Was this all some big mistake? She shouldn't have come here, though. That was clear.

'I'm sorry,' she said to Octavia. She felt so ashamed.

Octavia looked confused.

'Are you absolutely sure you haven't at least got a document saying you are free to pass between the worlds? Your grandfather didn't give you anything?'

'Positive,' said Effie.

'Then why are you even here?'

Effie shrugged sadly. 'I don't know,' she said.

'I can't let you cross over without your documents,' said Octavia. 'As well as a passport you should really have your M-card and the mark. If I did let you go, it would be a disaster. The Guild would revoke my licence.'

'Where do I get the documents?'

'Now, that I don't know,' said Octavia. 'Liminals – the people who come in here – are a bit of a mystery, to be honest. I don't know what happens to them in there,' she gestured towards the door to the Otherworld, 'but they aren't half blooming secretive about it. As far as I understand it, you have to have been in once to be allowed back, but how you get in the first time without any documents or anything, I don't know. I must admit I did wonder how you'd have the mark – but you do hear stories. Your grandfather was so well-connected that nothing would really surprise me. He didn't always do what the Guild said, that's for sure. And he had all those boons . . .'

Effie wiped a tear from her eye. She couldn't cry here. She had to just . . .

Octavia patted Effie's shoulder kindly. 'Look, it's not the end of the world if you don't get to the other side,' she said. 'I've never been there either. Lexy would love to go, but she's never had the opportunity, poor thing. There's no shame in not going. Some people say it's terrifying anyway, and completely different from here. Although it does seem a shame that you've got your magic ring and all that M-currency and you can't even use it. Maybe you can sell it all to someone for krubles or Realworld money? Or you could try to find another way in, although I don't know how you'd do that.'

'Well, I'm sorry for putting you to the trouble of trying to let me though this way,' said Effie. 'I'd better get home. I'm late as it is.'

She felt so sad and, now that the embarrassment had faded, sort of cold and alone. She started putting her cape back on.

Octavia said goodbye and went back into the kitchen.

'Do you want a tonic before you go?' said Lexy.

Effie had tears in her eyes. 'What will it do?'

'Help you out there. You said you were hungry, and you looked a bit weak when you came in. The buns are sort of magical. It's complicated, but they don't give you much actual Realworld energy. And after all that stuff with the ring . . . A tonic will help you get a bit of strength back. Maybe help you stay up and read? After all, you've got that book, *Dragon's Green*. Maybe that's got some answers in it.'

'OK,' Effie said, wiping her eyes. 'Thanks.'

'The only thing you have to do is give me a tiny amount of Realworld money. It doesn't matter how much. It can be five pence or two pence. It's just that we're not allowed to give away tonics for free. There's a Guild rule and . . .'

Effie reached into her schoolbag to try to find her battered old purse. But . . . How odd. Something was vibrating somewhere inside. She wasn't allowed to have a pager until she was fourteen, and unlike many of the other children she didn't carry an old phone to use as a calculator, dictionary and torch. What could it be? She put her bag on the table and the vibrating got stronger. It seemed to be coming from the drawstring pouch that Dr Black had given her this morning. Effie reached in and found the clear crystal she'd originally taken from her grandfather's secret drawer. When she put her hand around it, the vibrating stopped.

'What's that?' said Lexy, leaning forward.

'It's the crystal I got from my grandfather,' Effie said. 'It seemed to be vibrating for some reason. It's stopped now.'

'Could I . . .?' Lexy reached across the table. 'Could I see it? If it's what I think it is, then, well, I'd love to just look at it for a moment. In fact . . . I might even be able to use it to make your tonic stronger if I can just hold it for a few seconds.' She blinked shyly. 'But only if you don't mind.'

Effie shrugged. 'OK.' She held it out. It was a large oval-shaped clear quartz crystal mounted in a silver circle with a dark green stone set in it. There was a hole you could put a chain through so you could wear it around your neck, but no chain. It was very beautiful to look at, and heavy and reassuring to hold, especially now that it had stopped vibrating. It didn't make Effie feel anything particularly different when she touched it. To her, it didn't seem like a magical object at all – just a very nice one. And it didn't seem like something she'd wear herself, more like something she'd admire on someone else.

Lexy's eyes grew bigger and bigger.

'Oh my goodness,' she said. 'Wow.'

Effie put the crystal on the table between them so that Lexy could pick it up and look at it properly. As soon as she'd put the crystal down, it seemed to do a little hop in Lexy's direction, and then began vibrating again.

As Lexy's hands got closer to the crystal she started giggling uncontrollably. 'It's so tingly!' she said. 'Ow! It tickles. Stop it. Come here, you . . .' She started talking to the crystal as if it were a small, recalcitrant animal that she wanted to coax into its hutch so that she might give it its supper. Her words got softer and more jumbled until Effie could have sworn she was hearing some kind of magic spell. Lexy's small hands came close to the crystal, then moved away, then closed in on it. 'Got you!' she said, finally, as she picked it up.

'What's going on?' asked Effie.

The crystal now sat in the palm of Lexy's hand. Lexy herself looked as if a very flattering light had just been shone on her, as if the sun had come out above her head and no one else's. Suddenly, she seemed so much more alive, vibrant and powerful than she had before, although with a strange touch of melancholy too. The crystal wriggled around on her palm as if it were trying to get comfortable, moving this way and that before it finally stilled with – unless Effie was simply imagining this – a happy little sigh.

'It's so beautiful,' said Lexy. 'And it does fit me. I wondered.'

'What do you mean? And why do you look so sad?'

Lexy frowned. 'It means I really am a true healer. It's a healing crystal – the only one I've ever seen. The only one I'm ever likely to see.' She handed it back to Effie. 'Thank you for letting me try it. I can add a bit more oomph to your tonic now, at least.'

The crystal clearly didn't want to go back to Effie. It arrived in her hand feeling cold, heavy, and sort of sulky. It then got heavier and heavier until Effie had to put it down again. Once it was down, it started shuffling back across the table towards Lexy.

'Don't,' Lexy said to it. 'You belong to her.'

'It wants to go to you,' said Effie.

'Well . . .' said Lexy. 'I suppose it does. I'm sorry, I didn't think that would happen.' She looked down at it fondly. 'Shoo,' she said. 'You don't belong to me.'

The crystal simply threw itself into her lap and crawled into one of her pockets.

'I'm so sorry,' she said to Effie, taking it out and putting it back on the table. But the same thing happened all over again. 'Look, I'll get your tonic and then I'll think of some way to persuade it to go back with you.'

While Lexy was in the kitchen Effie tried to make sense of what had happened today. It seemed clear to her now that the crystal had brought her here so that it could find Lexy. That was the only explanation. Why else would her new abilities have brought her to a portal to another world that she wasn't even allowed to access?

Effie couldn't help feeling a bit disappointed that she had inherited these wonderful objects from her grandfather and the only one that worked on her had almost killed her. The pleasure that Maximilian had in the glasses, and that Lexy had in the crystal – Effie herself had felt none of that with the ring. Well, it had felt amazing when she was playing tennis. But then she'd been so very drained afterwards – and, if Maximilian was to be believed, she had almost died. And something about the ring just felt wrong. As if it weren't really meant for her. But hadn't her grandfather said he'd found it specially?

Lexy came back a few minutes later with a silver flask.

'It's not enchantment-free, I'm afraid,' she said, with a twinkle in her eyes. 'It'll give you a bit of strength and help you read in the dark if you have to. I hope you like it.'

'Thank you,' said Effie.

Lexy took the crystal from her pocket and offered it to Effie. The crystal seemed to duck, cower and try to hide, then it turned and rushed up Lexy's sleeve.

'Oh dear,' she said.

'You'd better keep it,' said Effie.

'I can't. It's worth thousands and thousands of . . .'

'I don't care about that.'

'And it's illegal to give away a boon unless you register it with the Guild.'

'Well, why don't you borrow it, then? We're friends now, and friends lend things to one another. Like a long-term loan. Who knows? Maybe you'll be able to use it in some way to help me find my grandfather's books and get them back.'

Lexy rushed over and threw her arms around Effie.

'I'll be your healer,' she said. 'Just like in the stories. You won't regret this. Thank you, thank you. I'll start working now on remedies and tonics to help you get the books back. Something to make Leonard Levar a bit sleepy, perhaps.' Her eyes were sparkling. 'Actually, wait here a moment,' she said. 'I'm just going to go and get . . .'

When she got back she was holding a box with two brand-new walkie-talkie radios inside it. Effie had seen these devices plenty of times before but had never touched one. Only well-off children had two-way radios. And you needed to have a best friend to share one with anyway. After the worldquake, radio waves were the only thing you could really count on, and some of the richer and more popular children now had three or four of these devices in their bags – one for each friend. But it was more common to carry only one, which was connected to your best friend, and use your pager (if you had one) for everything else.

'This was my Christmas present last year,' said Lexy. 'But I hadn't found anyone to give the other one to before now. They've got a ten-mile range, so we can stay in touch always. And you can give me instructions on what sort of healing tonics you want.'

'Are you sure?' said Effie.

'Of course I am,' said Lexy.

'Thank you.'

Effie put one of the radios in her bag, thanked Lexy again for her tonic, and left.

13

So far, this was the best day of Maximilian's life. Well, sort of. Well, it would be, were it not for . . . But he wasn't going to think about that. His horrible secret.

Anyway, he'd done it. He'd done what he'd always dreamed about. He'd epiphanised.

Maximilian lived with his mother on the other side of town from Effie and Lexy. It would take about half an hour, if you had a really fast bike (or, in days gone past, a broomstick), to get from Mrs Bottle's Bun Shop to the university. After that, you'd cycle (or fly) past the Tusitala School for the Gifted, Troubled and Strange, where Mrs Beathag Hide was currently feeling cross and rather baffled, past the Old Rectory with its brand-new locks, past the hospital and the cemetery and the botanical gardens. You'd go down a road with big houses and ancient trees and around a corner. And then you'd get to a block of flats with concrete stairs, where a boy was currently pacing up and down the length of his room wondering what to do about everything.

If you carried on past these flats to the end of the road, you'd get your first view of the sea. And there, around the corner and opposite the bingo hall, in a small bungalow with a pretty front garden, was Maximilian, with his magic freshly awoken, happier than he'd ever been.

Except for, well . . . *that*. The thing he wasn't going to think about.

He'd spent the first hour after he'd arrived home simply looking at things through the Spectacles of Knowledge. Everything in his room was different. He could see the contents of his drawers and cupboards without even opening them. The spectacles helpfully provided an inventory of every item he owned and, until he asked them to stop, started working quite hard on finding new ways of ordering his socks, underwear, school uniform and so on, shuffling the items around this way and that in hypothetical scenarios that seemed entirely unnecessary to Maximilian.

As well as looking at items in his room like this, he could, if he wanted, see into the ground beneath the house, and examine all the artefacts that had been buried there over the years. He could check on the battery life of his pager, his scientific calculator and his radio. If he opened a book, the spectacles would tell him all sorts of interesting facts about it, and could provide dictionary definitions or translations of any words Maximilian chose. It was a bit like the way old people said the internet had once been, only more so.

Also, intriguingly, the spectacles seemed to give a set of statistics on every book in the room; a bit like the stats he'd seen hovering around Effie and Wolf. Like Effie and Wolf (but not like the neighbour Maximilian had peered at through the window

110

just now), each book had two status bars – one green, one gold – that seemed to indicate energy or physical strength, along with something else. But books didn't have energy or strength, did they? And as for the something else, the gold bar . . . Well, if that was (as Maximilian suspected) some kind of way of tracking magical power, or M-currency, as it was called on the dim web, then that was just bananas. How could a book have a life, and a magical energy of its own? The neighbour had no magical status bar at all, which was no surprise to Maximilian. But for a book to have one? It didn't seem right, somehow.

After his tea, Maximilian settled down to read old issues of *The Liminal* on the dim web, to see what he could find out about Leonard Levar and Griffin Truelove's library. You usually needed a password and subscription to get into *The Liminal*'s Bulletin Board System – which cost a thousand krubles a year. But the spectacles had kindly supplied him with a lifetime subscription and unlimited access to the back issues.

Maximilian was supposed to be searching for news items, but he kept getting distracted by adverts for exclusive and rare boons – for example, an archer's bow made from silverwood and unicorn gut, complete with fifteen enchanted arrows, all tipped with dodo feathers. It could be shipped from the Otherworld in just three hours for a total cost of 1.5 million krubles, or around a hundred thousand in M-currency.

Also distracting were all the true-life stories of spells gone wrong, disastrous trips to the Otherworld, creatures from the Otherworld currently said to be on the loose, without papers, in the Realworld (these included obvious deviants like the Loch

Ness Monster, the beast of Bodmin Moor, the faeries in the New Forest, Bigfoot, the man in the moon and the Bermuda triangle, plus all the usual yetis, ghosts and so on, as well as less obvious interlopers like the Northern Lights, three royal babies, one prime minister, a scientist and four world-famous athletes). Each issue of *The Liminal* also carried a recipe for a healing tonic as well as a free spell. And there was also a very diverting problem page.

But he had promised Effie.

An initial search for Leonard Levar brought up numerous articles, mainly from the news section of the paper. Although the reporters avoided saying so directly, Leonard Levar was something of an international book thief, involved in almost every major book heist of the last three centuries. He was alleged to own the original Voynich Manuscript – a secret document whose meaning had eluded scholars for centuries – along with a guide to the code it was written in. He allegedly had the minutes to every secret meeting ever held by the Rosicrucians, the Knights Templar and the Speculative Society. He had an unpublished play of Shakespeare's. He had John Dee's diary, a selection of never-seen letters written by Queen Boudica, the lost journals of King Arthur and several unknown tablets from *The Epic of Gilgamesh*. The rarer a book was, the more likely Leonard Levar was to have it.

If he did have any of these books, he had hidden them well. Multiple raids on his antiquarian bookshop had found none of the items he was alleged to have stolen. He had properties in France, Morocco and New Zealand, but searches of these properties had found nothing. Several years before, *The Liminal* had done a special investigation into Leonard Levar, but it found no evidence of the books he was meant to have stolen ever being sold on to anyone else. But what was the point of being an international book thief if you didn't make money from your operation? It was as if every high-profile book acquired by Leonard Levar simply disappeared into some kind of black hole.

Perhaps he just couldn't bear to part with them. He certainly did seem to be a book lover. A *bibliophile*, as he described himself (which is Greek for 'one who loves books'). As well as running his antiquarian bookshop, he currently had a 20 percent stake in the Matchstick Press, an up-and-coming publisher. Perhaps the Matchstick Press was how Levar made his money, as he didn't seem to sell any books from his shop. His tax returns showed a dreadfully poor man making a loss every year, scraping to survive . . .

None of which explained three strange things about Levar. First, if all reports about him were true, he would have to be at least three hundred and fifty years old. Second, whatever the tax inspectors believed about his bookshop, he was clearly very, very rich. A small gossip column piece from the year before seemed to imply that he had recently bought one of the most expensive objects in the Otherworld – a dragonstooth dagger called the Athame of Althea, which had an enchanted platinum handle studded with precious gemstones from both worlds.

The last strange thing was that, for a book lover, Levar did an awful lot of pulping. Pulping, Maximilian had discovered, was a process where unwanted books are melted down into a milky liquid and then turned back into blank paper. And Levar owned 75 percent of a book pulping business in the remote

Borders. Why would such a bibliophile be interested in pulping books? It didn't make sense.

Just then, there was a tap on the window. Maximilian jumped. He wouldn't have been surprised to find Leonard Levar himself standing there, all shrivelled and tiny and frightening, perhaps wielding the dragonstooth dagger Maximilian had just been reading about. Would he murder him slowly, or would it be mercifully quick? People who messed around with Levar's business didn't tend to survive very long, on the whole. *The Liminal* had recorded at least seven suspicious deaths that were connected in some way to Levar. Of course, nothing could be proven, and . . . Maximilian looked up, his heart beating wildly.

It was Wolf.

Maximilian opened his window and Wolf climbed in. He was breathless and wet from the rain and kept looking behind him. He looked as if he'd just played seventy-nine minutes of intense Under 13 rugby, except that he wasn't bleeding. He did, however, look more frightened than Maximilian had ever seen him look before.

'What are you doing here?' said Maximilian.

Wolf tried to catch his breath. He was holding a key, Maximilian noticed: a large ornate brass key with rusty turquoise smears on it. The spectacles scanned first Wolf, and then the key. Wolf's energy was about 50 percent of normal, which the spectacles assured Maximilian was fine, given that he had probably just run halfway across the city. Wolf's M-currency was looking quite low for someone who had recently epiphanised, at around four hundred. The key had no stats at all, which was odd, given that even a pair of Maximilian's socks generated several numbers and a heartfelt suggestion that they be either washed or destroyed immediately. Perhaps the key was cloaked or blocked in some way.

'It's for where he's keeping the books,' said Wolf. 'Effie's books.'

'OK . . .' said Maximilian. The key was was actually more useful than all Maximilian's research. Which made him feel slightly put out. 'So you're on our side now, are you?' he said, sulkily.

'I'm not on any side. I just want Effie to have her books.'

'So where are they?'

'Under the city. You go down to the basement of the old guy's bookshop – you have to go through a secret door behind a false bookshelf to get there – then after that you have to go through an old tunnel until you get to another door. This is the key for that door. Behind the door there's a kind of small cave that leads to a bigger cave full of loads of crates wrapped in plastic. Me and my uncle had to wrap up all Effie's books individually – all blooming 499 of them – he made us count them – and put them in crates and then lock the door behind us. My uncle's going to go totally ape when he finds out I've nicked the key. We're meant to give it back to the old bloke tomorrow when we drop off all the rest of the stuff from the Old Rectory.'

'Well,' said Maximilian. 'That doesn't give us much time.'

'Yeah, well, it was the best I could do. My uncle is literally going to beat the crap out of me when he finds out that— '

Just then the door opened and Maximilian's mother walked in.

'Oh,' she said, pleased. 'You've got a friend here.'

'Sorry, Mrs Underwood, I was just going.'

'Stay for supper,' she said. 'It's homemade cottage pie.'

14

When Effie got home, everything was horribly quiet. Normally there was the sound of the TV or radio and the whirring of the blender and the washing machine and the microwave and the bang-crash of baby Luna in her playpen while Cait did something – even if sometimes this was just blending – about dinner.

Effie walked in and shut the door quietly behind her.

'She's here,' she heard her father say. 'It's all right.'

The next thing Effie heard was a terrible wail, like a sort of primal scream, coming from the sitting room.

'ARRRGGGHHHH . . .'

Effie approached the sitting room. Cait was on the sofa, wrapped in about four different blankets. On the table was an empty pizza box, a half-finished bottle of wine and a dog-eared paperback romance novel – the one that had come with the latest tub of Shake Your Stuff. Effie's father was standing there, holding baby Luna, who was chewing his tie. Perhaps that was all the nourishment she'd had today.

'IT'S ALL SO SAD,' wailed Cait.

'Effie's back now,' said Orwell, throwing his daughter a glance that partly said *I am going to kill you* but also partly said *Help me*.

Effie threw back a glance that said *If you wanted my help you shouldn't have sold my books*, and then she looked away.

'BUT GRIFFIN ISN'T COMING BACK.'

'No, but . . .'

Effie was startled. Was Cait actually crying over her husband's dead wife's father? Cait hadn't seen Griffin for years, and they hadn't exactly been on the best of terms. And Cait had agreed with Orwell that all Griffin's talk of magic and other worlds was 'mumbo jumbo', despite one of the magazines she read reporting a study that said that magic in the world had increased by 10 percent since the worldquake. Well, Effie now knew that her grandfather's eccentric ways had been connected with real magic, and that his library was even more important than she'd thought. She still had to work out some way of rescuing his books and . . .

Effie's stomach grumbled again. Where was her dinner? Since Cait had thrown out all the food, there wouldn't even be any cheese in the fridge for cheese on toast. There'd be no milk to make a cup of hot chocolate . . . although Effie couldn't imagine tasting anything quite as wonderful as the hot chocolate in Mrs Bottle's Bun Shop ever again.

The room smelled of pizza. Cait must have ordered one when she got hungry after realising there was no real food in the house. This was typical of her lately. And she used to be quite nice.

'Is there any more pizza?' Effie said hopefully.

'AND I THOUGHT EFFIE WAS DEAD . . .'

'How could you?' said Orwell to his daughter. 'You've almost given Cait a nervous breakdown. Where on earth have you been?'

'My grandfather died, or have you forgotten? And then someone decided to sell the books he'd left to me. I was a bit upset, and so I'm home a little later than I thought I'd be. It doesn't look like I've missed anything interesting. Well, apart from pizza. Is there any more?'

'You are a cold, callous . . .' Orwell raised his hand, but at the last minute decided he didn't want to be the sort of father who hit his daughter. 'Look at what you are doing to us. You are destroying this family.'

Baby Luna started to cry. She didn't like it when her big sister got into trouble.

'Don't be so dramatic,' said Effie. 'And I don't know why Cait's crying over Grandfather Griffin anyway. She never even liked him.'

'ARRRGGGHHHH!'

'Right. That's it, madam. I've had it with you. You can go straight to bed without any dinner. And take Luna with you.' Orwell passed the baby to Effie. 'I'm going to try to comfort my poor grieving wife.'

Before Effie put Luna to bed she gave her a spoonful of the damson jam she'd taken from her grandfather's kitchen – the jam he said he kept for emergencies. He had once told Effie, with sparkling eyes, that it was 'medicinal'. Well, this certainly seemed like an emergency. Had Luna had anything real to eat today? Effie gave herself a big spoonful of the jam as well. It made her feel warm inside, and even quite full, almost as if she'd had a roast dinner this evening, rather than nothing at all.

Effie took all the important things out of her schoolbag – the walkie-talkie, the Sword of Orphennyus, the wonde, the candlestick, the candles and her grandfather's black book. And of course the ring. She turned each object over in her hands carefully before putting it into the wooden chest her grandfather had given her last Christmas. She opened the black book and saw line after line of her grandfather's handwriting – all in blue ink, and all in Rosian.

Then she got into bed with *Dragon's Green* and the flask of tonic that Lexy had given her. If the damson jam had made her feel that she'd just had a roast dinner, the tonic made her feel as if she'd just followed it with a lovely big steamed chocolate pudding with ice cream. She felt content and restored as she opened the book. Well, almost. Something was wrong. Of course – her grandfather was dead. And on top of that she was worried about the argument she'd had with her father, and found she was still furious with him because of the books. But maybe it wasn't really his fault. Maybe he was just doing what he thought was best. Effie resolved to apologise in the morning – well, sort of apologise, and only if he did too – and turned her full concentration to the book.

Once upon a time there was a girl who . . . it began.

Effie yawned. Oh dear. What with the damson jam and the tonic and the difficult and long day, she had begun to feel sleepy.

But the tonic was supposed to help her stay up and read – even read in the dark, Lexy had said. Effie took a deep breath and started again. Maybe the enchantment needed time to kick in.

Once upon a time there was a girl who was very, very sleepy, the book seemed to say now. How ridiculous. Effie prised her eyes open and started again. *Once upon a time there was . . .* The words blurred. The lines all started dancing around. And then, before she knew it, she was fast asleep.

The first thing Effie heard the next morning was a car horn beeping. There was some conversation that she couldn't pick up and the sound of a car door opening and closing. Then there was the sound of a very powerful and expensive engine turning over quietly outside. The car seemed to be waiting for something.

There was a knock on the door and her father came in.

'Breakfast is in ten minutes,' he said. 'Do you want it in bed?'

Breakfast in bed? What? And why wasn't her father at work?

'OK, thanks,' said Effie. Was this his way of apologising for the night before? 'And I'm sorry for last night. I was just really tired and upset and hungry.'

'Never mind that,' said Orwell. 'How do you want your eggs? Boiled or poached or fried? Sunny-side up? Hard, medium or soft? And would you like toast or soldiers? Brown or white bread? Grapefruit? Cereal? Maybe a bowl of porridge before your journey?'

Effie sat up and rubbed her eyes. 'What journey?'

'You've been invited to Dragon's Green,' said Orwell. 'Your driver's waiting outside. It must be something your grandfather arranged. You've got a private car and then overnight accommodation in the Green Dragon Inn, before . . . Well, the next bit's a surprise. Anyway, breakfast?'

'OK. Thanks. Can I have two boiled eggs with white soldiers, please? And a bowl of porridge. And some grapefruit would be lovely. Thank you.'

'Right away,' said Orwell, with a smile. 'Would you like brown sugar on your grapefruit and clotted cream and honey on your porridge?'

'Yes, please,' said Effie.

While Orwell was cooking breakfast, Cait came in.

'Sorry about yesterday,' she said. 'I've bought you something to make up for it.' She brought in a brand-new suitcase.

'It's all packed for you,' she said, 'with new clothes. It's a capsule wardrobe for a . . . Well, for a trip to a house in the countryside. And here,' now she presented Effie with two boxes, each tied with a silk ribbon, 'is your travelling outfit. I hope it's all right. The lady said it should fit you.'

But Effie had to wait to unwrap her travelling outfit, because just then her sumptuous breakfast arrived. Her father had brought her a cup of hot chocolate as well as all the food, because he knew it was her favourite drink.

When Effie came to put on her travelling outfit she was absolutely amazed. Where had Cait found this stuff? There was a delicate pink skirt with layers and layers of petticoats. It was the lightest, softest thing Effie had ever held, and must have been

121

made of the purest silk. It was the sort of thing that very rich girls might wear for a wedding or a party, but Effie had never seen anything like it before. As if knowing that Effie didn't like to look too girly, whoever had chosen the outfit – could it really have been Cait? – had added a distressed black denim jacket and a dark grey t-shirt with a gold star on it. There was even fresh underwear and a pair of soft grey cashmere tights. In the second box there was a pair of biker boots, and a thick studded belt.

When Effie was dressed she felt like someone else. She'd never worn a pink skirt in her life. Did she like it? She wasn't sure. But she did like the jacket, and the boots. She brushed her hair for the first time in about a week and then pulled it into a loose ponytail.

It was only when she had completely finished dressing that she looked down and noticed the ring on her thumb. She didn't remember putting it on. Should she take it off? But when she tried, it wouldn't budge. Never mind. It went with her outfit. And if – as Effie suspected – she was dreaming all this, it wouldn't matter anyway. In fact, if this was a dream, Effie didn't want to ever wake up, because so far it was the best dream she had ever had.

When she was ready, her family assembled in the thin hallway to wave her goodbye. Even baby Luna looked pleased to see her sister go off looking so glamorous, on such a mysterious adventure. What had Griffin arranged? No one seemed to know. Orwell helped Effie with her suitcase, and then kissed her goodbye, while the driver loaded the case into the boot of the car.

'Write to us?' said Cait.

Effie climbed in and got comfortable on the huge back seat of the car. She carried on waving to her family until they were out of sight.

'Music, miss?' asked the driver. 'I've got R&B, alternative folk, experimental jazz, East Coast hip-hop or drum and bass, if you please.'

'No, thanks,' said Effie. 'How long will the journey take?'

'Around four hours, miss.'

'Well, I might have some music later. Thanks.'

'My name is Percy, miss.'

'Thanks, Percy.'

Although it was still autumn, and quite grey as they drove out of the city and into the Borders, soon they were travelling down bright country lanes lined with meadows. Several of these meadows were full of buttercups, as if it were the height of spring. There were also ox-eye daisies, birdsfoot trefoil, black medick, white campion, clover, self-heal, yarrow, musk mallow and red campion, among all sorts of different grasses. The sun came out and sparkled on little streams and lakes. There were animals grazing contentedly everywhere. There were horses in paddocks and ducks on ponds.

The journey went quickly and did not seem to take anything like four hours. Soon, after turning left and then right and then travelling along an improbably tiny, leafy lane, they were approaching the Green Dragon.

The Green Dragon was an old-fashioned inn of the sort you might find in medieval English stories featuring highwaymen and wild boar. Or one of those very, very old plays that Mrs Beathag

Hide was fond of, where everyone went into a mysterious forest and came out married to the wrong person. The inn was made of yellow brick and its arched entrance was covered in pink clematis. Its windows were almost hidden behind great folds of pale blue wisteria.

Percy didn't drive right up to the entrance, however. Instead, he stopped just before a small wooden bridge that crossed over a winding stream.

He took Effie's case out and placed it on the ground by the bridge.

'I can't cross the water, miss,' he said. 'You're on your own from here.'

This seemed like an odd thing to say. But odd things did happen in dreams. Although Effie wasn't at all sure this was a dream. It seemed so real.

'When will you be back?' Effie asked.

'Can't say, Miss,' said Percy. 'My booking was one-way only. Good luck.'

And then he drove away, leaving Effie standing by the bridge, quite alone, listening to birdsong and the trickle of the stream.

She picked up her case and stepped onto the bridge. As she did, everything became foggy and cold for just a moment, and then went back to normal. After the fog cleared Effie could see she was no longer alone.

A boy a bit older than Effie was walking towards her, but paying her no attention at all. He was dressed in what looked like riding clothes, and carrying a large sword. He looked baffled but pleased as he strode by Effie and off in the direction from which she had come. It was as if Effie were invisible to him. How odd.

She picked up her case and walked towards the Green Dragon Inn, wondering again what her grandfather had arranged for her here. And wasn't she supposed to be saving his books? Maybe she should go back. But Percy had gone and the only way she could move was forward.

Effie wasn't alone for long. Soon a stout woman in an apron came bustling out of the inn.

'Welcome, welcome,' she said. 'Greetings to you.'

'Hello,' said Effie.

'I'm Mrs Little, the landlady. Call me Lizzie.'

'I'm Euphemia. Well, Effie. Do you know when . . .?' she began. She wanted to ask about how long she would be staying; when someone might be coming to pick her up. It had only just dawned on Effie that she had no idea what she was doing here. But Lizzie Little was now looking Effie up and down and touching the material of Effie's skirt as if to check whether or not it was real.

'Another batch of new princesses. Always so exciting!'

'Sorry?'

'Only two of you overnighters this year. Still, you'll meet all the others up at the big house tomorrow.'

Just then, a large car pulled up outside the inn. It stopped, but for a while no one got out. Effie could hear quite a lot of shouting and crying coming from inside. Eventually a door opened, and a girl of Effie's age emerged, looking shaky. She was tall, almost impossibly thin and dressed in a pale cream satin dress that looked like a ballerina's outfit. Her hair was pulled into a high ponytail and tied with a cream ribbon. She was pressing a white handkerchief to her face.

'Please,' she was saying. 'I don't want to . . .' Then a suitcase was handed to her by an unknown person inside the car. 'Please,' she said again. But the car hastily reversed, turned and drove away.

'Oh dearie, dearie me,' said Lizzie. 'This won't do.'

'Is she OK?' said Effie.

'She'll be fine once we get some blackgrain trifle into her,' said Lizzie. 'Anyway, you're sharing a room, so maybe you'll be able to cheer her up. You might need to remind her that it's a great honour to be chosen for an audition at the Princess School . . .'

'Princess School?' said Effie, but Lizzie Little was already striding inside carrying both girls' cases, saying something odd like, 'Doesn't like muscles, of course. Doesn't like them stringy.'

'Are you all right?' Effie asked the girl.

She tossed her ponytail like a horse trying to shake off a fly. 'You seem just fine,' she said to Effie. 'So, yeah, whatever, me too.' She dabbed her eyes. 'Let's suck it up.'

Effie had no idea what the girl was talking about.

'I'm Effie, by the way,' she said to the girl, who had now thrown a leather jacket over her ballerina dress and looked even more stunning than before – except for her red eyes from all the crying.

'Crescentia,' said the girl. 'I'd like to say I'm pleased to meet you, but I really would rather not be here at all. I never wanted to be pretty, you know.'

126

Effie didn't get the chance to ask what she meant, as they were both called in for afternoon tea. The girls were ushered into a cavernous room made entirely of wood, with long polished tables that looked as if they'd been used for thousands and thousands of years. The end of one of the tables was laid for tea. There were cakes, sandwiches and a big trifle. The only odd thing was that almost everything you'd expect to be white, or possibly pale brown – like the bread, the scones, the cakes and the sponge in the trifle – was black. It looked very peculiar indeed. The sandwiches were made with black bread and the scones looked like they were made with the darkest chocolate. But when Effie tried one they weren't chocolatey at all. They simply tasted like normal scones, only much more delicious.

'I don't want anything,' said Crescentia.

'Come on, girly,' said Lizzie. 'Blackgrain's good for you. And let's face it, you're not going to get much chance to eat trifle after tomorrow.'

Crescentia took a tiny helping of trifle and one scone. Effie watched as she broke the scone up into smaller and smaller pieces until her plate was covered in crumbs. She hadn't actually eaten any of it. She managed about one spoonful of trifle and pushed the rest around in her bowl until it turned into liquid.

Effie was about to bite into her third scone when Lizzie went to the kitchen for more tea. Effie had already eaten four cheese and pickle sandwiches and a cream bun. She had a helping of trifle in a bowl, and was very much looking forward to trying it.

'You do know it's drugged, don't you?' said Crescentia.

'What?' said Effie.

'The trifle. I can taste it.'

'Why would they drug the trifle?'

'To make sure we don't run away. Not that there's anywhere to run to.'

'Crescentia,' said Effie. 'Please tell me what's going on. I really have no idea why I'm here. I thought that my grandfather had arranged a trip for me to go somewhere special because . . . Well, he died and left me this book, called *Dragon's Green*, and I was supposed to be rescuing some of his other books, but then a car came to pick me up to take me to a place called Dragon's Green and so I just assumed that something important might happen here. He told me before he died that I had to come here, to Dragon's Green. But I don't know why.'

'Amazing,' said Crescentia, shaking her head. 'So your folks didn't even tell you where you were going. That's neat. Mine have been preparing me for years, ever since I was born so pretty. At one point I tried to run away, but they found me. Then I tried to get too fat to qualify. But apparently they take fat girls occasionally in case the dragon wants to binge.'

'What dragon?'

'What do you mean, what dragon?'

'I don't know. I mean, not a real dragon, though?'

'Do you live on the moon?'

'Well . . .'

'Do you seriously know nothing about why you're here?'

'Truly. And if you could explain what's going on I'd be really grateful.'

Crescentia sighed. 'OK. Look, once this is over we'll try to get out for a walk. I've been here once before with my sister, so I know where to go. We'll tell Lizzie we want to have a look at the dragon. He's pretty spectacular. Then we can talk properly. I'm sorry I was horrible before.'

'That's OK,' said Effie. 'You weren't really. You just seemed upset.'

After tea, Lizzie showed them up to their room. It was a tiny space in the attic with two beds and a small wardrobe.

'Get your audition outfits hung up,' said Lizzie. 'Don't let them get crumpled at the bottom of your cases. And get your wash bags out ready for the morning. It's an early start. The car's coming for you at seven in the morning.'

'Audition outfits?' said Effie quietly. But she was sick of asking questions and so she just copied what Crescentia did. Well, more or less.

She couldn't believe what she found in her suitcase. All the clothes inside it were made by famous designers that Effie had actually heard of. There was a silvery evening gown, a pair of soft black leather jeans, a pair of diamanté sandals with small heels, a cream silk pussy-bow blouse, a cashmere shawl and several other expensive items, all made of silk, cashmere or the finest leather.

'What do you think?' asked Crescentia. She was holding up two dresses. One was very similar to the one she was wearing now, except in pale pink. The other was black and made from a sort of soft suede material. It looked extremely expensive.

'The black one's a bit short,' said Effie. 'But I love it.'

'I could wear it with leggings, maybe? They like you to look sort of classic-contemporary, I've heard. Like, not too girly and princessy exactly, but very refined. A bit fashion. Like a foreign beauty going to a nightclub, or a bohemian dinner party.'

'Do you know what all that even means?' said Effie.

Crescentia grinned. 'Not exactly. But I've seen pictures in the papers.'

Effie watched while Crescentia expertly created an outfit from the clothes she had in her case. The black dress with black leggings – or sheer tights, maybe? No, cashmere tights. The same boots that Crescentia had on now? Or maybe the ankle boots with heels? A long silver necklace with a big mushroom on it? Or maybe the choker with the dragon's tooth. Not a real dragon's tooth, obviously. And long black gloves.

'I'm going to backcomb my hair for tomorrow,' Crescentia said. 'How about you?'

'Let's go for that walk,' said Effie. 'I really need to know what's going on.'

'Oh yes. Silly me. I totally forgot.'

'I need to know why I was supposed to come to Dragon's Green. And then I need to get back home somehow and rescue my grandfather's books.'

'Good luck trying to leave,' said Crescentia, ominously.

The girls borrowed some wellies from Lizzie. They looked really quite strange as they walked down a beautiful green hill towards the village centre. They were still wearing their fine clothes, of course, and Crescentia had put on some lipstick.

From here they could see two big houses, one on top of a hill and the other by a dense forest. There was also a castle that

130

seemed to be made entirely of battlements and looked a bit like a cake that had sunk.

The house by the forest seemed very attractive to Effie, although she couldn't really say why. She could see that it began with an impressive gatehouse, and its two ornate gates were currently shut. A long driveway led up to a fountain, and beyond that, the big house, made from soft yellow brick with a grey slate roof. The house looked warm and inviting. It had lots of large sparkling windows and several mysterious-looking round turrets and small towers all attached in a higgledy-piggledy fashion to the main rectangular building. Effie desperately wanted to go there. But Crescentia wanted to go the other way.

'That's where we're going tomorrow,' said Crescentia, pointing at the house on the hill. 'The Princess School. And down there is the village hall and the mill and the sunken castle. And all those fields beyond – that's where they grow all the blackgrain that's used for miles around.'

'And the dragon?'

'In the sunken castle, of course. Follow me.'

The girls walked past the village hall and down a short tree-lined lane. There in front of them was an old-fashioned village green with a maypole at one end and a cricket wicket marked out in its middle. The village green was surrounded by cosy cottages, all covered in flowers. It was an idyllic scene. People bustled around carrying flowers or baskets full of vegetables or buckets of water from the well. When the villagers saw the girls they oohed and aahed. A couple of the women shyly approached and asked to touch the girls' clothes. A couple of the men said

131

things like 'Thank you for your sacrifice', and then walked embarrassedly on. A boy a bit younger than the girls burst into tears as soon as he saw them and had to be comforted by his mother.

And then there was a terrifying roar.

It had come from the dragon. The roar was not terrifying because it was particularly loud or fierce. In fact, it was hard to say why it was so terrifying, but it was. It was a sound unlike anything Effie had ever heard, low and deep – the satisfied purr of a creature who would really quite enjoy killing you and eating you, who might even play with you a bit first. The dragon roared again – creating a small burst of flames – and then walked over to the edge of his vast garden, sniffing the air.

The girls ducked behind a tree. Effie could not take her eyes from the dragon. He was about twice the size of an ordinary man, with a reptile's face and green eyes that were strangely human. He was dark grey, with shiny scales all over, except for his arms and legs which, apart from being grey, huge, and very muscular, looked almost like a normal man's limbs. His wings, which were folded against his body, were slender, almost silky-looking, the thin grey flesh stretched over their bone structure like the skin on a drum. They gave the impression of vast paper fans, and Effie found herself imagining being cooled by them on a hot night and . . .

'A real dragon?' whispered Effie, still unable to look away.

'Yep,' said Crescentia. 'Handsome, isn't he? They say only a true princess – or a true hero, not that there are any of those – finds him attractive or interesting. To everyone else he's a

132

repellent monster. We mustn't go too close. They say he really can't resist beautiful maidens of any sort. I think he's already smelled us. They say that if he put his mind to it he could bust out of his castle grounds whenever he wanted and rampage around doing anything. It's only because of the work of the Princess School that he sticks around at all.'

Effie forced herself to look away from the dragon.

'Why do they want him to stick around? Why does no one just kill him?'

'Kill the dragon? You must be joking. What planet do you come from?'

'Er . . .'

'The dragon fertilises all the blackgrain fields for miles around.'

'What, like . . .?'

'Dragon poo is the only thing that will fertilise the soil in the right way to grow blackgrain plants. Most people around here can't tolerate any other grain apart from blackgrain. If they didn't have it, thousands of people would probably starve, especially through the winter.'

'So . . .'

The dragon roared again.

'He can definitely smell us,' said Crescentia. 'Let's go and find somewhere to talk privately.'

15

The girls found a spot under a rowan tree just outside the village, near the walls of the big house with the forest beyond. Effie wanted to look at her watch, to see what time it was so she could work out how to get home. But she didn't have her watch on. She'd been so surprised about her new outfit that she must have forgotten it.

'So you've really never heard of the Princess School or anything?' said Crescentia. 'I suppose that's one approach, keeping you completely in the dark. They say it's hard for parents to know how to handle it. And if you come from a long way away . . . I guess they must have sold you just for the money, rather than the glory.'

'*Sold* me?'

Effie felt tears come to her eyes. But she quickly blinked them away. This was almost certainly a dream. But wasn't it supposed to be a nice dream? And anyway, her grandfather wouldn't . . . But what about her father and Cait? They'd already sold her books. And they hated her so much they probably would sell her, given half a chance. But what for? Was it a punishment? Or was it just to stop her from wrecking their stupid deal with Leonard Levar?

'OK, I'm going to pretend you're an alien or something and start from the beginning.' Crescentia tossed her ponytail again. 'So, once upon a time, this village, and all the villages around it, were very, very poor. Every winter, people starved to death because there wasn't enough food. A long way away from here, in the western valleys, a farmer discovered this miracle crop, blackgrain, which, as I've already said, can only be grown in soil fertilised by dragon poo. He sold everything he owned to buy just three small bags of seed from an old magician who happened to be passing through. The magician also threw in a large blue egg, which he said would be useful. The first batch of seeds came to nothing, but that spring the egg hatched. It was a baby dragon. The farmer did a bit of research, consulted another magician or some wise man who was passing through, and found that he could fertilise his crop with the poo he collected from the dragon. With me so far?'

Effie nodded. 'How do you know all this?'

'Literally everyone in the world knows this, apart from you. Anyway, the dragon grew, and so did the crops, and everything was fine for a while. The farmer had a beautiful daughter who helped feed the dragon. On her thirteenth birthday she went out as usual with his bucket of blackgrain and, well, the dragon ate her.'

'He *ate* her?'

'He ate her. Then he ate all the other girls in the village. A couple of the girls' brothers made swords and tried to fight the dragon. He ate them, too.'

'Wow . . .' said Effie. 'That's pretty gruesome.'

135

'Yeah, right? Anyway, to cut a long story short, the dragon was somehow banished from the village. By then, he'd eaten pretty much everyone under the age of twenty anyway. He travelled across the land until he found a community that was willing to take him in. He basically struck a deal. If the village would provide him with one maiden, ideally a princess, every two weeks, then he would leave the rest of the villagers alone and live peacefully, allowing the local farmers to collect his poo to fertilise their blackgrain crops. It was seen by everyone as a win-win.'

'Except for . . .'

'Oh yeah. Except for the princesses.' Crescentia gulped. 'That's us, now, or might be after tomorrow, if we get through the audition.'

'Why exactly would we want to audition for that?'

'Oh, because it's very prestigious to go to the Princess School. Girls who get accepted are virtually guaranteed to become rich and successful in later life. You spend all your time there being taught how to be even more beautiful than you are already. You learn fine conversation skills, how to talk about art and poetry and literature. You learn the great ballads, and all the main healing potions. You learn to identify the most fragrant flowers, and use them to make perfume. You learn to enjoy fine wines and chocolates – although you never get to actually swallow them until the end. You learn to be a refined, rare beauty. Which is exactly what the dragon likes to eat. A princess, basically.'

'So are you saying that the school provides princesses for the dragon to eat every two weeks? That's awful. That's . . .' Effie searched for the word. 'Immoral.'

'It's what they call practical. The dragon would be eating people anyway. This way at least it's controlled. Parents who send their daughters to the school are paid a vast amount in return. Enough to give their other children an exclusive education and buy a big house and all the food they need for the rest of their lives. If you are born pretty, you are almost expected to want to sacrifice yourself for the good of your family and your community. I come from a place that relies on exports of black-grain from here. There are no beautiful girls in the whole place. They all come here to serve their people.'

'But what you said about girls from the Princess School going on to be rich and successful in later life? Surely if they are going to be eaten . . .?'

'Oh,' Crescentia laughed. 'Not everyone gets eaten. The school deliberately takes twice the amount of girls that they need. The dragon's taste changes week by week, and he's always trying different things with his diet, so they need a good stock of brunettes, blondes and red-heads, for example. Girls with pale skin and dark skin. So you can survive. There's no sixth form. If you make it through fifth form without being chosen then you get released back to your family. Although it's supposed to be really exciting being chosen by the dragon. Like, who wouldn't want to die young and beautiful, wearing the finest clothes and draped in the most expensive jewels? And apparently he drugs you first so you don't even feel it.'

'It still sounds terrifying.'

'Yeah, right? Now you know why I didn't want to get out of the car. My sister passed her audition two years ago. She used

137

to send me letters, until . . .' Crescentia's voice started to falter, and it seemed as if she might cry. Then she pulled herself together and carried on.

'Girls who go to the Princess School end up wanting to be eaten, apparently. They actually compete to be chosen by the dragon. The most creepy bit in my opinion is that the girl who's chosen has to spend the night with the dragon before she is eaten the next morning. Apparently that's what all the conversation classes and art appreciation is for. You have to go to the dragon's lair, right to the very heart of the sunken castle, where apparently you are served a fine meal and given the most exquisite wines, flowers and chocolates, and then you have to spend the whole night there, with him. And then . . .' Crescentia drew one finger across her throat. 'That's it. You get up the next morning and prepare to die.'

'So presumably we should just fail the audition on purpose. Get there late or something and just be sent home.'

'Ha! Sent home? If you fail the audition they put you out into the forest to run wild, and you just end up being killed or eaten by something else. A wild boar, perhaps, or a wolf. They have wolves around here, you see. There are also all kinds of weirdoes in the forest. Bandits, vagabonds, people who have been cast out of their villages. They say that some of them have formed tribes and if they find children lost in the forest they catch them and force them to act as their slaves for the rest of their lives. Trust me, you don't want to fail the audition.'

'Right.'

'Also, when you think of how much our parents have spent

on our dowries, like, you know, the extremely expensive clothes we take with us, and all the endless audition preparation – nails, hair, eyebrows, teeth, skin – they want something back.'

Effie looked down at her hands. Nails? She had never had her nails done in her entire life. Eyebrows? She wasn't even sure what that meant. She brushed her teeth every day, but she couldn't remember the last time she'd been to the dentist. But someone had bought her all those amazing clothes. Effie touched her skirt. What if . . .? What if she got to keep the clothes, and learned those skills that Crescentia talked about, and didn't get chosen by the dragon? Surely then the Princess School would be sort of fun? Except . . . What was she thinking? How could you enjoy anything while other girls were being eaten? The whole thing was so horrible.

Effie touched her silver ring, twisting it on her thumb. It felt warm and comforting, and she knew she was stronger than usual because of it. But she also felt it would not save her if she were faced with being eaten by a dragon. How would it even feel, to go off to spend a night in a dragon's lair, knowing that you were going to be lavished with great luxuries and then killed? It would be awful, unbearable. Effie was suddenly overcome with a feeling of wanting to put a stop to this unfair situation. But how could any one person do that?

Effie also still felt strongly drawn towards the big house by the forest. She longed to go through the gates and explore the grounds. After a while, Crescentia fell asleep in the warm afternoon sunshine and so Effie slipped off to look at the gates. They were locked with a huge brass padlock, which seemed unnecessary as they also had two men guarding them. Each man was wearing a uniform and had a sword in a scabbard by his side.

Again, Effie wondered where exactly she was. Was this the Otherworld? But she hadn't gone into the Otherworld. She hadn't been allowed. And, OK, here there seemed to be dragons and swords and maidens in peril – but there hadn't yet been much talk of magic. It felt more like the past than another world. Not that Effie knew anything for sure. This was so confusing.

She touched the lock on the gates. If only it would open . . .

'Halt and state your business,' said one of the armed guards.

'Sorry,' said Effie. 'I was just looking. Who lives here?'

'I can't give you that information,' said the other guard. 'Although,' he dropped his voice and she could see his eyes twinkle a tiny bit, 'if you look more closely at the gates you'll probably find out.'

Effie stood back so she could see the gates properly again. They did remind her of something. Their shape, the ornate, complex structure . . . They were also very beautiful. They were made of dark black metal with gold detailing. There were swirls and flowers and spirals and little pictures of moons and planets and suns, all picked out in delicate filigree. She looked closely until she began to see names made out in faded gold at the top of each gate. *Clothilde*, it said on one side. On the other, the name *Rollo* was spelled out. Rollo. That reminded Effie of something, although she couldn't think what. But she almost missed the most crucial detail. Underneath both names, and linking the two gates together, was one very familiar word.

TRUELOVE, it said, and then underneath that, the word HOUSE. TRUELOVE HOUSE. So this was . . . This meant . . .

'Please,' Effie said to the guards. 'I think I might be related to whoever lives here. My name's Euphemia Truelove, you see, and— '

'Do you have a calling card?'

'A what?'

'They only accept calling cards. Or, of course, an invitation.'

'Um . . . Could you just tell them that I'm here?'

'No.'

'Why?'

'Because those are the rules,' said the first guard.

'Just come back when you have a calling card,' said the second guard.

'I don't even know what a calling card is,' said Effie, feeling tearful.

'Well, we can't help you then.'

Just then, Effie felt a tap on her shoulder. It was Crescentia.

'What are you doing?' she said. 'You should have woken me up. We have to get back. There's a *lot* to do before tomorrow.'

'I just . . .' Effie realised that she couldn't really explain anything to Crescentia. She resolved to find some way of getting a calling card so she could return to this place. Her grandfather had told her to come to Dragon's Green, and this must have been why. *Rollo*. Where had she heard that name recently?

16

'Doesn't make any sense,' said Wolf.

Maximilian had finished telling him what he'd learned on the dim web about Leonard Levar. The boys had enjoyed their dinner – after their cottage pie they had been given three scoops each of Nurse Underwood's homemade chocolate fudge ice-cream – and gone back into Maximilian's room. Nurse Underwood had told Wolf to call her Odile and stay as long as he liked. Wolf certainly wasn't in any hurry to get back to his uncle, who by now would be extremely angry, pacing around their cold, damp, carpetless flat and thinking up painful new punishments to teach Wolf not to steal keys. Wolf shuddered at the thought. Although since this afternoon he had felt a bit stronger, as if he had changed somehow.

'Which bit?' said Maximilian.

'All of it, really,' said Wolf. 'So you've got this bloke who really loves books. Why would he want to pulp them as well?'

Maximilian shrugged. 'I don't know.'

His pager emitted a series of beeps and he picked it up.

'Aha,' he said.

'What's that?' said Wolf.

'Messages from a storage company. They say they're going to send a quote in the morning. I've been making a plan. Now we have the key, we can get the books easily. We just need somewhere to put them. There's M-storage as well of course, but that's really expensive.'

As well as explaining about Leonard Levar and all his nefarious activities in the world of rare books, Maximilian had also told Wolf all about magic, or, at least, as much as he knew. Wolf hadn't understood all of it, but he had grasped that the world was full of secretly magical people and that he was now one of them – he had epiphanised, or something weird-sounding anyway, and was maybe some sort of 'Neophyte'– since he first touched the Sword of Orphennyus. And he understood that anything with the prefix M was enchanted or magical in some way. But M-storage? What on earth was that?

'It's more secure,' said Maximilian, as if he were reading Wolf's mind. 'I saw an ad in *The Liminal*. They basically ship your stuff to the northern plains of the Otherworld and keep it there. Obviously no one apart from liminals can get to it if it's in the Otherworld, which makes it more secure for a start. Well, Otherworlders can get to it too, but they don't care about property the way we do . . . And the locks are magic, of course. And there's some kind of cloaking or secrecy that they turn on at night and . . .'

'Can't you just stick the books in your garage?' said Wolf.

Maximilian sighed. Surely he was supposed to be the practical

143

one and Wolf was just supposed to provide the muscle? Maybe life wasn't that simple.

'That's actually not a bad idea,' he admitted. 'At least, in the meantime. The only thing is that we're going to have to work out how to get them here.'

'Have you got any money?' said Wolf.

'No. Wait. Yes.' Maximilian remembered the twenty-pound note he'd taken from Leonard Levar for Effie's books. He explained to Wolf how he'd obtained it. 'Do you think . . .?' he began. 'I mean, would it be immoral to . . .?'

Wolf shrugged. 'I reckon for twenty quid we could get my brother to come and drive us over to the Old Town and help us break into the main shop and load up the car, no questions asked. He's an apprentice locksmith. He'd probably do it for a tenner.'

'Well . . .'

'I think Effie would rather have her books back than the twenty quid,' Wolf said. 'And anyway, if one book's worth twenty, think what 499 are worth.'

'You're probably right.'

And, Maximilian remembered with a gulp, he wasn't exactly a moral person anyway. Before he could protest any further, Wolf had started paging his brother.

'Where's your dad?' asked Wolf, when he'd finished.

Maximilian shrugged. 'I haven't got one,' he said.

'Really? Me neither.'

'So the charity man is . . .?'

'My uncle,' said Wolf. 'He took me in after . . .' He paused. 'What happened?'

'My mum walked out on us after an argument with my dad. Then my dad got a new wife but then he walked out on her. Then she got a new husband and he hated me. Used to beat me up. So my uncle took me in, although he's not much better, to be honest. How about you? What happened to your dad?'

Maximilian looked at his hands.

'I just don't have one,' he said.

'You can't not have a father.'

'I know. It was . . . I suppose I do have a father, but I just don't know who he is.'

Maximilian had often dreamed that his father was a great space-traveller or millionaire or inventor, but he really didn't know.

'I think it was basically a sort of brief love affair,' he said. 'My mum has never even admitted it. I thought my mum's ex-husband was my dad for years even after they divorced, but then I overheard them rowing and, well, you know. It sort of became clear that they split up because she was pregnant with me and that my dad was someone else entirely . . .'

'Pretty rough,' said Wolf.

'Please don't tell anyone.'

Just then there was the sound of a car pulling up outside, the heavy thrum of the engine indicating that this wasn't one of the neighbours arriving home from their yoga class or the Women's Institute in their sensible, quiet hatchback, but a boy racer from – horrors – Middle Town in his low-slung antique car with huge speakers and an old-fashioned cassette deck that everyone agreed produced a better bass sound than digital music ever had. This cassette deck was currently playing a recent Borders hip-hop tape with a lot of swearing in it.

'Oh God,' said Wolf. 'It's Carl. He's never quiet.'

Maximilian turned towards the window, where he saw a young blond man sitting in a souped-up VW of a sort they definitely did not make any more. The spectacles told him that Wolf's brother Carl was twenty-three years old and currently suffered from lower back pain and an injured Achilles tendon. His energy was relatively high. He didn't have anything magical about him at all, not even a flicker of M-currency or the potential to carry any.

Wolf was indicating out of the window for him to quieten down, while Maximilian stuffed his bed with the spare pillow.

'It probably won't work,' he said. 'But who cares?'

'Cool,' said Wolf. 'Let's go.'

'Are you sure you've thought this through?' said Carl, once they'd filled him in on their plan and were driving towards the Old Town. He'd accepted ten pounds as payment for helping his brother and the nerd with the weird glasses.

'Why?' said Wolf.

'Well, don't you think this Levar geezer is going to work out where his books have gone and come and get them back? Or he'll just get the Old Bill to, I don't know, look up Max's address or whatever and probably arrest him too.'

Maximilian had not introduced himself as Max, and wasn't sure he liked it. He also didn't like the idea of being arrested. This plan had been all very well when it was just a plan. As a reality it lacked something. In fact, it lacked several things. It lacked safety and security and the warm feeling of being at home just thinking.

'Yes,' said Wolf, 'but they're not going to think Maximilian's involved, are they? The prime suspect'll be Effie. And since she doesn't even know we're getting the books, we'll all be in the clear. We can tell her at school tomorrow and . . .'

'I could store them for you,' said Carl.

'Yeah, right,' said Wolf. 'You'd sell them back to this Levar bloke before we can even blink. No thanks. And you'd better not tell him where Maximilian lives, either.'

Carl grinned. 'You know I sell my services to the highest bidder.'

'But I'm your brother. That should count for something.'

'He's not.' Carl gestured at Maximilian.

'All right, what if we give you twenty quid?'

'Done.'

'Really, Carl, you can't tell anyone where we take the books.'

'Yeah, well, you've got to get them first.'

Carl parked the car at the bottom of the steep cobbled alley leading up to Leonard Levar's Antiquarian Bookshop. The caves under the shop also had some kind of exit just beyond – Maximilian had found this on some old plans he'd looked at with the Spectacles of Knowledge. But when the boys looked now, they could see that this exit was heavily boarded up and covered with posters for last year's circus and this year's book festival. They would have to go in through the shop, as Maximilian had originally thought. But

147

how were they going to get the books out without anyone noticing?

'How did you load them in earlier?' asked Maximilian.

'We parked up there outside the shop entrance in the loading bay.'

Maximilian frowned. 'Well, we can't do that now.' He started scuffing his shoe against the kerb, something he did when he was thinking by a roadside (which admittedly wasn't often). After a few moments he became aware of a grille in the wall just below knee height.

'What's that?' he asked.

'What's what?' said Carl.

'There . . .' Maximilian looked with the spectacles and saw that the grille was part of a ventilation system from when the caves had been used to store ammunition in one of the old wars. 'Where does that lead?'

He brought up a selection of historical maps on his spectacles until he found the right one.

'Aha,' he said. 'Right. Carl, you break us in through the main bookshop door and then wait for us out here. We'll go in and use the key to get to the storeroom. We should be able to get back to this hatch and then pass the books through to Carl. All you need to . . . Carl?'

A woman with very high-heeled boots was negotiating the cobbles. Carl watched her curvy body as it bobbed up and down. Then she disappeared around the corner into a smaller alleyway. The only thing there was the Funtime Arcade. She didn't look like the sort of person who'd go to an arcade, but . . .

148

'Carl?' said Maximilian again.

'Sorry, mate.'

'Have you got a screwdriver?'

'Flat-head or Phillips?'

'I don't know. But can you get this grille off?'

'Yes, mate.'

'Brilliant.'

'And you won't just drive off with the books?' said Wolf.

'Not sure,' said Carl, scratching his head. 'Got any more money?'

This was ridiculous. The only person Wolf knew with a car was also completely unreliable. There was only one thing for it. Maximilian scanned himself. His M-currency stood at 468. It seemed that he had been given around five hundred in M-currency when he had first put on the spectacles and epiphanised, but since then using the spectacles was slowly draining his power away. Once it was gone, what then? The dim web wasn't completely clear on how you increased your M-currency. It certainly wasn't like buying new batteries for a radio. In those Laurel Wilde books he'd read when he was younger, the 'chosen ones' had seemed to have unlimited power to do whatever they liked. But in real life his power seemed to be running out, and he needed more.

Could you un-epiphanise? Change back? Maximilian would rather be dead. But what could he do? If he wanted to keep the spectacles, he needed to help get Effie's books back. But it seemed as if this were going to cost him. He would have to gamble some M-currency on . . . well . . . *what*? He had to get Carl under control, but how?

17

Maximilian knew how to cast a spell, of course. Anyone who spent as much time as he did on the dim web knew how to cast a spell. There were, he understood, two main ways of doing it.

The first way, mainly used by Neophyte or Apprentice hedge-witches with limited access to M-currency, was to spend a great deal of time thinking about your spell, the exact wording of it (*The Liminal* always contained lots of examples of poorly worded spells and the disasters that followed), the exact personage or spirit in the Otherworld to whom it should be directed, along with the best mode of flattery to persuade them to help you. This request would then be written down, ideally in one's own blood (though ink from an elegant fountain pen was also acceptable), on extremely nice paper, during a full moon, and then burnt. The ash would then be buried at a sacred spot from where the resident faeries would convey the request to the Otherworld, where it may or may not be granted.

Spells cast in this way often had unexpected results. Given

the natural resistance of the Realworld to magic, and the habit of Otherworlders not to do magic in the Realworld, anything not worded precisely enough was bound to go completely wrong. Requests for money would often be met with a death in the family ('Oh? You mean you *didn't* want to get rich through inheritance? You should have said so in the spell!'). Requests for fame could often lead to someone growing the biggest ever toenail or developing the worst breath in the world or something along those lines ('Oh? You mean you wanted to be famous for something *attractive*? Why ever didn't you say?'). The Otherworld frowned on requests made for oneself, but it was also seen as bad form to request something for someone else.

So this way of doing magic was quite hard.

The second way of casting a spell was officially only supposed to work if you were an Adept or Master in your ability and had some amazing boon. But in theory, if you had enough M-currency for what you wanted to achieve then you could simply use your mind to achieve it. If, for example, you wanted to light a candle using magic (which only a fool would attempt, given the low Realworld price of a box of matches), you would look at the wick, concentrate in a special way, think 'flame' and, as they say, *abracadabra*. It would light.

That was the theory. In reality, learning to light a candle using just M-currency was about twice as hard as learning to ride a bike. Not impossible, but tricky. Once you had the ability, you had it for ever, like a two-handed backhand or joined-up writing. But developing the knack required practice. And ideally, guidance. A few Monday evening sessions in St George's Hall with

Dr Green, perhaps. Maximilian had not practised, nor had any guidance. He had not even thought of casting a spell before. Not really.

Carl was walking up the cobbled alleyway with a selection of strange-looking hooks and bits of metal and a book called *Easy Pickings*. Maximilian and Wolf were alongside him.

'You *have* done this before?' said Wolf.

'Yes, mate. I'm an apprentice.'

'But . . .'

'This is my textbook. Be good practice, this. I failed my last test and—'

'Wait. You failed a lock-picking test?'

'Only by ten marks. Well, eleven.'

'How many marks did you need to pass?'

'Pass mark was twenty-nine out of forty. I got eighteen. Not bad, eh?'

Maximilian sighed.

Another problem with using spells in the Realworld was that they could easily start clashing with each other, jostling for position, elbowing one another out of the way, as they all hurtled chaotically together through the thinnest part of the Luminiferous Ether between the Realworld and the Otherworld. (The Luminiferous Ether is, as everyone knows, the main substance that conducts magical energy through the universe.)

For example, right now, several spells were working on

Maximilian. There was the spell cast by Effie's grandfather, Griffin Truelove, as he fought for breath not far from where Maximilian was now. It had not been a very strong spell, given the power he had left, but had been intended to protect his books and get them to Effie. Magic cast in this vague way uses the nearest and most obvious resources to achieve its aims. In a sense, then, Maximilian was simply one of these resources. But elsewhere in the Luminiferous Ether lurked another spell, also quite weak, cast by Odile Underwood when her son was born, that asked for him to live a normal, unremarkable, unmagical life that should be neutral if it could not be good.

This spell, which had been rather badly worded, especially given that the Luminiferous Ether often ignored prefixes like 'un', was partly responsible for Carl. (Although, of course, in another quite random way, Carl was just Carl.) There were also other, less significant spells working on Maximilian. Somewhere in the west a farmer had prayed for rain and so Maximilian, along with everyone else in the city, was breathing approximately 0.0000007 times faster than usual to create the moisture so requested. Such is the way of the world.

And then there was the spell being cast right at this moment in the grounds of a dark folly (a sort of pretend castle built by rich people long ago) in a small village to the south of the city by a girl in a black nightdress who really should have been finishing her homework and going to sleep.

Raven Wilde found it hard to sleep when her mother was still downstairs 'entertaining', which had so far involved many bottles of expensive wine and a live jazz band (well, the gamekeeper's son and his friend on tenor sax and double bass). Raven had been part of the dinner party until ten when Torben, a poet from the valleys with long, wild, grey hair, had taken out a bottle of dessert wine and a guitar and given her 'the wink' that meant she should go upstairs and allow him to try to serenade her mother in peace. There were other guests to get rid of too, of course, including Skylurian Midzhar, Laurel Wilde's glamorous publisher who had been holding court at this particular dinner party for what seemed like hours. Or maybe Torben actually planned to serenade her? At the folly it was often unclear who exactly was being serenaded by whom. And if it meant a chance of Torben actually getting his poetry published – he'd probably do *anything*.

Raven Wilde needed friends. That's what her spell was for. Like Maximilian and Wolf, she had no father – he had been a lot older than her mother, and had died when Raven was only five. She had no brothers or sisters or cousins and so she spent a lot of time alone. Her mother, being a famous writer and therefore quite temperamental, was prone to locking herself in the folly's keep (a kind of small tower in which you could in theory hide from your enemies, or amorous poets) in order to plot for long periods of time. Laurel Wilde was also often to be found standing on the battlements, her red hair flying in the wind, sobbing over lost love and the fact that someone else was at number one in the hardback fiction charts.

This week she was particularly upset because her latest book had just sold its one hundred thousandth paperback when the Matchstick Press had announced that it was not going to print any more copies. Where was the logic in that? Skylurian Midzhar had not been very forthcoming on this issue. Rather confusingly, she'd even brought along a magnum of champagne to toast Laurel's success.

Raven had spent months thinking about her spell and researching it, just as her spell book had said. She had even bought a special fountain pen with which to write it out – having read that this was the correct way to present a spell (after being edited, the book had no longer mentioned that these spells should ideally be written in blood).

In Raven's mother's books magic just happened, almost of its own accord, to the select set of attractive people born with the ability to use it. Laurel Wilde wrote about magic but did not believe in it, although she never admitted this to her many fans. Raven believed in her heart that magic did exist and that it didn't work the way her mother wrote about it, but she had no real idea how it did work. She'd been trying the invisibility spell for months now and nothing had happened, except that thing with her pencil. But Raven now suspected that the pencil had just been lost or stolen.

The friendship spell was much more important. And it was going to work.

Dear Luminiferous Ether, she had written. *Please help me. I am choosing this day to bring friendship into my life. I send this heartfelt request that I will soon find new friends, that these friends will be human children* (Raven had read about people who had asked for friends but forgotten to specify their species), *ideally from my school, and that we will share life in a beautiful and meaningful way together for many years, helping each other through any difficulties and problems we encounter. In order to help facilitate this spell, I will try my best to bring friendship into my life using normal means – for example, I will try to talk to people more often. And I will continue to make offerings and give aid to any other troubled beings I encounter, in the spirit of Love and Life. Thank you. Yours faithfully, Raven Wilde.*

The Luminiferous Ether was quite touched by this. No one ever usually wrote to it. It was hardly ever seen as a magical personage in its own right, only as the vague 'stuff' used to carry magic around. But this Realworld girl had chosen it as her way of connecting with the Otherworld. It had been chosen as her special helper. Well, all right, what was it she wanted? *Friendship*? Hmm. The Luminiferous Ether had quite a few spells flowing through it at this moment that could just be shifted a little here, and there, and rearranged just so, and, well . . .

After a lot of swearing and much consultation of *Easy Pickings*, Carl managed to get the door open. Maximilian and Wolf walked into the dark interior of Leonard Levar's Antiquarian Bookshop.

'So we're going to pass you the books through that grille I showed you before,' said Maximilian to Carl. Wolf had the antique brass key all ready. All they had to do was go to the back of the shop, where Wolf would show Maximilian the secret bookshelf that would open onto . . .

'Right,' said Carl, distractedly.

'And then you're going to wait for us and drive us back to Maximilian's,' said Wolf. 'And help us unload the books into his garage.'

'Right.' Carl scratched his head. 'Unless . . .'

'What?'

'Are you sure you haven't got any more money? If someone else comes along and offers me more I might just . . .'

'Carl!' said Wolf.

'All right,' said Maximilian. 'I really didn't want to have to do this, but . . .' He looked hard at Carl, who had now started putting his hooks and other implements in a battered leather pouch. 'Carl?' Carl looked up at him. 'I haven't done this before, so apologies if . . .'

Maximilian looked deep into Carl's eyes. He thought something in his head like, 'You are sleepy. You are now in my power.' Carl started swaying slightly, but his eyes remained fixed on Maximilian, a little as if he were a baby duckling and Maximilian were his mother.

'You will now do my bidding,' Maximilian said with his mind. Carl carried on swaying, looking at his new master with just a touch of confusion. He nodded slightly. Yes, he would do whatever Maximilian told him. But . . .

There were so many problems with this spell that it is hard to even know where to begin describing them. This particular spell had occurred to Maximilian in the first place because he'd read something about a similar attempt to overpower a mind that had gone disastrously wrong. He could not remember how it had gone wrong, nor what could have been done to make it right. He had just remembered the idea. And then there was the problem that attempting to overpower someone's mind was not permitted by the Guild of Craftspeople, which meant that officially Maximilian was now dabbling in what Laurel Wilde would probably call 'the dark side'. Third, the overpowering of another's mind, as well as being unethical, is very costly.

It was hard to tell how much of Carl's mind had been overpowered before Maximilian gave him his main command.

'You will wait for us to pass you the books and then you will take us to my house and help us unload them. Is that clear?'

Carl's eyes were floating around like two eggs in a pan.

'Yes, mate,' he managed, before turning to walk unsteadily back to the car.

'Is he all right?' asked Wolf.

'I think so,' said Maximilian. 'Right. Where's this bookshelf?'

Carl staggered like a zombie down the alleyway until his mind (which was unaccustomed to holding magical instructions) decided it was indeed very sleepy, and he settled down for a snooze just by the turning to the Funtime Arcade.

Maximilian and Wolf managed to find the secret door hidden among Leonard Levar's dusty bookshelves. There was a first edition of *Summer Lightning* by P.G. Wodehouse that you had to sort of push, and then . . . They were through. Maximilian and Wolf groped around until they found the switch that dimly lit the passageway down to the caves. Then they crept down the passageway and used the old brass key to open the large wooden door into the first small cave, and then they made their way into the final cave, which was full of crates.

And then all the lights went out.

'Good evening,' said a cold, thin voice. 'I see you have come for my books.'

18

The evening before the audition went very quickly. After a hearty blackgrain stew, most of which the girls left uneaten, Crescentia lent Effie her clear nail polish and showed her how to file her nails into perfect ovals. She also taught Effie how to exfoliate her skin all over, which was not just extremely boring but painful, too. In her wash bag, Effie found a vial of golden oil. Crescentia explained that this was the very, very expensive Oil of Perfection and that Effie should put it on in the morning, first thing, before getting dressed.

At seven o'clock in the morning, they were ready. Crescentia was wearing the black suede dress with cashmere tights, and Effie was in her black leather jeans with the cream silk pussy-bow blouse and the diamanté sandals. She didn't like this outfit as much as the one she'd travelled in the day before, but Crescentia had assured her it would go down well with the judges. Crescentia had back-combed her hair and put on a lot of make-up – pink lips and black, smoky eyes. Effie didn't have any make-up, but the Oil of Perfection had meant she didn't really need any. She sort of glowed all over.

As they waited for the car, Effie took in just how calm Crescentia now was, compared with the day before.

'Are you OK?' Effie asked her.

'Sure. Why wouldn't I be?'

'Well, it's just that yesterday, when you arrived . . .'

'I was a different person then. I'm ready for this now.' She tossed her back-combed hair. 'I'm ready to be a princess.'

Effie couldn't help wondering whether something in their breakfast had been drugged. She felt a bit soft and relaxed and not quite so desperate to go home and get on with rescuing her grandfather's books. She found she'd even started to forget what and where home really was. She touched her silver ring and willed some of her normal self to come back. Yes. She had to get into Truelove House somehow. That was what she was here for, she remembered. *Find Dragon's Green*. That's what her grandfather had said. She had found it. Or at least she thought she had. She just had to get through today and then she could find a way to escape and get a calling card, whatever that even was. *Rollo*. Again she tried to remember where she had heard that name before.

The car arrived and drove them through winding leafy lanes and up towards the big old house on the hill. Effie again wondered where exactly they were. This place was so much like something from the past, with all the villagers looking like peasants and no sign of anything like a pager or a radio or even – Effie scanned the landscape – any kind of electricity pylon. But there were still cars and fashion. Maybe the girls were just very deep in the countryside.

When the car pulled up to the house they were greeted by one footman who took their luggage, and another carrying a large parasol.

'Well, cover them, cover them!' called a large woman in a black velvet dress.

'Sorry, Madame McQueen. Immediately, Madame McQueen.'

'Do not let the sun touch them!' shouted Madame McQueen. 'Hurry, girls, inside, inside. We don't want freckles.'

'Good luck,' whispered Crescentia to Effie.

'You too,' said Effie.

Then they were whisked inside. They ended up separated in a room with dozens of other girls, all waiting to take their turn in the audition room. Talk was mainly about make-up, fashion and hair, although two girls in the far corner seemed to be having a more passionate discussion about the ethics of the dragon.

'Yeah, well,' one was saying to the other. 'My mum says that in Dragon's Wold – and in loads of other places, actually – the dragon insists on having his princesses force-fed with dried apricots, sage and breadcrumbs. He likes them to come pre-stuffed, apparently. The girls in the school there have to live in crates so that they never see the sun and never develop any muscle at all. That dragon can't bear even the tiniest bit of gristle. Imagine that. So we're lucky to be here, in fact. It could have been so much worse.'

Effie's audition was over more quickly than she'd imagined. It took place on the stage in the big hall. When she entered she

161

could see that there were four other judges apart from Madame McQueen.

'Walk,' said one of them, a very thin man. 'Stop. Turn. Approach the desk.'

Effie did these things.

'Hands,' said the woman next to the thin man.

Effie showed her hands.

'Not bad, but you'll need more hand cream.'

The next thing Effie had to do was explain her beauty regime. Of course, she didn't have one, so she simply described what she'd seen Crescentia doing the night before.

'Excellent,' breathed Madame McQueen. 'Stunning.'

Effie gulped. No one had ever called her stunning before.

'The hair,' said the thin man. 'May I smell it?'

Effie approached and let him smell her hair.

'Adorable. And the colour – it's extreme.'

Extreme? Effie's hair was, she'd thought before, a very normal colour. It was mainly brown, but had blonde bits from when she'd been in the sun. It was very, very long, mainly because no one could ever be bothered to take her to the hairdresser. Sometimes, when she didn't brush it for a long time, it went into tendril-like curls.

The judges started to mumble amongst themselves. Effie heard the words 'fast-track' and 'younger than ever' and 'stringy'.

'Go and wait in the room over there,' said Madame McQueen, pointing in quite a different direction from where Effie had seen the girl before her go. Did this mean that she had failed the audition, despite her 'adorable' hair? Would she now be cast out into the forest to die?

The room was cold and small. A display on one wall explained how you should never wear a low-cut top with a short skirt and how you should always take off the last accessory you put on before you leave the house. It was like being in a giant magazine – one of those things you would read at the dentist (if you ever went to the dentist).

Across the room was a display of Polaroid photographs of beautiful girls. FORM 2C, it said at the top. Under each image the girl pictured had written her aim for the year. A girl called Jodene had written *to learn to use blusher properly*. Another girl, Bonita, was aiming *to learn to blow-dry my own hair*. Did any of these girls have any academic or sporting aims? No. The closest thing Effie could see was someone called Lisette who wanted to learn to speak the ancient language of dragons.

The door opened and Crescentia came in.

'Well,' she said, without smiling, 'top marks to us.'

'Why?'

'We've been fast-tracked.'

'Which means?'

But Crescentia didn't get the chance to explain, because the door opened and a short man with glasses and a bald head entered the room.

'Ooh, fast-tracking,' he said. 'I love it. L. O. V. E. I. T. Come on, darlings, if we hurry we can get you in tomorrow's catalogue. It'll be extreme. Got your things? Where are your things? No things. Did someone take them? Someone took them. OK, girlies, *followez moi.* Are you following? You're following. Good. *Allons-y, les petites femmes. Allons-y.'*

He carried on talking to himself in this way until they reached a small set of winding stairs, at the top of which was a photographic studio. Inside the studio was a photographer with three different cameras and several silver reflectors set up around a bright white backdrop. The girls' cases were there, and their clothes had been unpacked and hung on rails. One was labelled *E. Truelove* and the other was labelled *C. Croft.*

A short, fat woman bustled in and before Effie knew it she was being dressed in every possible outfit you could make from the clothes she had brought, and photographed in each one. The leather trousers with the star t-shirt, the pink skirt with the cream blouse and so on. Then Crescentia went through the same process. She seemed to enjoy having her photograph taken. Effie thought her pictures would look beautiful.

Then the girls had to give all their clothes back to the short fat woman. They were given big pots of cold cream and told to take off all their make-up, even though Effie didn't have any on. Their outfits were re-hung on the rails and wheeled into a huge cupboard with the words 'Current Catalogue' on it. The fat woman bustled back out and gave each of them a shapeless blue smock with the number three on it.

'What's this?' said Crescentia.

'Welcome to form 3A,' said the fat woman. 'Third-form common room is down the stairs, turn right, turn left, round the corner, up the back stairs to the first floor and you can't miss it. If you hurry you'll catch the last half hour of lunch break.'

The girls tried their best to follow the instructions but soon ended up lost in the basement. Effie kept looking for some way out, but there didn't seem to be any.

'What does fast-track actually mean?' she asked Crescentia. 'And what's this catalogue?'

'It's like we've basically come top of the class without really doing anything. We've been moved up to the third form. We should be first-formers, obviously.'

'But why . . .?'

'Some law stops the dragon from choosing anyone from below third form. But as you can see, that doesn't stop the staff putting whoever they want in the third form. Anyway, we're in the catalogue now. Start praying.'

'What exactly is the catalogue?'

'It's what he uses to choose which princess he's going to eat and what he wants her to wear. Like I said, cross your fingers. Where is this stupid common room?'

Around another corner came the smell of burnt toast, cigarette smoke, perfume, incense and hairspray. There was loud, bass-heavy R&B playing. Effie and Crescentia approached. This could not be the third-form common room, surely? FIFTH FORM ONLY KEEP OUT said a sign on the door. At least, that's what it used to say. Someone had crossed out FIFTH FORM and written in the word SURVIVORS instead. There was a little glass panel in the door and through it Effie could see girls dancing. The girls looked – well, it was almost impossible to describe – but Effie immediately wanted one of them as a big sister.

They were completely different from the girls waiting for their auditions, with their tiny arms and legs and their long hair brushed just so. These girls were bigger, for a start – but not just because they were older. Their clothes stretched over them in ways that made them look like real, grown-up women. Although they were wearing the same smocks that Effie and Crescentia wore, they had taken theirs in with darts and pleats so that they were extremely flattering – each in an individual way. They had embroidered them with various slogans, not all of them that polite. *War on Dragons* read one of the more repeatable ones. *Badass gristle* said another.

'Wow,' said Crescentia.

'I guess if you got to fifth form here you would want to celebrate,' said Effie.

'Yeah, unless the dragon decides he wants a more mature meat.'

The door opened and a tall girl with long black hair came out. She had a pierced lip and a tattoo across her collarbone that read *Make a wish, sucker*.

'Who are you?' she said.

'We're new,' said Effie. 'We're looking for the third-form common room.'

'If you're new, you want the first-form common room.'

'No, babe, they fast-track the most delicious little morsels now,' said another girl. 'Straight to third form, straight in the catalogue, straight in the mouth of . . .'

'God, they're disgusting,' said the first girl. She looked deep into Effie's eyes. 'Are you scared?' she said.

166

'Um, sort of.'

'Are you scared?' she asked Crescentia.

'Yes,' said Crescentia.

'All right, I'll give you a tip. They can't stop you doing press-ups. Even if they put you in a crate, you can squat. Get some muscle on you and you won't get chosen.'

And then she and her friend went back into the common room and shut the door behind them.

19

The rest of the day went quickly. Effie and Crescentia eventually found the third-form common room, but it was hard to make friends with girls two years older than them who already knew each other very well. So they stuck together. They stood in line together in the dining hall, and then ate their tiny salads together. They sat next to one another in double hairstyling, and when it came to practising using heated rollers, they did each other's hair. Effie found herself missing her real school. And she kept wondering how exactly she was going to get out of here and find her way back to Truelove House. And then go home.

'I think it's wearing off,' said Crescentia.

'What?'

'The effect of the drugs.'

'Why?'

'Because I really am very scared,' Crescentia said.

Effie looked at Crescentia. As the day had gone on she'd grown paler and paler.

'Don't worry,' said Effie. 'It's all right. We won't get chosen. Not on our first day. I mean, some of those girls in the fifth form must have been in hundreds of catalogues, and they're still around.'

But if they didn't get chosen, someone else would. Effie kept thinking about the fifth-form girls. They were clearly against what was happening, but hadn't worked out how to do anything about it. Or maybe they didn't care now that they were – more or less – out of danger. After all, bad things happened in the world all the time and you couldn't necessarily do anything about them. Effie was quiet for the rest of the day, thinking and thinking.

Why hadn't all the girls in the school just walked out? Together they'd be a match for any evil forest tribes. They could do what they liked, if they all acted together. They could walk through the forest together and . . . What then? Have to endure the shame of their families, who would probably have to give back the money the school had given them?

And there'd still be the problem of the dragon.

After supper, Effie and Crescentia were allocated a dorm. Although they were officially in the third form, the dorms with spare beds were all for first-formers, so they ended up with four girls Effie recognised from this morning. Each girl had a single bed, a small chest of drawers with a mirror on it and a bedside cabinet with a lamp. Each chest of drawers had a tub of thick white cold-cream on it, apparently for taking off make-up, and various expensive cosmetic products.

'Apparently it's all product placement or something,' said a girl called Blossom. 'Or, like, sponsorship or whatever. We were given a talk about it this morning while you were being photographed. When the papers interview you before you go off to be killed you have to say the dragon chose you because you used Oil of Perfection or Fourflower Lotion or whatever. Rich old ladies apparently lap up all that stuff. They want to pretend to be us. And the companies give your family money, too. After, well, you know.'

'You're so lucky, going straight into the catalogue,' said another girl, Nell. 'You know you were the only ones to be fast-tracked from first form to third form?'

'Yeah. Whoopee for us.' Crescentia got into bed and put a pillow over her face. It sounded as if she were trying to hide the fact that she was crying.

'Is she scared?' asked Blossom.

'Wouldn't you be?' said Effie. 'Why do you all – do we all – put up with this?'

No one answered. Everyone started brushing their hair – a hundred times, or you faced detention, apparently. Effie's last detention had, of course, been quite interesting, although it felt as if that happened in a different time or a different world from this. She remembered Wolf standing there with his sword. Could he be a match for the dragon? But Effie wouldn't even know how to get a message to him. And of course the last time she'd seen him he had been helping the horrible charity man take her books. But Maximilian would be out there somewhere using the spectacles to help her. And Lexy might be doing something with the crystal. She had two true friends, at least. They just seemed a very long way away.

Effie had expected to spend the whole night awake, but suddenly it was morning. There was one bell that told you it was time to wake up, and another bell for breakfast. After that all the girls got ready in their blue smocks and went to assembly. On the way there, Effie decided that she really had to find some way to escape today. She had to obtain a calling card somehow and then go to Truelove House. This was what her grandfather had meant her to do; she just had to work out how to do it. And after all that she still had to get home and rescue his books.

Madame McQueen stood up on the stage to address the school.

'I am extremely happy to report that we have broken a record today,' she began. 'For the very first time, the special honour of being the dragon's consort is going to a girl who appeared in her very first catalogue only yesterday.'

'What does that mean?' hissed a girl in front of Effie.

'The dragon's chosen a new girl,' said another girl.

Effie gulped. A cheerful pop song started playing up on the stage.

Then a picture flashed up. It was Crescentia, wearing the black suede dress that Effie had so admired the day before. This time she had paired it with leggings and high-heeled boots and the mushroom necklace. This was the outfit the dragon must have chosen. Effie could sense all the girls admiring it, making mental notes about it.

'Please come up to the front, the lucky, the beautiful, Crescentia Croft!'

Everyone clapped as Crescentia started walking towards the

stage. Effie noticed that she almost stumbled, and that she had to wipe a tear from her eye. But by the time she reached the stage she had composed herself, just as she had yesterday morning.

'Thank you,' she said. 'It's impossible to describe the honour I feel at being chosen. I will represent the school and my family with dignity and purpose.'

'And who will you choose to be your handmaiden?' said Madame McQueen.

'Euphemia Truelove.'

Everyone clapped again. The girls near Effie turned and smiled or touched her hands or said things like 'Yay!' or 'Good luck'. Effie had no idea what it meant to be a handmaiden, but as the girls all filed out of assembly she was asked to stay behind.

She and Crescentia were taken off to a different room, where they were instructed in what were chillingly called the 'final preparations'. Crescentia kept asking for more peppermint tea, because she was sure it was drugged and said she didn't want to feel anything. Effie tried not to eat or drink anything suspicious. She wanted to keep her wits about her. But what was she going to do? Time was running out to save Crescentia, and she'd have to do that before even thinking about escape herself.

The rest of the day was like being best friends with a celebrity. Effie helped Crescentia to prepare her bath of almond milk and rose petals, and arranged all the products that she needed before she got dressed. Oil of Perfection, obviously, as well as Moonflower Petal Lotion, which had tiny pieces of real gold and diamond blended in with it. Effie watched while Crescentia had

172

a manicure and pedicure, drinking peppermint tea all the while. The more she drank, the calmer she became. Then Crescentia dressed carefully in the outfit the dragon had chosen. Then it was hair and make-up. Then a press conference. It would almost have been quite fun, had this not been a preparation for death.

Effie bathed and dressed carefully as well. As Crescentia's handmaiden she would be travelling to the dragon's lair with her, to put any last finishing touches to her hair and make-up before she went in. As handmaiden she was expected to look beautiful as well, to represent the school to any villagers who turned up to watch.

At five o'clock Effie and Crescentia were picked up by a horse-drawn golden carriage. The carriage made its way slowly through the village so everyone could look at the latest young woman who had agreed to sacrifice herself to save the lives of the villagers and to ensure they would not starve this winter. People threw confetti, flower petals and even dried blackgrain, which apparently brought luck.

Too soon, the carriage had left the village, looped around the big dark forest and was entering the approach to the dragon's lair. The day before, the girls had looked at the dragon from the village green and had seen only the raised grounds and very top level of his sunken castle. Now they were about to start the journey down the twisting narrow lane, past the roots of the great trees of the forest, deep down to the underground moat and the sunken drawbridge over which Crescentia would go and never return. The carriage paused while the driver fitted something to the wheels to make them capable of such a steep descent.

Crescentia gulped and took out a small hand mirror to check her hair and make-up. Her hand was shaking so much she could hardly hold it.

Effie's silver ring started to grow warm. She suddenly felt strong and fearless and . . .

'Wait,' said Effie, before she could stop herself. 'Let me go instead.'

'But . . .' Crescentia clearly wanted to agree, but didn't know how she could. She was not a very brave girl really, and had no idea how she was going to face the dragon alone. 'How?'

Effie dropped her voice to a whisper. 'We just need a bit more time.' She raised her voice. 'Driver?' she said.

'Yes, miss?'

'Please could you drive around up here for a few more minutes. Our preparations are not yet complete. Avoid the villagers if you can.'

Then Effie drew the curtains of the carriage and, as it bumped over the uneven roads on the edge of the huge forest, she and Crescentia swapped outfits.

'I don't see how it's going to help if you get eaten instead,' said Crescentia. 'I mean, it's very kind of you, and brave, but . . . I'll probably get expelled when I go back to the school.'

'If my plan works, then . . .' What? The school was hardly going to be happy with Effie if she found some way of stopping the dragon eating princesses. After all, providing the princesses was the only thing the school did. But it simply wasn't right that this dragon should be allowed to eat as many girls as he wanted, that a school should exist to supply those girls and . . .

'You have a plan?' Crescentia's eyes widened in admiration.

In actual fact, Effie did not have a plan. She was still thinking of one. But she had her silver ring, which was somehow making her feel braver than usual. And she also had a strange, desperate urge to meet the dragon, to look at those wings again. To . . . to do what? She didn't know. To talk with him, to get him to see reason? But surely that wouldn't work. He'd probably just roast her to death instantly.

'Yes,' lied Effie. 'I have a plan. Sort of.'

The carriage looped around a section of forest and then approached the steep downhill lane again.

'Are you ready now, miss?' asked the driver.

'Yes,' said Effie.

Down, down, down they went. Crescentia squeezed her hand and thanked her again. 'Good luck,' she said, as Effie got out of the carriage and walked towards the drawbridge, where an elderly maid greeted her and took her into the castle. The drawbridge was raised behind her and the carriage drove away.

The maid took Effie down a stone passageway and through a thick wooden door. Then Effie was left alone at the top of a steep, wide staircase with thick red carpet. At the head of the staircase were two stone plinths with statues of the dragon with his wings spread. All the way down there were portraits of other dragons, each one ornately captioned in a language that seemed oddly familiar. Effie gulped and continued down into the main part of the underground castle, her way lit by candles.

At the bottom of the stairs she found a massive wooden door that had been left ajar. From inside came a flickering, warm light

175

and the smell of freshly cut flowers. Effie breathed deeply and went in. The room was quite small but had a very high ceiling. There was a vast candelabra full of white candles, all dancing slowly together. There was a roaring fire in the huge fireplace. The carpet was a deeper red than the one from the staircase, with swirling gold patterns in its thick wool pile.

There were paintings and tapestries on the walls, some depicting great fights between dragons and young men with swords. These differed from the normal style of such paintings, in that in most of them the dragon seemed to be winning. They also had what looked like the same caption as the portraits.

Spyrys – Pryder – Wythrés.

There were fresh roses in a great vase on the coffee table and bowls of fruit and chocolates and candied peel everywhere. Through another wooden door Effie could see a luxurious dining room with a table set for two. She gulped.

Where was the dragon?

20

'I suppose I am going to have to kill you,' said Leonard Levar. 'It would appear to be the only reliable way to make sure you don't get your hands on my books.'

He didn't switch the light back on. Instead, he lit several candles around the cold, dark cave. Although it is, of course, extremely uneconomical to use magic to achieve such a task in the Realworld, Levar wanted to impress on these puny boys just how magical – and dangerous – he was, and so he lit each one with just a snap of his thin fingers.

All of which was very costly for someone who had so recently done what he had done. But no matter. The rewards he would get from . . .

'Um . . .' said Maximilian. 'They aren't really your books.'

'I paid for them. Even for the five hundredth book that I do not have.'

Maximilian gulped. The five hundredth book must have been *Dragon's Green*. Oh well; at least Effie had that one. Now all that remained was to get these 499 books back to her as well. But that was probably going to be difficult, now that they had been captured by this . . . this . . . What was he? In candlelight, he looked more like a creature than a man: small, shrivelled, with slightly pointed ears and an air of something that had been pickled for a very long time. He was supposed to be over three hundred and fifty years old, Maximilian remembered, which would probably explain it.

'Effie didn't want to sell those books to you,' said Wolf.

Maximilian tried to scan Leonard Levar with his spectacles. He wondered what a man like him would have in terms of M-currency and—

'How dare you!' said Levar, spinning around. 'You are not just impudent, but stupid as well. You boldly try to scan one as powerful as me, without even trying to cloak what you are doing? And of course you find out nothing, because I have cloaked myself. And then you also give away the fact that you carry a great and valuable boon. Well, let me have them.'

Maximilian's heart jolted.

'WELL?' said Levar. 'Give them to me.'

'Give what to you?'

'Oh, you silly boy. You're not going to live much longer, but you might try to dignify your end by acting a little less backward.'

Levar took out a pen and a notebook and started writing something down. From the outside, it may have looked as if he were just a forgetful old man writing a shopping list or jotting down an aide-mémoire. But the more he wrote, the more sick Maximilian started to feel. It began in his stomach, but soon progressed to his head until all the organs in his body were swimming in nausea. Of course, being such a high-level scholar meant that Levar carried with him several quite powerful weapons. One of these was the Pen of Prescription with which he was writing now.

'Uh . . .' said Maximilian. 'Are you doing that? Please stop.'

'You've gone completely white,' said Wolf. He turned to Levar. 'Hey, stop it!'

'Silence,' said Levar. 'The spectacles, please.'

He walked over to Maximilian, who now felt so sick and unstable he was grasping around for something to hold on to. As the cave only contained shallow crates of books, there was nothing apart from the cold, stony walls. Levar took the spectacles without any trouble at all, and Maximilian fell back against the wall and slumped to the ground as if he had been punched.

'Give those back,' said Wolf. 'They're not yours.'

'Oh, but they are, pathetic boy, they are.' Levar put the spectacles on. 'Hmm. Not bad,' he said. 'The Spectacles of Knowledge. Where did the boy get these, I wonder? They are ancient. Beautifully made, of course. Crafted on the Western Plains perhaps even before the Great Split. One of only four pairs of this precise sort in the known universe.' He held them up to the light as if he were about to polish them. Their antique silver frames glinted in the faint candlelight.

And then he bent them with both hands until they were about to snap in two.

'No!' cried Maximilian. Even though he still felt sick, he

managed to haul himself up. He ran – well, stumbled – towards Levar. 'Please don't break them. Please . . .' he said.

'If you beg me, then I won't break them,' said Levar. 'Call me sir.'

'Please, sir,' said Maximilian. 'Please— '

'Don't,' Wolf said to Maximilian. Wolf knew something about how bullying worked. Not that he did it himself, well not very often, but he had hung around with enough 'troubled' boys – and indeed the crueller of the so-called 'gifted' ones as well – to know that there was absolutely no point ever doing what bullies want. And then, of course, there was his uncle, who often set Wolf impossible tasks just as an excuse to beat him when he failed.

'But . . .' said Maximilian.

'Too late,' said Levar, and snapped the spectacles in two.

'No!' wailed Maximilian. He threw himself to his knees. 'Please put them back together,' he said. 'Please, sir . . .'

'You disgusting coward,' said Wolf.

'Isn't he?' said Levar.

'No. I'm talking to you, you repugnant reptile.' Before Wolf had a chance to think about what he was doing, he had rugby tackled Levar to the ground. The pen went flying, and the pad fell out of his hands as well. For an eleven-year-old boy Wolf was extremely strong, with muscles like a well-trained fifteen-year-old.

Levar had not expected to be attacked. After all, what child in their right mind attacks an adult with such formidable magical powers? Still, all he had to do to bring this pathetic beast under control was reach for his . . . his . . . Drat. His pen had rolled away. Never mind, if he could just get hold of . . .

But the boy was stronger than Levar had thought. He had Levar's arms pinned down.

'Get the pen,' said Wolf to Maximilian. 'Write something.'

Wolf kept holding Levar down by his arms. In rugby, you make the tackle and then get on with the game. You are penalised for continuing to tackle someone who doesn't have the ball. Wolf was very used to bringing people down in rugby, but had no idea how to restrain or hurt people in real life. When his uncle beat him he just took it, although he wasn't sure why, especially now he probably had the strength to overpower him. So what should he do to Levar? Some voice was saying to him, 'Bash his head in. Beat it against the floor until blood comes out of his ears.' But Wolf knew he couldn't do this. He didn't want to go to prison. He didn't want to spend the rest of his life as a murderer. 'Bash his head in,' came the voice again. Wolf realised the voice wasn't in his head. It was Maximilian.

'Go on, Wolf,' said Maximilian again. 'Bash his head in!'

'I can't,' he said back. 'It's wrong. It's . . .'

'It's not wrong when . . . Oh, never mind. Hold him and I'll . . .'

Maximilian had picked up the pad and the pen. How would you use a magical prescription pad? Maximilian thought you would probably just write down whatever you wanted to happen to your foe, but how did you specify who exactly was your foe? He didn't want something bad to happen to himself or Wolf. Where were the instructions? If only he still had his

181

beloved spectacles. In fact . . . *Mend the spectacles*, he wrote. *Give them to me*.

Were his priorities right? Perhaps not. The spectacles did in fact mend themselves – spinning in the air with little fizzes and pops and the odd pink spark – and then return to him. But when he put them on, the world didn't change at all. It was as if their magic was gone.

'What have you done to them?' he shouted at Levar.

'Stupid boy,' Levar said. 'You've used up all your currency doing that, so you can't even use the spectacles any more, or cast any spells on me.' He looked at Wolf. 'I can feel that this boy has some magic in him, but he has no weapon. So . . .'

Levar closed his eyes, and Wolf found himself releasing his grip on Levar's arms. Then Wolf was floating in the air. He hovered for a few seconds, then hit the ground with a thud. It was like Saturday night with his uncle in slow motion.

'I do believe,' said Levar, 'that I have won this silly little battle.'

He stood up and looked down on Maximilian and Wolf.

'Why are you dabbling in things you do not understand?' he asked them. 'My business is of no concern to you or your pretty girlfriend. I bought some books, quite fairly, and now you have come to steal them. I wonder what the police would say about that? Or your parents? Or maybe they'll never find you, because . . .'

What could he do to them? Leonard Levar didn't want to use up too much more of his already very low M-currency, although he'd be able to exchange the spectacles for quite a lot of lifeforce at one of the Edgelands markets. Tying the boys up magically would cost too much, but there was no way he could do it with just his physical strength. Of course, throwing Wolf across the room had been easy. He had just used a simple deflector spell that turned the boy's own strength against him. And Maximilian's nausea was created entirely by a tiny misdirection of his stomach juices. That was the thing with magic. Sometimes the tiniest interventions could lead to the most spectacular effects.

So. Drowning. Levar really liked the idea of drowning. For example, if he had a nice big tub and a hosepipe and if he could tie these two up and put them in the tub and then put the hosepipe on . . . He imagined them fretting away, screaming perhaps, praying to be rescued, while the tub filled up and up and up. But to do all that in the Realworld, with M-currency? It would cost thousands. Hundreds of thousands, more likely.

What else was there? Spiders. Everyone knew that all young boys were afraid of spiders. And what did spiders cost? Nothing at all, if you happened to own an antiquarian bookshop next door to an exotic pet shop, and if there happened to be a secret door from one shop to the other, left over from the days when armies were based here during one of the old wars. So. You didn't always need magic at all. You simply needed keys. Two keys, to be precise. One to lock the boys into the empty cave with the grille (which was far too small for them to escape through), and one to open the door to the pet shop. Oh, and just a tiny little bit of magic to put the boys to sleep for a while, so they didn't try to escape before he came back with a book trolley to move them.

When they woke up, they would find themselves alone in the darker, smaller, empty cave, perhaps feeling relieved to still be alive. Levar would leave them some candles and matches. That would be nice. They wouldn't believe their luck when they found they had light as well. Alone in a bright cave. They may even start to feel cosy and comfortable and entertain hopes of being rescued. But then at some point they would notice the large Chilean six-eyed tarantulas that Levar was just about to go and get. That would keep them busy while he went to sell the spectacles. Then he could come back with a bit more power and, if necessary, finish them off. Then his precious books would be safe.

21

Effie heard a door creak from somewhere beyond the dining room. Then came the *click-click* of a creature's claws striking the tiled floor of the dining hall, which turned into more of a soft padding sound as the stone gave way to thick carpet.

The dragon entered the drawing room with a deep, satisfied sigh. He was just as majestic and beautiful as Effie remembered, his hard muscles glistening under his shiny grey skin. He sighed again, perhaps with enjoyment of the ambience of the room, or the tinkling piano music that was now coming from the dining room.

But then he noticed Effie, and started. He looked at her rather the way you might look at a pepperoni pizza when you were sure you had ordered a margherita. He blinked and looked again, taking her in, up and down and up and down, until he took a step back and frowned. The piano music continued as if this were the most elegant restaurant, rather than an appointment with death.

'Why have they sent you?' he asked, a little sadly. His voice was as smooth and dark as the finest melted chocolate. It was both comforting and terrifying at the same time. It was comforting because if this creature was your friend, you would be protected from anything else for miles. No human or beast from the forest could harm you. For this one night, you would be safer than you'd ever been. But terrifying because of course after this night, he meant to eat you.

'They didn't send me. I took Crescentia's place.'

'Why do they want me dead?' he said, with a touch of melancholy.

'Sorry?'

'You won't win. Gin and tonic? Martini? Aperol?' The dragon sat down slowly on a large sofa upholstered in a heavy gold fabric with a pattern of apples and pheasants on it. 'Maid!' he called. The elderly woman entered. 'A gin and tonic and a . . .?'

'Nothing for me, thanks.'

'Champagne?'

'I'm not old enough to drink.'

'Have it your own way.'

The maid brought in a glass tumbler full of ice cubes, clear liquid, mint leaves and slices of lime. The dragon took this in his hand and sipped from it. He looked almost refined, sitting there on his expensive sofa, drinking his perfectly prepared cocktail. If it hadn't been for his size, his shiny grey scaly skin, his wings, his tail and the fact that he breathed fire, he could have been a very handsome man.

'I wondered why they put you in the catalogue with the others,' said the dragon. 'I even wondered about choosing you, to see

what would happen. But Crescentia, Crescentia . . . How delicious she would have been. Ah . . .' The dragon made a kissing
sound with his lips, the way great gourmets do when they know
they have just been served something really nice.

'Crescentia. It could have been such a beautiful evening, you
know. The village put on a game of cricket for me this afternoon,
and the women brought baskets of flowers and buckets of mead
– not that I drink the revolting stuff, I give it all to the staff.
Still, it's a rather delightful touch. They want to make me happy.
Of course they do, since I appear to emit gold. But then someone
sends you.'

The dragon looked down at his drink, sipped from it, stirred
it with the little green swizzle-stick. He sipped again. 'Why?' he
said, quietly.

Effie didn't know what to say.

'WHY?' he suddenly roared, flames coming out of his mouth.

'I don't know what you mean,' said Effie, quite afraid.

'You have the ring,' said the dragon. 'But no weapon. Where
is your sword?'

'I don't have a sword,' said Effie.

'Then . . .?' The dragon sighed. 'How will we fight?'

'Fight? Why would we . . .?'

'Don't tell me you don't find me just a bit fascinating,' said
the dragon. 'Of course you do. You may think you're sitting there
all innocently, but perhaps you have forgotten that you are
wearing the Ring of the True Hero. Everyone knows a true hero
cannot resist a dragon. It's in your blood. The princesses are
naturally a little nervous, poor things, although I must say I

think they have a fine time once they get here. But you? I bet you couldn't wait. Did you kill her to take her place? Did you fight Crescentia for me?'

'Of course not. I don't understand . . .'

'Playing stupid is not going to help your cause,' said the dragon. 'What, did you think we were going to settle down to a nice dinner, with me believing that you were the princess I ordered, wearing her clothes, acting like her, even smelling like her? How many courses was I to have before you stabbed me in the back? A true hero can't keep away from the dragon she – or more usually he – is destined to kill. But the dragon in question does have an inkling of his own destiny as well. Do you think you can smell us, but we can't smell you? Do you not think that I yearn for your blood just as you yearn for mine?'

'Well . . .'

'You will be checked for weapons, then we will dine as if you were the princess. You will spend the night with me as arranged, as my guest. In the morning, we will fight. I had a modest battle arena constructed in my grounds in case this situation ever arose. How about that? Will you dine with me first?'

'You must know I can't eat anything here.'

'Well, as you like,' said the dragon. ' But it's a shame. They usually put on quite a good spread for the princess.'

'I've heard it's all drugged.'

'We usually drug the breakfast. Perhaps there is a bit of something in the dinner, too, just to help the princess relax. I can ask the cook to leave that out, although it may be too late. Please join me anyway.'

The dragon called for his butler, and a portly man entered the drawing room. He was wearing a long black dinner jacket lined with red silk. Effie followed the dragon and his butler through to the dining room, letting what he had said sink in. Was she really a true hero? What was it Crescentia had said the day before, when they had secretly watched the dragon from behind that tree? That only princesses and true heroes find the dragon attractive. But then she had said that there were no true heroes.

Was that why Effie had felt compelled to take Crescentia's place and come here? That was what the dragon seemed to think. And whether or not it was true, it would surely be better to have a chance to fight than just be eaten. But, as the dragon had pointed out, Effie had no sword. She hadn't even been able to use the sword that her grandfather had left for her. What on earth could she do?

Her stomach rumbled. She was still so hungry.

'Are you sure you will not eat?' said the dragon.

In front of Effie was a plate of meat and vegetables with roast potatoes and a thick dark sauce. The dragon had a similar plate in front of him, except that his was white china and Effie's was blue. And his sauce was more of a red colour. He also had a large goblet of very dark red wine, which he now sipped from.

'There are no drugs,' the dragon said again. 'Here, we'll swap plates.'

'Well . . .' Effie wondered if he had planned to do that.

'You should eat something.' His voice sounded almost tender. Was he as nice to the princesses as he was to the person he believed had come to fight him? 'I assume that if either of us wanted to kill the other right now, we would. We each have the power. But let's leave that until the morning. Let's enjoy this last supper.'

'OK,' said Effie. 'I'll eat, but on one condition. We'll toss a coin for who eats from the blue plate and who eats from the white plate.'

'Well, all right. But, *momentito* . . . Butler!'

The dragon and the butler had a whispered discussion and the white plate was taken away and a new blue plate brought out. Both plates were placed on the table. Now both sauces were dark. Then the dragon found a coin – an old doubloon from a strange-looking chest – that had two different sides (Effie checked). They tossed the coin to see who would eat what. Then Effie insisted on the plates being switched one more time. It wasn't perfect, but it would do.

Effie's food was delicious, and she ate it hungrily. Dessert was a big crystal bowl of trifle, which was offered first to Effie and then to the dragon. The bowl had writing on it. *Spyrys – Pryder – Wythrés*. The same three words Effie had noticed on the portraits and tapestries before. This time, the words were arranged around an image of a chariot with a driver and a horse. The chariot was labelled *Spyrys*, the driver was labelled *Pryder* and the horse was labelled *Wythrés*. The words looked Rosian, although maybe an older form than the one Effie had studied. *Spyrys*. What was that? A ghost, or spirit, or . . .?

'With the princesses, I normally discuss art and poetry,' said the dragon, sighing. 'I expect you are too coarse for such things. How about cricket?'

Effie nodded, remembering that her grandfather had liked cricket. She looked again at the caption on the bowl. *Spyrys* was a spirit, she was sure. And *pryder* meant something to do with thinking, Effie remembered. Thought, reasoning, or contemplation. And *wythrés* was action or battle.

The dragon began talking about the cricket match he had watched earlier. The villagers had put together two teams and one of them had done something clever, and then the other had done something cleverer and something to do with a leg break and a cut shot . . . While the dragon talked, Effie began to have an idea.

'What if we don't fight at all?' she suddenly said.

'Excuse me?' said the dragon. 'Not fight?'

'What if we found some other way to settle our dispute?'

The dragon scratched his scaly head. 'Interesting,' he said. 'But what is our dispute? Do we even have one? I always believed that when a true hero comes to the dragon, he – or she – means simply to kill him. It's then a fight to the death. That's what happens in all the stories. Of course, the true hero usually finds some way to win. But there are exceptions. My great-great-great-uncle Gregorius beat one of your lot back in the Middle Ages, I believe. And there was the great battle of White Horse Hill. Thank you, Elmar.'

The butler moved around the table and poured more of the very dark red wine into the dragon's crystal goblet.

'Our dispute is about you eating princesses,' said Effie.

The dragon looked taken aback. 'Well, what about it?'

'I think that the princesses would rather not be eaten.'

191

'Heavens! But why don't they say so?'

'Do they really not say or do anything once they're here that shows how frightened they are?'

The dragon considered this. 'Sometimes they do beg for mercy, that's true. But I thought that was all part of the service.'

'I think it might be real.'

'Oh.' The dragon looked sad. 'Gosh. But the school always tells me what a great honour it is for the girl who is chosen, how pleased she is.'

'That's just what they say. It's not true. Crescentia didn't sleep last night because she was so scared. You should have seen her hands shaking on the way here. She was very grateful when I offered to take her place.'

'Did she not want to see me at all?'

'Well . . .' Effie thought about this. 'She did say she thought you were handsome. But I really don't think she wanted to be eaten. And she is a bit young.'

The dragon thought for a little while.

'Do you think Crescentia would come here if I didn't mean to eat her? Do you think she might one day come just for dinner?'

'Perhaps when she's a bit older, yes. If you agreed not to eat any more princesses.'

The dragon looked down at his scaly hands, then back up at Effie.

'But what will I eat on my Princess Night? I LOVE princess. It's my very favourite food.' The dragon looked gloomier than ever. 'Have you ever tasted princess . . .? No, perhaps not. But you should, it's really . . .'

'Did you know that some princesses are kept out of the sunlight in crates to make them more tender? They have no lives at all.'

'Well, that's just wrong. Who does that?'

'Other dragons.'

'We'll need to put a stop to that. Princesses should be running free in the sunshine, full of light and air and the taste of summer meadows and . . . Oh dear. Are you saying they should not be eaten at all, by anyone?'

Effie nodded. 'Yes.'

'But what is a dragon to eat instead? Ooh – how about farmer's sons?'

'No.'

'Fallen women?'

'No.'

'Village idiots?'

'No. You can't eat any humans.'

'None at all?'

'No.'

'Oh dear.' The dragon sipped from his wine. 'But of course you haven't won yet. You haven't killed me, or felled me. You can't tell me what to do.'

'I don't want to fight,' said Effie. 'There's no point. And you did say that dragons usually lose. Perhaps there's another way? I think if I were to win the contest you would probably agree never to eat humans again, and then everyone would be happy.'

The dragon appeared to consider this. 'I did hear of one distant relative who was a tremendously good archer. When he came

across a true hero in a forest they agreed to a shooting competition. Perhaps something like that? We could round up some
villagers and see who can get more of them? I am rather deft
with a bow.'

'I think it would be nicer to do it in a way that nobody gets
killed.'

'How on earth would we do that?'

Effie thought for a moment. If she was going to have any
chance of winning a battle against the dragon, and saving
Crescentia and the other girls, she was going to have to find some
kind of competition that would appeal to him, but that she could
win. What was she good at? What had she practised? The words
Spyrys – Pryder – Wythrés came into her head again. Spirit –
Thought – Action. The image on the bowl had seemed to suggest
that the first two were superior to the last. Maybe . . .

22

'A thinking competition,' said Effie. 'We'll have a thinking competition.'

'Good heavens,' said the dragon. 'Well, I suppose I do have a great intellect, and you are a mere child. Surely a true hero relies on brute force, though?'

'Maybe not always,' said Effie.

'Right. Well, good. A thinking competition.' The dragon sipped his wine.

'Are you sure this is wise, sir?' said the butler.

'Yes, yes, yes. I'm fairly sure I can outwit almost anybody in a thinking competition. Ooh. This will be like the battle of White Horse Hill all over again, but with less blood. Right. Well. How do we do it? We'll need a referee. Elmar can do that.'

The butler bowed his assent.

'And we need rules. What are the rules? How do we play?'

'We could ask each other questions and . . .' Effie thought. 'They must be questions that you can solve just with your mind, not with facts or memory or anything like that. So you can't ask me your great-great-great-uncle Gregorius's middle name or something similar that I couldn't possibly know . . .'

'Dash it,' said the dragon. 'How did you know that's what I was going to ask?'

'Are you talking about riddles, miss?' asked the butler.

'I suppose I am,' said Effie. 'Some people call them Magical Thinking problems, or even lateral thinking problems, I think. But yes, let's call them riddles.'

'May I suggest the following format?' said the butler. ' I believe it is called "sudden death". You each pose one of these riddles and then go to bed. At dawn, you meet in the arena to provide your answers. If you both provide the correct answers, then you each pose a new riddle and the process begins again. But if one of you cannot answer the other's question then they lose. They are then "dead".'

'What if no one gets the right answer?' said Effie.

'Then that round is a draw, and you begin a new round.'

'Oh goody,' said the dragon. 'I already have my question.'

'There's just one final thing,' said the butler. 'We have already decided that if the dragon loses he will agree to eat no more humans. But what if he wins? What is his prize? He should name it.'

Effie wondered whether the dragon was going to say that he would simply carry on eating princesses for the rest of his life. But he considered the question for several minutes.

'You,' he eventually said to Effie, 'will be my bride.'

'What?' she said. 'But . . .'

'Yes. If you lose, you have to marry me and live here for ever.'

'But . . . I thought you preferred Crescentia?'

'Yes. But you should suffer if you lose. And you'd make an interesting wife.'

'Good,' said the butler. 'Then we shall begin.'

Even though the dragon had said he already had his question, he now closed his eyes, pressed his clawed forefingers to his temples, wrinkled his brow and started to emit a strange low humming sound. Effie looked at the butler.

'He is thinking, miss.'

'Oh. Right.' Effie started thinking as well. Although she knew what she was going to ask. Well, she was pretty sure. No, very sure. No . . .

The humming sound eventually stopped, and the dragon opened his eyes and looked at Effie.

'Begin,' said the butler. 'The dragon will go first.'

'Oh, good,' said the dragon. 'Right. There is a creature that walks on four legs in the morning, two legs at noon, and three legs in the evening. What is its name?'

'That is your riddle, sir?' said the butler.

'It is,' said the dragon. He smiled in a satisfied sort of way and sat back in his chair to wait for Effie's riddle.

'Go on, miss,' said the butler.

'OK,' said Effie. 'A man throws a ball . . .'

'Is it a cricket ball?' interrupted the dragon.

'Yes, if you like,' said Effie. 'A man throws a cricket ball some distance. The ball then turns and travels back to the man, and he catches it.'

197

'Ooh, ooh, I know the answer, I know the answer,' said the dragon.

Effie gulped. She thought of her grandfather, of his wise twinkling eyes as he first posed this question to Effie all those months ago. 'The ball has not hit any solid object, nor is it attached to anything,' she continued. 'And no one has worked any magic on it. How has this happened?'

The dragon put his head in his hands.

'I don't know!' he wailed. 'I was going to answer that it had been hit with a cricket bat. But then you say it has not been struck with an object. It's an impossible question!' He put his head down on the table and began a long, loud groan.

'May I remind you, sir,' said the butler, 'that you have all night to think about the question. Perhaps the answer will come to you later.'

The dragon frowned. 'Oh well. Never mind. You probably don't know the answer to my riddle either.' He yawned. 'I'm going to bed. To think.'

Shortly after the dragon left the dining room, the maid arrived to show Effie to her bedroom. It was a large, square chamber three flights of stairs further underground, with a huge four-poster bed with gold silk sheets and what seemed like hundreds of pink and gold pillows. There was a fire just dying in the hearth. Someone had warmed an old-fashioned hot water bottle – it was a real thick stoneware bottle – and left it on the bed, along with a silk nightgown embroidered with complex patterns. Effie sat on the bed for a long time, just thinking.

She knew the answer to the dragon's riddle. Well, she almost did. It had been in one of the first plays that Mrs Beathag Hide had made them read. Effie remembered Wolf Reed playing an ambitious young king who had ended up blinding himself with a badge with the words 'Neighbourhood Witch' on it that had been pinned to Raven Wilde's rucksack. The badge was a prop representing a brooch belonging to the ambitious king's wife. His wife had also, unfortunately, turned out to be his mother.

Effie remembered Mrs Beathag Hide imploring them all not to overact, to remain calm in the face of great tragedy, to allow themselves to be cleansed and purified by it. 'Let your emotions flood out,' she had said to the perplexed children, who were still wondering why exactly the poor king had to blind himself with the brooch and cast himself out into the wilderness and . . .

But what about the riddle? Effie remembered that the young king had faced some sort of monster, early in the play. A sphinx. That's right. The sphinx had asked him the riddle and the answer was . . . The answer was . . . Before she knew it, she had fallen asleep. When she woke up she was inexplicably under the sheets and clothed in the nightdress. The maid must have helped her. There were no windows in the underground castle, and Effie had no watch, but soon someone knocked on her door and told her that dawn would be breaking in half an hour.

Effie got out of bed and splashed water on her face and brushed her teeth. Crescentia's case had been brought up into the room. Effie wondered what Crescentia was doing now. Had she gone back to the Princess School? Effie was glad, though, that Crescentia wasn't facing being eaten this morning. How awful, to have to get up and get dressed and have breakfast while

199

knowing that you are soon going to die. The outfit that Crescentia had been going to wear for this morning was neatly packed in her bag. It was the simple pink silk dress that Effie had seen before. This didn't seem like the right kind of thing to wear for a battle, however, even if it was a battle of wits. Effie noticed that there was a large wardrobe in the room. Perhaps she might find something more suitable in there?

When she opened it, she gasped. Here were the clothes of all the princesses who had ever been here – or at least rather a lot of them. There were satin ball gowns and silk slip dresses and mini-skirts and leather trousers and even the odd pair of jeans. There were silk blouses, cashmere cardigans, soft t-shirts, wrap dresses and perfect white cotton shirts. There were pencil skirts, full pink tutus, and a lot of shoes, including high-heeled diamanté sandals and soft pink leather ballet pumps. Effie hurriedly threw together an outfit she thought more fitting for a true hero: a pair of dark blue jeans with a black t-shirt and a grey wool blazer. She didn't have time to do her hair, so she scraped it up into a messy ponytail. Then she slipped on a pair of black studded ankle boots and left the room.

The maid showed her up the stairs to the main part of the castle, explaining that breakfast was to follow the event in the battle arena. The dragon, she said, felt too sick to eat. And anyway, the maid went on, they wanted to get this private battle out of the way before the more bloodthirsty villagers started turning up expecting to see a princess being eaten. For many of the villagers, this was the highlight of their fortnight. The maid didn't know what was going to happen today when they discovered that the dragon seemed to have stopped eating princesses – at least for the time being. She hoped there would not be an uproar. Effie followed the chatty maid up the flight of stairs with the red carpet that she had been down yesterday. The drawbridge had already been lowered and Effie walked across it and into the fresh morning air.

It was a misty and still morning, with pink streaks across the sky. Effie followed the maid up some stone steps and past a pond and across some grass. There was the arena. It looked like a small Roman amphitheatre. There were weeds pushing up around the stone seats, however, and moss had grown over much of the round central area. It was clear that there had never been any fights here.

The dragon was pacing around the arena, mumbling to himself. He was holding a bright red cricket ball in one of his clawed hands, tossing it up and down. Oh no. Did he have the answer? But he wasn't acting like a dragon with the answer. He was trembling and pacing and muttering and, occasionally, stamping his clawed foot. Fire shot from his nostrils a couple of times as he sighed and groaned.

'Good morning, miss,' said the butler.

'Good morning,' said Effie.

The dragon plodded over. 'Your question is impossible,' he said.

Effie took a deep breath. 'I have an answer to yours,' she said.

'WHAT?' boomed the dragon. More fire came out of his nostrils.

'Calm yourself, sir,' said the butler. 'Let us commence.'

The butler repeated the rules that they had agreed the previous night, and then, after taking a sheet of blue paper from the inside pocket of his jacket, he read out the questions.

He looked at the dragon first. 'Do you have an answer to Euphemia Truelove's riddle?' he asked.

The dragon sighed. Breathed out a little bit of fire. Frowned. 'Dash it,' he said. 'No.'

'And do you, Euphemia, have an answer to the dragon's question?'

'I do.'

'State it.'

'The answer is man,' said Euphemia. 'Well, humans. In the morning of their lives humans crawl, which is the four legs bit. At noon, in other words, in the middle of their lives, they walk on two legs. But in later life they often use a stick, which gives them three legs.'

The dragon growled.

'Is that correct, sir?'

The dragon nodded his head. 'Yes, dash it all. I should have picked a harder one. It was only the first round! We should start again. This isn't fair.'

The butler cleared his throat.

'I will ask again. Do you, Dragon, have an answer to Miss Euphemia Truelove's riddle?'

'No.'

'Then we will declare Miss Euphemia Truelove the winner!'

'Wait,' said the dragon. 'We should hear the answer first. This ball that is thrown and comes back without hitting any objects.' He tossed the ball to Effie. 'Show us how it's done, then.'

'All right,' said Effie. She threw the ball into the air and caught it. 'Like that,' she said. 'I have thrown it a distance and it has come back to me, without hitting any objects and without being attached to anything. I have not used magic. It's just gravity. See?' She threw the ball up and caught it again.

'Oh, bravo,' said the butler. Then, 'Sorry, sir.'

The dragon didn't say anything for a few moments. Effie wondered if he was going to eat her after all, or just roast her to death with the flames that were now steadily coming out of his nostrils. He tipped his head to one side. The flames stopped. He took a step towards Effie. Then another one.

He held out his clawed hand.

'Very clever,' he said. 'You win. What is it about true heroes? They always find some way to defeat the dragon.'

'So you promise you won't eat any more people?'

'If you insist,' said the dragon.

The butler clapped, and so did the maid, and the cook, who had come to watch. And soon there was the sound of someone else clapping. It was Crescentia.

'Oh my God,' she said. 'I don't believe it!'

'Crescentia,' said the dragon. 'More beautiful even than your picture.'

'Now I know I'm not going to be eaten, I thought I'd come and say hello,' she said. 'And to put our dinner date in my diary for . . . Let's say three years' time? If you're still interested, that is.'

The dragon looked pleased but confused.

'Oh, the maid told me everything,' said Crescentia.

23

The sound of clapping grew dim and echoey and it suddenly seemed to Effie as if the sky were full of shooting stars. Was she collapsing from the excitement? No. She stayed upright, but the world began swirling gently around her. Soon there was only darkness, and then, for a moment, only light. Some words seemed to be forming in faint fireworks above her head.

THE END

The words were drawn in little puffs of light and smoke. *The end*. What did that mean? It was as if Effie had just finished reading a book. Perhaps it should have felt frightening, but it didn't. It felt quite comfortable and satisfying. In fact, it felt almost exactly the way finishing a good book feels.

When things went back to normal, Effie found that she was standing outside the big ornate gates of Truelove House with a calling card in her hand. It read *Clothilde and Rollo Truelove would be honoured to entertain Miss Euphemia Truelove at her convenience*. There was no sign of the dragon, or Crescentia or anyone from the last few days. It was almost as if Effie was now in an entirely new world. Perhaps she was. Everything felt different, although she couldn't have explained quite how. But the grass around her was a slightly different shade of green than it had been before. It was brighter. More vivid.

All was still and quiet, except for a robin singing loudly in the rowan tree. The sound was more clear and real than anything Effie had heard in days. Perhaps more than she'd ever heard. Beyond the rowan tree, the whole landscape had changed. All the grass was the new shade of green. The Princess School was no longer there on the hilltop, and the village had gone, too. Even the air around her felt different. It was a bit like when spring becomes summer, or when a flower opens.

'Can I help you, miss?' asked a guard.

Effie turned and handed him the calling card. He looked at it, smiled, nodded, gave it back to her, and opened the gates.

'Straight up the driveway, Miss Truelove,' said the guard. 'Can't miss it.'

Just inside the gates was a strange swirling mist that was cold and thick and smelled faintly metallic. Effie walked through it, hearing the robin's song grow dim and then disappear entirely. After a few seconds, she emerged into the most beautiful garden she had ever seen, with a pathway leading through it and up to the big house with its smooth turrets and circular towers. It was warm and bright, and the sun was high in a perfect blue sky.

There were birds, bees and butterflies everywhere, and a smell of lavender, jasmine and rose. Dragonflies flitted here and there, along with some other creatures that Effie couldn't name, little round glowing orbs that darted up and down. Were these fireflies? Mayflies? But they seemed like creatures from another universe. Where was she?

There was a young man standing by the door waiting for her. He was oddly beautiful in some way she couldn't fathom. He had shoulder-length dark hair and glasses and was wearing a loose white silk shirt and long beige linen shorts.

'Beautiful day,' he said to Effie, smiling.

'Am I in a dream?' she asked him.

And then everything seemed to hit her all at once. Her grandfather's death, followed by a long, horrible day with hardly any food, the argument with her father and Cait, Lexy's tonic, and then trying to read the book *Dragon's Green*. Then falling asleep in her bed, and the next day being brought to the place Dragon's Green and finding she had been sold to the Princess School. And then discovering she was a true hero and finding a way to overcome a dragon and bring peace to a village and save a lot of girls from being eaten. It had been an intense few days. In fact, now that she was here in this relaxing place, with this calming person looking at her in quite a loving way, perhaps she could just . . . could just . . .

The next thing Effie knew she was waking up on a beautiful mauve velvet sofa in a large, light drawing room with delicate white curtains billowing softly in the warm breeze.

The young man was looking at her with concern. There was a young woman with him as well. They were both in their late teens or early twenties. The young woman had long blonde hair and was wearing a yellow silk dress. She was holding out a turquoise teacup and saucer.

'Fourflower tea,' she explained, handing the teacup to Effie. 'It'll restore you. I hear you've had quite a journey to get to us. My brother believes you came through a book.' She sat on the edge of the sofa and gave Effie the most friendly, warm smile Effie had ever seen. 'I'm Clothilde, and this is my brother Rollo. We're your cousins, sort of. We'll explain in a moment. But first, tell us everything,' she said.

So Effie did. Right from the beginning. It took a long time, because her beautiful cousins kept oohing and aahing and asking her to repeat bits. They both expressed great sadness to hear of Griffin's death, although what they said about it was very odd – 'It will take a long time for him to reach us now.' They had clearly known him very well. When Effie got to the parts about the Princess School the cousins became quite excited, laughing and clapping and asking her to repeat even more things.

'You actually faced a dragon, alone!' said Clothilde. 'Trueloves are known for their bravery, of course, but did you have any idea how dangerous that was?'

Rollo shook his head, but looked quite admiring. 'Insane,' he concluded.

'Pretty risky, if you ask me,' Clothilde said to Rollo. 'Getting her here through a book.'

'Clever, though,' said Rollo. 'There's no way she could have been followed.'

'True. But if she hadn't decided to take on the dragon, she

could have been stuck in the book for ever. She could have been at the Princess School for *years*.'

'Griffin must have known she'd come through. He taught her everything she needed to do so. And, of course, he knew that only a true hero could have made it through that particular story. It was certainly clever. After all, how many true heroes are there? None among the Diberi, certainly.'

'But he didn't teach her everything. She had to rely on her own knowledge as well.'

'I suppose he couldn't have known that she was going to need the book so soon . . . He probably meant to teach her the other things later. But any true hero would find a way through that book, I'm sure.'

Effie was now feeling quite well again, although some of the things Clothilde and Rollo were saying made it seem even more likely that she was in a very long and complicated dream. She pinched herself a couple of times – she'd read stories in which people do this to try to wake themselves up. Clothilde had been looking very serious as she talked to Rollo. But now she laughed.

'What are you doing?' she asked Effie.

'Checking to see if this is a dream.'

'Would you want to wake up, if it was?'

Effie smiled. 'Maybe not. If this is a dream, then it's the most interesting dream I've ever had. But if it's not a dream, then where am I? And what do you mean when you keep talking about me coming "through a book"?'

'Ah,' said Rollo. 'Yes. Where to begin.'

'Do you know where you are now?' said Clothilde.

'Am I still in Dragon's Green?'

'Yes. Sort of. A different Dragon's Green from the one you were driven to, though. But you do realise that you are now in the Otherworld?'

'The Otherworld? But I couldn't get through. I didn't have the right papers.'

'You came through the book.'

'You keep saying that. What does it mean?'

Clothilde sighed. 'There's so much to tell you, I don't even know where to begin,' she said. 'You don't know much about the Diberi, clearly, and you don't know about the great war with the Book Eaters and . . .'

'When you started reading *Dragon's Green*,' Rollo said, 'and you fell asleep . . . You remember that?'

'Yes. I was in bed. I'd just had the tonic my friend made me.'

'That tonic will have helped you a great deal. You should thank your friend when you see her.'

'But it was supposed to keep me awake! I just fell asleep.'

'You didn't fall asleep,' said Clothilde.

'You fell into the book,' said Rollo. 'Well, in a manner of speaking.'

'I don't understand,' said Effie.

'When you are the last person to read a book,' began Clothilde. 'Oh – but I'd better not start with that, because there's a *lot* of explanation about being a Last Reader. But it was so clever of Griffin to think of that and find a last edition of a book that would bring you so close to here, that only someone like you could survive . . .'

'For reasons we won't go into now,' said Rollo, smiling at his sister, 'when you are the Last Reader of a book, lots of special magical things happen. The main one is that you enter the book. If it's fiction, you experience it as a character, rather than reading it normally. You go inside the book and experience it from within.'

'You live it,' said Clothilde.

'And at the end you usually come out somewhere interesting in the Otherworld. I've heard before how difficult it is to get from your world to the Otherworld, although it's even harder to go the other way. Being a Last Reader gets you straight here. As well as a number of other things. But you have to get to the end of the book and out the other side.'

'And when you say "Last Reader" you mean . . .?'

'The last person ever to read the book in the whole universe. Most books won't have their Last Reader for centuries yet, or even millennia. Who knows when the last person will read *Hamlet*, or the Bible. But it will happen eventually.' Rollo pushed his glasses up his nose and continued. 'Reading a last edition is such a strange and singular thing that it awakens any magical abilities a person might have. And there are also great boons that they receive after completing their adventure and— '

'Or it's all just a scam by the Diberi,' said Clothilde. 'And they invented the whole Last Reader thing for their own ends, as a way of giving themselves unlimited power.'

'Let's not confuse our young cousin,' said Rollo. 'If that did happen, it would have been centuries ago. The whole thing is true lore now, anyway.'

'So, when I read *Dragon's Green*,' said Effie, 'you're saying that I entered its world somehow? So falling asleep wasn't real, but just part of the story? And when I woke up and Cait and my father were nice to me, that was part of the story too, and being taken to Dragon's Green in that car was all part of the beginning of the story?'

'Exactly,' said Rollo.

'But how could a book buried under my grandfather's floor-boards know that I was going to have an argument with my father and Cait and work that into its story? It was already written. I mean, how . . .?'

'All readers and books merge in various ways,' said Rollo. 'You know when you read a book that's set in a big house, and you get a description of the house, but your imagination makes up its own description anyway? And if you think about it, the house you picture is actually somewhere you visited when you were five, or your neighbours' place or something like that? Books are used to having their meanings shaped in these ways by readers. In fact, the most powerful ones find all sorts of ways of adjusting to accommodate you. And the more of your own self you put into a book – not just descriptions, but emotions, feelings, anger, sadness, love – the more you add to its magical charge, the thing you call M-currency. It's one of very few things that have remained the same in both worlds since the Great Split. Oh dear. Of course you won't know about the Great Split either . . . Anyway, if ten thousand people all read a book and love it, and add their own descriptions, locations and feelings and so on, the book absorbs all that energy and becomes extremely powerful. The Last Reader of that book will have a

211

particularly strong experience of it, and at the end he or she will absorb all of that power . . .'

'Which is exactly what the Diberi exploit for their own ends,' said Clothilde.

'Which we'll come to *later*,' said Rollo, pointedly. 'Books mould themselves to you just as you shape them with your mind. If you are to become the main character of a book then it will shuffle a few meanings and details this way or that to accommodate you. It's easy to slip into a character when reading a book – you must have experienced that anyway, even before you became a Last Reader.'

'Yes,' said Effie. 'I suppose I have.' She remembered reading that play of Mrs Beathag Hide's, the one that helped her with the dragon's riddle. She had imagined herself as Oedipus, that young would-be king, standing before the sphinx, faced with what seemed to be an impossible question. Only by imagining herself as him, as the poor tragic hero, had she been able to feel anything about the story at all – and remember the riddle.

'How's the tea?' asked Clothilde.

'Delicious,' said Effie. 'Thank you.'

'We'll have proper tea on the lawn later with cakes and little sandwiches and everything. Pelham Longfellow is coming. We told him you were here. But would you like any more tea, or anything to eat now?'

'No, thanks,' said Effie. 'I'm still trying to understand all this. Where am I? I know this isn't a dream exactly, and I'm in the Otherworld, but am I in some way still at home in bed?'

'No. You're really here. Later, Pelham will show you how to get home.'

'And have I been here for days? Will everyone be searching for me at home?' Effie quite liked the idea of this in some ways, although it would mean she'd be in even more trouble. 'Or . . .' She gulped. 'I heard a story once where a man went to a magical land and when he got home hundreds of years had passed.'

Clothilde laughed. 'Don't worry. It's actually very convenient for you Realworlders to come to the Otherworld. A day here – we call them moons, by the way – is equivalent to around 19.1 minutes of your time. An hour in the Realworld gives you just over three days here: 3.14, to be precise. A long weekend.'

'What about the time I spent in the book?'

'Books and any liminal spaces work on mainland – sorry, Otherworld – time. So from what you said, you've been here for around three moons so far. Just under an hour.'

'Look,' said Rollo. 'I know you must have thousands of questions, and we have a lot to tell you as well, but we've done enough talking for a little while. We'll show you to your room and you can rest before tea.'

'Oh, and take some Fourflower Creams up with you,' said Clothilde, reaching over to the corner cabinet and then passing Effie a turquoise box with a pink ribbon around it. 'I find one of these always makes me feel better.'

24

The key rattled in the lock and Maximilian sat up slowly in the dimly lit cave. Leonard Levar's unconsciousness spell had not worked. Maximilian had not gone to sleep as he was supposed to. Wolf had, but something in Maximilian's system had simply refused to accept Levar's magic.

The first strange thing was that he'd actually *felt* the spell approach him. Did people normally feel spells as they approached? It seemed unlikely. When Maximilian was younger, his mother had taken him to see the sights of London. Whenever he'd stood underneath one of those tall monuments and looked up, it had seemed as if the monument were falling on him. Down, down, down, until splat, he was dead. Although, of course, that had been just in his imagination. A sort of optical illusion. But it turned out that the falling-monument sensation was very similar to how it had felt having a spell approach him and then fail. Down, down, down, until splat, he was unconscious. Except he was not. He was quite awake.

Maximilian had no idea where Levar had gone or what he was doing. He had taken the spectacles with him. Maximilian's precious, beautiful spectacles, without which the world made even less sense. Maximilian sighed. At least it wasn't completely dark. There was some kind of skylight in the ceiling and the moon was almost full. Could he climb up to the skylight and escape? No. Could he get out through the door? No. Could he wake Wolf up by shaking him a lot? No. But Wolf did have a beaten-up old phone in his pocket with a torch function, which Maximilian was sure Wolf wouldn't mind him borrowing. So now Maximilian could explore, and read. And there was lots of reading material around: crates and crates of books that had belonged to Griffin Truelove, the famous Master scholar.

Most children who had just been locked in a cave by a dark mage on an evil mission would probably cry, scream, beat their tight little fists against the thick wooden door. But Maximilian was not most children. If only Mrs Beathag Hide could have seen him now, her so-called Bottom of the Class. Calmly, he used the torch to help him see to open one of the crates. Calmly, he chose a book – a dark blue cloth-bound hardback with silver lettering on the front called *Beneath the Great Forest*. Then, calmly, he sat down with his torch to read it. If he was going to die, then he was going to die doing the thing he most loved. He was going to die reading. But not just any old book, either. Maximilian knew these books were in some way powerful, he just didn't know how.

Once upon a time . . . began the book. Maximilian found he was oddly sleepy. Sleepier than he usually was when reading. *Once upon a time there was a boy in a cave with no hope of escape.* Well, that was a coincidence. *Once upon a time . . .*

When Maximilian woke up, the cave felt colder than it had before. There was still no sign of Levar. Wolf remained unconscious on the floor. He was breathing, but Maximilian still couldn't wake him, however hard he tried. He looked at his watch. He hadn't been asleep for long at all; no more than five minutes or so. But things had changed. As well as being colder, the cave was also a little darker now. A little, well, *greener*. There was also, suddenly, a smell of damp earth and leaves.

Maximilian looked around and found the reason. A large tree was growing up through the uneven cave floor and out of the skylight in the ceiling. Its vast, aged trunk now took up most of the far corner of the cave. Had Maximilian simply not noticed it before? It was possible. Sometimes we do choose to ignore the biggest, densest, most gnarled things that surround us. The tree had thick roots, some of which were now visible as bulges under the cave floor. And at the bottom of the trunk was a sort of hollow that looked like an entrance to somewhere.

The hole was surrounded by thick, twisted bits of trunk that almost looked like an ancient carving. Maximilian even fancied there were words written there, too, in the old brown bark, but he could not read their language. One of them seemed to say something like *bitteren*; another said *dirre*. Maximilian wished he had the spectacles for a translation, although he wasn't entirely sure they would work on these words.

He crawled into the hole, and, after passing through a strange kind of grey mist, found himself in a low passageway lit by candles. The ground underneath his feet was soft and earthy and felt quite pleasant. But the darkness here was blacker than anything he had ever encountered before. Without the small candles he would have been completely lost. Soon Maximilian heard singing coming from somewhere ahead of him. It sounded deep and dusky and strange: sad one moment, then betrayed, then angry. But it was still very beautiful, unlike the noises emitted by his tuneless school choir and the old ladies in that church his mother had once made him go to.

Soon the passage opened out into a night-time forest still lit by small, flickering candles. Maximilian had the uncanny sense that although other children would be terrified in this place, he was not. He felt there was something for him here, although he had no idea what it would be. Something had happened before – around the time he picked up the Pen of Prescription – that had made him feel different, almost as if he had epiphanised again. It was odd, but this new feeling was somehow connected to that.

He walked on. Soon he came to a little cottage, with smoke curling out of its chimney. The cottage was on the bend of a thin, twisting river. Just beyond it was a rowing boat tied to a small jetty on the riverbank. If Maximilian was going to go any further he would need to cross the river. Perhaps there was someone in the cottage who would take him across? Maximilian had never rowed in his life. And there was no point in stealing a boat if he didn't have to.

He knocked. There was no answer. He tried again. Nothing. Perhaps now was the time to go and get Wolf. It was likely that Wolf could row that small boat. Although he'd have to wake up first, and who knew when that would happen. Maximilian knocked and knocked. There was still no answer from the little cottage, so, for the first time, he looked back the way he had come.

Everything was gone.

There was no path. No candles. Nothing visible in the deep blackness. Maximilian knocked on the door again, this time with desperation.

'All right, all right,' said a voice inside. 'Keep your hair on.'

The door opened. There stood a thin young man of around twenty, dressed entirely in black, with black braces over his black polo neck. He was smoking a thin black cigarette.

'Stately, plump Buck Mulligan . . .' said the young man seriously. Then he laughed. 'Ahahaha . . .' He fake-swooned. 'I think he died for me . . .'

Maximilian had no idea what he was talking about.

'You'd better come in,' said the young man. 'My name is Yorick. As in "Alas, poor . . ." and so on. Although no actual relation, I'm pleased to say.'

'O William?' called a woman from inside. 'Is that William? Has he brought a pineapple?'

The cottage opened onto a thin hallway, rather like something you'd find in an urban terraced house. On the walls were many

218

posters and handbills advertising bicycles for sale, poetry reading groups and art exhibitions, as well as an 'existentialist support group', whatever that might be, and a man who was promising to shoot himself on the 9th of September as long as nine or more people came to watch. There was a WANTED poster for someone called Woland.

Maximilian followed Yorick past a pram and into a sitting room, in which there were seven people – all as thin as Yorick, all dressed in black, all smoking the same black cigarettes – and a blue Persian cat.

There was a fire glowing in the small brick fireplace. One of the men was feeding sheet after sheet of a manuscript into it. He was muttering something about turning thirty and going to a sad aircraft hangar and burning whatever remained of his work, which looked as if it wouldn't be much.

Two of the other young men were standing up and looking at each other solemnly. One was reading to the other. 'And they both realised that the end was still far, far away, and that the hardest, the most complicated part was only just beginning,' he said.

One of the women was writing in a notebook. She read out what she appeared to have just written. 'No paper or envelopes, of course. Only a morsel of pink blotting-paper, incredibly soft and limp and almost moist, like the tongue of a little dead kitten, which I've never felt.' Maximilian couldn't make any sense of what was happening. It was like one of those adult jokes that go on for too long.

The table in the centre of the room had bowls containing

olives, gherkins, hard-boiled eggs, anchovies, fish mousse, coffee creams, rye bread, very smelly cheese, liver sausage, lambs' kidneys, caviar, coriander salad and one huge pale quivering white blancmange. Maximilian felt sick just looking at it all.

'Coffee?' said Yorick, producing a small cup and saucer.

'I don't really like . . .'

'Any of it. Of course you don't. What child likes olives and coffee? What youngster can stomach liver sausage? But you have to eat it all before Isabel takes you across the river. That's the rule. Don't blame me.'

'I have to eat all that?'

'Yes.'

'Where exactly am I?' said Maximilian, still feeling sick at the idea of eating even one thing from the table.

'We are condemned to be free,' said the man by the fire.

This didn't seem like much of an answer.

'Drink the coffee,' said Yorick. 'Before it gets even darker outside.'

'Hurry, dear William,' said the woman Maximilian thought was called Isabel. 'I do hate to row in the dark. Although, of course, it always is dark here.'

'Why does she think I'm called William?'

'Drink the coffee and maybe she'll tell you while she rows you across.'

Maximilian took the small cup. The smell made him feel a bit sick. But adults liked coffee, didn't they? And this seemed somehow to be the most coffeeish coffee you were likely to find anywhere. An adult who liked coffee would probably love this,

Maximilian realised. It was thick and black with a sort of pale cream on the top from being so strong. The little cup it was in was also black, with a delicate silver handle. He sniffed the coffee. It smelled grown-up, dark and complicated, rather like the place he seemed to be heading for. He sniffed once more and then drank it all.

After that, the olives actually tasted quite nice. They were black, wrinkled and very, very salty. But after the coffee they made a sort of sense. Maximilian almost liked them. Well, at least he didn't completely hate them. He didn't vomit. He looked at the remaining dishes on the table. The trick, he thought, was to have the things in the right order. To balance something salty with something sweet. Now that he almost liked coffee, the coffee creams might not be so bad. He should save them for last, to take the taste away from everything else. And . . . He approached the table again. Smelly cheese on rye bread. Yes, not a bad combination: the sourness of the bread blending with the pungent depth of the cheese. After that, the liver sausage wasn't so terrible. And the anchovies could have been nice if it hadn't been for all the little bones Maximilian had to crunch through.

'Can I have another cup of coffee?' he asked Yorick.

'Well, that's a first,' Yorick said, pouring it. 'No one's ever asked for seconds before. In fact, barely anyone has ever managed to complete this task before. Not that very many have tried, for, well, obvious reasons.'

25

Maximilian didn't know what he was doing, but he kept on doing it. The coffee seemed to make everything else taste better, so he kept asking for more of it. All he had to do was pretend he was a grown-up – yes, maybe like his mother's French friend Henri with the beard that smelled of cabbage – and think himself into liking all these strange foods. Caviar. Yes, OK, it *was* fish eggs, but some adults paid a lot to eat it. He spooned it all out of the bowl and tried to enjoy the way each black egg popped in his mouth like a small salty balloon. Then the lambs' kidneys, which were quite sweet and creamy, once you forgot what they were.

After he'd eaten all the remaining savoury things he had to face the blancmange. It was slimy and pale, like the tongue of the little dead kitten that the woman on the couch seemed to keep talking about (although that was pink and this was a ghostly white). After all that, the coffee creams did seem like quite a treat. Maximilian ate them slowly.

'Right,' he said, once he was finished. 'Now can I go across?'

The woman who kept calling him William got up off her chair and stretched.

'Take the gift from him, poor Yorick,' she said. 'And then we can go.'

'You may give us your gift now,' said Yorick to Maximilian.

'Gift?' said Maximilian. 'You never said anything about a gift. Come on. I did as you asked. I ate every piece of food on that table. Now please will someone take me to the other side of the river?'

'Not until you give us a gift.'

'I don't have anything with me,' said Maximilian, irritated.

'Yes you do. You have thousands of gifts with you, and we only want one.'

Maximilian frowned. Perhaps he shouldn't have been surprised that the rules kept changing in a place such as this, whatever it was. But what could they mean? What did he have thousands of with him? Bacteria? Atoms? Did they want him to brush off some skin cells or something? Or pull out some of his hairs? He thought back to everything they had said since he'd arrived. These people seemed to like spouting things in that way adults do when they are quoting Great Works of Literature. Indeed, rather like Mrs Beathag Hide had said 'O Maximilian, O Maximilian' earlier. So perhaps that was what he could give them. A line from a great play or poem or something. It had to be something weird or disturbing in some way, though, he guessed. They wanted the literary equivalent of the foods they had just made him eat. He realised that, because . . .

He suddenly found that part of his mind, which he hadn't been aware of until very recently, had stretched out and was now reaching inside Yorick's mind and looking around, the way you might rifle through a drawer for something if you'd just broken into someone's house. And he discovered that he knew the sort of thing Yorick and the others wanted. They wanted something like in that book of his mother's. The one she read every year around Maximilian's birthday. The big battered hardback that looked wrong among all her medical books and cheap holiday paperbacks.

Maximilian had explored his mother's books often, and had memorised parts from most of them. He wasn't fussy. They were all interesting. From his mother's books you could learn about really disgusting diseases, and the cruel courtship rituals of celebrities. This other book had always been harder to understand, though. But he had read bits. And something here had reminded him of it, although he wasn't sure what.

Deeper into Yorick's mind he went. He had no idea how he was doing it. Down here in this forest, wherever that even was, he seemed to have more magical energy than he'd had before, when he had been trying to overpower Carl's mind. Although, of course, Maximilian was not trying to overpower Yorick's mind, just read it a little. Maximilian remembered more bits of this book of his mother's. It had a talking cat, and the devil, but the devil wasn't all bad and in the end everyone lived happily ever after. Well, in a way.

And suddenly Maximilian found himself quoting part of the end of the book he didn't even know he had remembered, but realised he had rather liked.

'Can it be that you don't want to go strolling with your friend in the daytime under cherry trees just coming into bloom, and in the evening listen to Schubert's music? Can it be that you won't like writing with a goose quill by candlelight?'

As Maximilian spoke, a deep calm came over Yorick's face.

'You found something happy,' he said, a tiny smile beginning to appear on his lips. 'You found something happy that we can accept. A rare gift indeed. For that, we will give you a lot of . . .'

Then came a furious banging on the door. BANGBANGBANG. It didn't stop, so Yorick hurried to answer it. A few seconds later Leonard Levar strode into the room, his chin quivering and his eyes blazing. He pinched Maximilian's ear between his forefinger and thumb and dragged him out into the hallway and then out of the cottage altogether. The cottage then disappeared, leaving Levar and Maximilian in almost complete darkness.

'Ow!' said Maximilian. 'Let go of me.'

'You stupid boy.' In his other hand, Levar was carrying a candle in a glass holder. 'What on earth do you think you are doing?'

'Whatever I'm doing is none of your business,' said Maximilian, unable to get out of Levar's grasp.

'It certainly is my business, since you have stolen, and entered, one of my books.'

'I haven't stolen anything,' said Maximilian.

'You are like me – I recognised it when I first saw you – but stupid. It's a terrible combination, and I won't let you . . .'

'I am nothing like you,' said Maximilian.

'Oh, really?' said Levar. 'How peculiar, then, that you seem to find yourself on the well-worn path to Faery, a place where only dark mages can usually go.'

Maximilian released himself from Levar's grasp somehow. He took one step away from him. Then two. A dark mage? Maximilian? No. It couldn't be true.

'Or the Underworld,' Levar continued. 'Whatever you want to call it, it's the same place.'

'I'm a scholar,' said Maximilian.

'Oh yes. Scholar. Your secondary ability, like mine. They call it your art; the thing you dabble in. But your true nature, your *kharakter*, is engraved on your soul. You are a mage, boy, perhaps even a powerful one.' Levar paused. 'I can smell dark magic on you now. Yes . . .' He sniffed the air. 'Toffee apples and rust and smoke. Peculiar, but distinctive. I never took an Apprentice,' he said. 'But perhaps now is the time. Come back with me. I can make you powerful.'

'I would never go anywhere with you.'

'Oh, really?'

Maximilian felt an odd pang. For a few moments he imagined himself as Levar's Apprentice. He saw a dark but comfortable town house full of beautiful artefacts and ancient relics. He heard complicated piano music playing on an old-fashioned record player. He saw a room full of glass jars full of interesting powders and liquids, because he had no idea that mages don't in fact use such things. He saw room after room of rare books that he could study whenever he liked. He saw Mrs Beathag Hide and Coach Bruce and Mr Peters – and a few other people who had been mean to him lately – all locked in his own private torture chamber. Coach Bruce was stretched out on some sort of medieval rack. Maximilian crept forwards and turned the wooden handle that meant . . .

'Stop it,' he said to Levar. 'Whatever you're doing to my mind, stop it.'

It was the same feeling he'd had before. The monument falling on him, but not really falling. The fantasy disappeared. He had somehow resisted Levar's magic.

'I don't know how you keep blocking me, boy,' said Levar. 'But all you do is make yourself more interesting. Join me. I know how much you want what only I can give you.'

'Why do you want me to join you?' said Maximilian, suspiciously. 'And why would you be trying to help me when you only want the books? It doesn't make any sense. You meant to kill me up there anyway. Why would you be rescuing me now? If this Underworld is so dangerous, why don't you leave me here? I was just about to be taken across the river. Why didn't you let me go?'

Levar said nothing.

'It's something to do with the books,' said Maximilian. 'But what?'

'You know full well,' Levar said. 'You can't be so stupid that you don't understand the power of the book you are in, and what reading it for the last time means. But perhaps, on the other hand, you are just as stupid as I first thought. What do you think would happen to a Neophyte who tried to take control of the Underworld? You would go over that river and into a complex web of darkness from which you would never return.

227

You would remain lost and confused for all eternity. I am saving you.'

'You are not saving me from anything. I'd rather be lost in the Underworld than dead, anyway. No. I think I understand,' said Maximilian. '*You* want to take control of the Underworld. Whatever I'm doing is ruining it somehow for you.'

'You know full well you are inside the book,' said Levar. 'And that over on the other side of the river is the character you will release, whose place you will take. I have wanted to own this book for a very, very long time. And I, not you, will be its Last Reader. It's clear that the universe has not yet decided. That is why we can both be here, on the same path, suspended like Schrödinger's Cat . . .' Levar started speaking in some sort of incomprehensible scientific language that made Maximilian feel a bit sleepy.

'Come with me, boy. I'll give you the spectacles. And your own beautiful athame. I will give you an Apprenticeship, as I promised. I will teach you how to be a truly gourmet Book Eater – but you will need to begin with simpler volumes than this one. A nice detective story. Or something with a lot of romance. Would you like to fly, boy? There are books that will enable you to do just that. Would you like to rule over great lands? You could do magic beyond what you can even imagine now. Just come back with me. You will see wonders, have riches, know great beauty . . .'

Maximilian had not realised that while he was talking, Levar had been leading him slowly back up the pathway towards the hole through which he had entered this world. Before he knew it, they were both standing in the cave storeroom again, with Levar holding the blue cloth-bound book that Maximilian had chosen: *Beneath the Great Forest*.

Maximilian yearned to be back in the book again. He so desperately wanted to know what was across that river. Even if it was dark and confusing, he felt it would be important and worthwhile. But now Levar had taken the book from him, and Maximilian felt lost, sad, and as if he had failed in some dreadful way.

This time Levar doubled the unconsciousness spell, and the monument really did fall. Soon Maximilian was asleep next to Wolf, dreaming of a very long, very wide river that he couldn't seem to cross, however hard he tried. And on the other side of it, waiting patiently for his chance to be back in the Realworld, was a man he was sure he knew.

26

Effie's room in Truelove House smelled of clean sheets and very old wood. There was a big bed made up with blue and white striped linen, and the walls were covered with pale blue wallpaper with a pattern of silver birds and stars. There were no signs of electricity anywhere. The pale wooden desk had a beautiful lamp – a fresh white candle in an intricate brass holder with a glass dome around it. Next to that was a ceramic jar filled with quills, a pot of ink and a stack of pale blue writing paper.

There was also a peculiar kind of silence, quite different from the creepy quiet of the greyouts at home. This new silence sat softly under all the other sounds of birdsong and summer insects and, from somewhere not so far away, the sounds of croquet mallets hitting balls and the clinking of ice cubes in glasses. In the Realworld there was a constant hum of machines and cars that existed under every other sound. Here, there was nothing.

Effie looked at the square turquoise box that Clothilde had given her. *Fourflower Creams*, it said on the front in gold leaf and pink foil. She untied the ribbon and lifted the lid to reveal three layers of mauve waxy paper. Nestling at the bottom of the box were six chocolates. Each one was round and black with a turquoise candied petal on the top. Effie picked one out. It was strangely heavy. She bit into the thick black chocolate, which made a low cracking sound as she did. Inside was a pale white fondant that tasted like sweet flowers of a sort that didn't exist in Effie's world. It was delicious.

Effie took off her studded boots and lay down on the bed. But she was not at all sleepy. She twisted her silver ring on her thumb. Was she a true hero in real life now? Or was that just within the story? Rollo had said that she wouldn't have reached the end of the story at all had she not been a true hero. But what did it all mean? Effie shuddered when she thought of other ways the story could have gone. She could have been trapped in the book for ever – or worse, eaten by the dragon.

Effie sat up and got off the bed. She felt restless. Perhaps her cousins wouldn't mind if she explored the house a little, maybe went downstairs to get a glass of water. It was still very warm, and the sound of ice cubes in glasses was making her thirsty.

Her room was one of several surrounding a sort of gallery from which you could look down the grand staircase to the entrance hall below. The drawing room had been off to the right, but Effie had no idea what other rooms there were. And how far up did the house go? There were more stairs at the end of the gallery to the left of Effie's room, leading to a smaller landing and then the beginning of a thin spiral staircase with worn purple carpet and wallpaper with faded golden moons all over it.

The stairs seemed to go on for ever; up, up, up, they wound and coiled and twisted. Effie realised she was almost certainly in one of the circular towers she'd noticed when she'd looked at the house from outside. At the very top of the stairs, Effie found an oval-topped wooden door with intricately carved details of plants and animals on it. Something told her she should knock, so she did. When there was no response, she knocked again, more loudly.

'All right, all right,' said a gruff voice from inside. 'I'm coming.'

The door opened and there stood – Effie gasped – her grandfather!

'Grandfather . . .' she began, her voice catching in her throat.

'Hush, child,' said the man, patting her on the head as she rushed to embrace him. 'There, there. It's all right. You are safe here.'

He reached inside his long purple robes and pulled out a very large white handkerchief, as if he were expecting her to cry. But she didn't.

'Grandfather?' Effie said again.

'No, child, no. I am simply his cousin. My name is Cosmo Truelove. And you, I believe, are the famous Euphemia. I hear you've had quite an adventure reaching us here. Clothilde told me everything. Come in, child. Sit.'

Cosmo Truelove did look like Effie's grandfather, but, as they say, even more so. In fact, if Griffin Truelove had grown his beard another foot, doubled his eyebrows, tripled his wrinkles, quadrupled his moustache, painted his fingernails silver and then put on a wizard's costume, this is exactly what he would have looked like. Cosmo's robes were slightly too big for him, or perhaps there were just a lot of them, because he seemed to be around 60 percent swirling robe and only 40 percent man. On his head he wore a soft grey hat with a pattern of silver stars and gold crescent moons. It was pointed at the end, like all wizards' hats. His eyes were the brightest green and sparkled in his face like two moonlit emeralds.

'Well, come in,' he said again. 'Sit down.'

His circular room was almost entirely lined with bookshelves. They were only broken by a black cast-iron fireplace with two armchairs and one rocking chair in front of it. In the centre of the room was a desk and a very old-looking wooden chair. A large hardback book was open on the desk. It seemed like some sort of atlas. A black cat was asleep on the rocking chair, so Cosmo gestured to Effie that she should sit on one armchair, and he then sat down on the other.

'Water, dear universe,' he said quietly, and a glass of water appeared on the table next to Effie.

'You said you were thirsty,' Cosmo explained.

'Oh, I was sure I just thought it, but, well, thank you . . .'

'Oh dear. Forgive me for reading your thoughts. Such an invasion of privacy.'

Effie didn't know what to say. This person was not just dressed as a wizard, he appeared to actually be a wizard. Despite all those years asking her grandfather, Effie had never actually seen magic happen before, right in front of her, so casually. She picked up the water and sipped it. It was, it was . . .

'Lemonade,' she said. 'Well, still lemonade. Thank you.'

'But I asked for water! Oh dear. Never mind. This happens – you'll get used to it. I must have said water but *thought* "lemonade". It is a very lemonadey sort of a day, which is probably the reason. Maybe I actually fancy lemonade and that's why . . . Lemonade, dear universe,' he muttered, and a ceramic jug appeared with liquid so fizzy you could hear it cracking and popping. Bubbles were bursting out of the top of it as if they were full of joy and longing for exercise. 'Oh my, I really was thinking of lemonade,' said Cosmo. 'Perhaps you'll join me? I fear what I ordered for you may be neither quite one thing or another.'

Cosmo flicked his hand and Effie's glass of flat lemonade disappeared. Instead, he poured her a glass of the most fizzy, lemony, refreshing lemonade she had ever tasted.

'That's better,' said Cosmo. 'Now. You knocked on my door, which means you must have some questions. People without questions do not go knocking on strange doors.'

Effie didn't know where to begin. Her mind filled with things she wanted to know about her grandfather, and her recent adventures, and being a true hero. But one question quietly pushed all the others away and put itself right there in the front of Effie's mind.

'What happened to my mother?' she asked.

Her eyes pricked with tears as she remembered Aurelia dancing in the kitchen with Orwell and chatting so happily with Griffin. Effie knew now that her mother must have come here, too. She had been magical as well. But what had gone wrong?

Cosmo said nothing.

'Did she come here on the night of the worldquake?' Effie asked. 'Did she get lost somehow? My father always says she's dead, but at first he said she'd run away. I heard him telling my grandfather. I just want to know the truth. Is she still alive? And if not – what happened?'

There was a long silence. Cosmo blinked and frowned.

'I suppose I should have realised you would ask the most difficult question first,' he said. The old wizard pushed his fingers together to make a sort of triangle of his hands and sighed. 'Unfortunately, it is the one question I cannot answer. Nor can I explain why. Not yet. In time, perhaps.'

Effie felt a single tear slip down her cheek. She wiped it away.

'There, there, dear child,' said Cosmo, offering her the hand-kerchief again. 'Have faith. You will know everything you need to know, but all in good time. There are more pressing issues at hand. We must try to find Griffin, if he is out there somewhere. The Diberi will be stronger as a result of their attack on him. I hear they have Griffin's books, too. If they are not stopped, the Diberi will be able to derive great power from them. Possibly even enough to launch a serious attack on us here. Perhaps you already know, but here at Truelove House we are Keepers of a very, very great library that must be protected at all costs. The Trueloves have always guarded and maintained this library, and in time you will learn how to help us. But before that, you will need to go back and rescue your grandfather's books. They are not important in the same way our books are here, of course. But they are a potential source of power for the Diberi. I wish it were

235

not so. You are still too young to be involved in all this. But once the books are safe, you will be out of danger. For a while.'

'Is my grandfather still alive?' Effie asked.

'We don't know for sure,' Cosmo said. 'From what you told the others, it seems that he found a magical surgeon to help him try to cross over permanently. But we fear that even if he did make it here, he may be thousands of moons away.'

'Moons?'

'Days of travel. Your grandfather may be out there on the plains somewhere, safe enough, but by himself he might not reach us for hundreds of years. This world is vast. And we are deliberately very difficult to get to, because we must keep the Great Library concealed.'

'But won't everyone be . . . I mean, in hundreds of years . . .'

'Oh, *dead*? No, child. We try not to die here.'

'Then . . . You're . . .' Effie tried to remember the word for never dying.

'Immortals? No, not quite. But we do live for a very long time. The worst that can happen if we die here is that we have to begin again in your world. Although we try to avoid that, because it means becoming a baby again and learning everything from scratch – and trying to remember that we belong here. It's a long hard road back.'

'Have I come back?' Effie asked.

Cosmo frowned. 'What do you mean, child?'

'Like you just said. Did I start here and end up in the Realworld by accident? I feel like I belong here. Much more than I do at home.'

Cosmo shook his head. 'Your spirit did not originate here,' he said. 'You're a traveller, though, which means you can spend time in both worlds. And your *kharakter* is a very rare one. It should be very interesting finding your art and shade and working out what to make of them. But your true home is the Realworld. For now, at least.'

'I wish it wasn't my world,' said Effie. 'I want this to be my world.' Effie had only been in this house for a few hours, but already she ached to stay. She wanted to remain here and learn to do magic and help her cousins and Cosmo. She wanted to sit in the sunshine and feel that the people around her truly loved her.

Cosmo nodded wisely and then sighed.

'I do understand. But most travellers from your world simply don't have enough lifeforce stored up to remain here for very long. The problem for you islanders is that you don't store lifeforce as easily as we do. You can get better at it, of course. And with the Ring of the True Hero . . .'

'My ring?' Effie said, looking at it.

'Your grandfather did well to see that you are a true hero – we haven't had one for a very long time – and to find the ring . . . I believe it will help you to generate and store lifeforce. You'll need to work out how. You only truly learn the complexities of what a boon does by using it.'

'If I got enough lifeforce I could stay here for ever?'

Cosmo smiled. 'No one stays anywhere for ever. But once you've secured your grandfather's books you'll need to find ways to generate enough lifeforce to visit us regularly.'

There was suddenly a loud miaow from the rocking chair. The black cat stood up, stretched, shook, miaowed again and then jumped down onto the floor and up again onto Effie's lap. It turned itself around in about five circles one way and five the other before settling down on her lap and purring like a lawn-mower. Not that they probably even had lawnmowers here. In all likelihood they mowed lawns – and did everything else – with magic, just as Lexy had said.

'Moonface agrees,' said Cosmo. 'Ever since we heard you'd been born and that you showed, well, the right signs, we've all been tremendously excited. But Griffin kept telling us to be patient, that you weren't quite ready yet. And then . . . Well, here you are. You must have more you want to ask, but we must be conscious of not overloading you. You may ask me one more thing, and then you really must rest before tea.'

Effie stroked the cat. Her head was still full of questions.

'What is the Great Split?' she asked.

'Aha. Good question.' Cosmo sipped on his lemonade. Some bubbles got caught in his beard and fizzed and popped there for a while. 'Well, a long time ago our two worlds were one. Magical creatures roamed the Earth, which was, at that time, quite flat. The Earth was flat because it was infinite – well, almost infinite, but we can't go into all that now. In any case, there was magic and adventure and, well, I suppose it all looked a lot like this world does now, but with the beginnings of the world you come from buried within it. History is always hard to get a proper hold of. For one thing, it's usually the victors that write it. For another thing, people in power tend to lie a lot. Then there are the Diberi, who will have hidden whole volumes of true lore . . .'

'Who are the Diberi?'

'A group of very powerful dark magi, scholars and alchemists. They are extremely dangerous. They are against everything we stand for here. Well, except magic, of course, which they want for the power it gives them. Some people even believe they were responsible for the Great Split, although it's hard to imagine how they could have been. No mortals would have had the power to make something like that happen.'

'What *did* happen?'

'The Earth – the original Earth – split into two different worlds. No one knows exactly when. But the cracks had been forming for a very long time. Science versus magic. Technology versus the old religions. Money versus kindness. When one world contains two such strong world-views, eventually the strain gets too much and it splits into two separate dimensions. That's what happened. One world – yours – curled into a ball, like a galactic woodlouse. Ours remained flat. Well, flattish. Some people think this happened mere hundreds of years ago. Some believe it was thousands of years ago. But in any case, as a result we now have what we call the mainland – us – and the island – you. And you call them the Realworld and the Otherworld. One is a world of cold fact and reality; the other is a world of magic and adventure.'

'I want to stay in this world,' said Effie.

'Wait until you see more of it,' said Cosmo. 'I like it, but it does have flaws.'

'But you can do magic here. Proper magic.'

Cosmo chuckled. 'You can do proper magic in your world, too. Granted, it is a bit different, and the inclination of magical energy is to be pulled towards our world. But I hear that many people in the Realworld still communicate with animals, for example. Sportspeople use magic all the time, I have heard. Writers and other bards use a very ancient magic. And I also understand that you have a certain type of Master healer who cures very sick people only with words. If that isn't magic, I don't know what is.' He finished his lemonade. 'Now you must go and rest before tea.'

'But . . .'

'Please, child.'

'But when you said the Diberi...'

'We'll discuss all that later. Go and rest.'

27

Back in her room, Effie lay on her bed, trying to put together everything she'd learned so far. She would have to go back and rescue her grandfather's books, that was clear. But she hated the idea of leaving this beautiful, magical place. Luckily, time moved faster here than in the Realworld, which meant she wouldn't have lost too much time when she did get back.

When the bell rang for tea, Effie went downstairs and discovered a large conservatory full of very green, feathery plants and stone statues, with its doors thrown open to a walled garden. Out on the lawn were several wooden trestle tables with lavish cake stands and delicate-looking teapots, china plates, teacups and saucers.

Clothilde was sitting there in the sun, her eyes sparkling with kindness and intelligence. Rollo looked more serious, and appeared to be saying something of great importance that Clothilde didn't seem to be listening to. Then there was another person Effie had not yet met. He was a long-legged man with pointed black shoes that looked both very old and very new, perhaps due to the number of times they had been polished. He had a tiny, tidy red beard, which perched primly at the bottom of his face as if it were just politely ignoring the mess of strawberry-blond hair going on above. He had tortoiseshell glasses, which were quite normal-looking, and a bright cerise suit, which was not.

'Ah, Effie,' said Clothilde. 'Come and join us. This is Pelham Longfellow.'

The man in the cerise suit stood up and bowed.

'A pleasure,' he said, shaking Effie's hand solemnly. 'I have heard so much about you. And you have had quite an adventure to get here, I understand. It seems you came to us through a book.'

'Yes,' said Effie. '*Dragon's Green*. It was . . .'

'But you no longer have the codicil?'

'No. Well, I never actually— '

'That's a pity. Your grandfather's original wishes were that you should inherit all of his magical estate, of course, most of which it seems you have been given already, although the books seem temporarily to have fallen into the hands of the Diberi. We must do something about that. But I wonder what on earth he meant by adding a codicil. I deeply regret,' Pelham Longfellow went on, pushing his glasses up his nose, 'that I hadn't known he was so injured. He can't even have had enough lifeforce left to call for me, poor Griffin. I can't fathom what happened in those last few days, nor what he meant to give you. Unless . . .'

'What?' said Effie.

'Back on the island – sorry, in the Realworld – there is something being kept for you, for when you come of age. I wonder if . . .'

'If what?'

Pelham Longfellow frowned. 'Yes,' he said quietly, partly to himself and partly to Rollo. 'Perhaps he wanted the child to have it now, if she was to be coming here and taking her place in the family early.'

'What is it?' asked Effie.

'A great boon. I can't say more without the codicil. You already have several boons anyway, I believe. The Spectacles of Knowledge, for example. The Ring of the True Hero.'

'Yes.'

'The calling card you got when you finished *Dragon's Green* is a boon, too, a very special and rare one. Make sure you keep it safe. It's your way of getting back here whenever you want.'

Effie's heart skipped slightly. 'How does it work?'

'Oh, you simply take it out when you want to come here. You should be transported easily enough – it opens a portal wherever you are. Just make sure no one sees you do it, or you'll create trouble with the Guild. And make sure you leave yourself enough time and energy to get out again.' Pelham Longfellow scratched his head. 'I'll show you how to get back to the Realworld after tea. I really must advise you never to enter the Otherworld by any means other than the calling card. You must only come here to Dragon's Green to help with the library and so forth. Don't try to go off adventuring on the plains. Or if you do, and it goes horribly wrong, don't come crying to me.'

'OK,' said Effie.

'Unless it's an emergency,' he added. 'I will always help a Truelove.'

While this conversation was going on, Clothilde and Rollo had been arranging cakes on a plate. There were miniature Victoria sponges held together with dark red jam and cream, chocolate cakes covered completely in chocolate icing, and tiny lemon cakes with cream in the middle and a thick layer of lemon icing on the top.

'And of course,' said another voice, 'you must destroy the book.'

'Uncle,' said Clothilde. 'How nice of you to join us for tea.'

'Cosmo,' said Pelham Longfellow, offering his hand. 'Blessings.'

'Blessings to you, young Pelham. How goes the new life abroad?'

'I dislike the air most of all,' said Longfellow. 'The food is odd, although a convenient enough way to obtain energy, I suppose. People are bewildered when you do magic, and then you have to do more magic so they don't call the police – or worse, the Guild – and then it becomes very hard to keep the lifeforce ticking over, so to speak, but I get by.'

Clothilde passed Effie a small plate on which she had placed one of each type of cake, and a beautiful cup and saucer for her tea.

'Pelham has taken a job on the island,' she explained. 'In your world.'

Effie didn't like hearing the Realworld described as hers. She wanted to live here so very much. She wanted *this* to be called her world. And she wished everyone would stop translating things all the time. Already, in her mind, she thought of the Realworld as the island – just like a proper Otherworlder, or mainlander, would do.

'Most Otherworlders can't travel between the worlds,' said Cosmo. 'We have no way of converting lifeforce into your kind of energy. Pelham has the capacity, it seems. So he's now a travelling solicitor. He deals with estates that cross between one world and the next, and does a bit of investigation work on the side, I believe . . .'

'Mainly I deal with boons that have been smuggled onto the island,' Pelham said. 'Ownership claims and wills and so forth. The odd murder case, when someone has decided that they cannot live without their neighbour's Sword of Clear Water, for example. The Guild only really tolerates me because I promised to try to get all the boons back here and help close the portals. It's all been rather chaotic since the worldquake.'

'But he doesn't try very hard with those bits,' said Clothilde.

'Well, I suppose that's true,' said Pelham. 'Although, to be honest, if we could close off this world it would stop the Diberi from trying to get their hands on the Great Library.'

'They'd find some way in anyway,' said Clothilde.

'Why do they want the Great Library?' said Effie.

'Oh, that's a long story, child,' said Cosmo. 'We'll tell you everything when you come back. But suffice to say that the rarer a book is, the more the Diberi want it, and the library we have here holds the very rarest books in the whole universe. It is our job to guard them. As I said earlier, the Trueloves have always been Keepers of the Great Library.'

Cosmo stood up and reached for a large yellow teapot. Everyone was quiet for a few seconds, and Effie listened again to the strange and beautiful silence that moved softly around the garden and into the forest beyond.

'So, we hear that Griffin left some sort of codicil,' said Cosmo, 'but it was destroyed. That's a pity. With all the Diberi in her world, the child probably needs . . .'

'The original will forbids us from telling her what the boon is, of course,' Pelham said.

'Of course. But if the codicil has indeed been destroyed, then . . .'

Pelham sniffed the air. 'The original has,' he said. 'But I can smell a copy.'

Cosmo laughed. 'From here? You really are a talent. You were wasted on the mainland.'

Pelham smiled wryly. 'I always thought so.'

'So the child needs to find this copy of the codicil,' said Cosmo, looking at Effie. 'Can we help her somehow?'

Pelham shook his head. 'I don't imagine so,' he said. 'Now. I need a lot more cake before I have to go back. I fear my London supper club is not open tonight.'

Clothilde took Pelham's plate and added three more cakes to it. Effie noticed that her hand shook ever so slightly as she poured him another cup of tea. Their eyes did not meet once, but their hands did lightly brush one another as Clothilde passed Pelham the cup and saucer. After that, Clothilde blushed and went off to refill the large teapot.

'Right,' said Pelham suddenly, once he'd finished his last cake and drained his final cup of tea. Get ready to say your goodbyes. We need to be off very soon.'

Effie still didn't want to leave. There were so many things she wanted to ask. And she felt as if, after she had asked all the questions she wanted to, she could just lie on the lawn and look at this endless blue sky for ever and be perfectly content. The air smelled of flowers, and hummed gently with the sound of bumblebees collecting nectar. Over on the far side of the lawn was a croquet set, ready for people to begin playing. And from her bedroom window earlier on, Effie had seen a completely clear blue swimming pool. What she would give for a swim now, a game of croquet (not that she knew how to play, but she felt sure she'd learn quickly), and then . . .

'Effie?' said Clothilde. 'Did you hear Cosmo?'

'Oh dear,' said Effie. 'No. I think I was daydreaming.'

'You must destroy the book,' said Cosmo.

'Which book?' she said.

'*Dragon's Green*,' said Rollo.

'But why?' For some reason Effie couldn't explain, she suddenly wanted to cry. The idea of going back to her world and having to destroy the book that got her here . . . It was horrible. She loved books, and her grandfather had taught her always to show them the greatest respect. She could not imagine ever destroying something as precious as a book.

'It's to make sure that you remain the book's Last Reader,' Clothilde explained. 'You might have wondered how your grandfather knew you were going to be the last person ever

247

to read *Dragon's Green*. Well, he knew because he trusted that you would get through the book and arrive here, and we would explain what you have to do. Destroying the book after you read it makes sure you were its Last Reader, and then you definitely receive any boons, honours or prizes that it has inside it.'

'In this case, a very rare calling card,' said Pelham.

'But I've already got the calling card,' said Effie, a little confused.

'That's because time is very wise,' said Cosmo. 'It knows that in the future you have, as it were, already destroyed the book. It's best not to think about these time issues too much. Of course, if you didn't destroy the book and someone else were to read it, then they would get the calling card instead – well, if they could finish the book, that is. But in any case, all knowledge of your visit here would vanish from your memory.'

'I still think . . .' said Rollo, frowning.

'Shhh,' said Clothilde. 'It worked. It doesn't matter.'

Rollo didn't look very happy. 'But if it's not all right for the Diberi to destroy books, but all right for us . . .' he began.

'It's just once,' said Clothilde. 'It was an emergency.'

'That's what the Diberi probably think, too,' said Rollo crossly.

This was the point where normal people in a different kind of world would probably have an enormous argument, but instead Rollo took a deep breath and smiled at his sister.

'I respect your point of view,' he said. 'Blessings to you.'

'I respect yours, too,' said Clothilde. 'Blessings returned.'

'So, child,' said Cosmo. 'Do you understand?'

Effie did not in fact understand much of what had just been said. But she could not miss the main point.

'I must destroy the book,' said Effie.

'As soon as you return. You can't hesitate, or stop to do something else. It doesn't matter how you do it, as long as the book cannot be read by anyone else after you.'

'OK,' said Effie.

'And then you'll visit us again soon?' said Clothilde, squeezing Effie's hand.

'Of course,' said Effie. 'I just wish I didn't have to leave.'

'As well as destroying the book as soon as possible, you need to restore your energy,' said Rollo, 'which you cannot yet do here. At the moment, just being here will be draining your life-force – your M-currency, or whatever they call it out there. You need to have enough to return as well. You may need to find someone from your world to help you work it all out. It's such a shame Griffin isn't there to help you.'

'You might try and look up a fellow called Professor Quinn,' said Pelham Longfellow. 'Fine chap. Perhaps he can help you get the books back somehow? I might beep him when I return. I'd help you myself, only I have to be in London this evening for some urgent business. Now, everyone, I think it's time I escorted young Miss Truelove to the portal. Especially as darkness will soon be upon us.'

This didn't seem to be the sort of place that ever got dark.

'And,' said Longfellow, mysteriously, 'we'll need to try to get a post office to appear.'

Suddenly everyone was standing up and saying goodbye, and Pelham Longfellow was shaking everyone's hand, and Clothilde was kissing Effie on both cheeks and Rollo was patting her on the arm and Cosmo was patting her on the head and murmuring something that could have been 'There, there, child', but could also have been a gentle spell to keep her safe as she travelled.

And then they were off down the long driveway. Pelham Longfellow set quite a formidable pace, with his extremely long legs, and Effie almost had to jog to keep up with him.

28

Outside the gates of Truelove House, the landscape looked different yet again. The first time Effie had seen Truelove House had been when she was inside the book *Dragon's Green* and looking at something she couldn't yet access that lay beyond the end of the story. At that time there had been the Princess School and the peasant village and all the other places from inside the book. And after she'd finished the book, there had been the empty landscape and the cold, metallic mist, and then the calm summertime atmosphere of Truelove House.

Now, when the guards closed the wrought iron gates behind them, Effie found that she and Pelham were on a wide, dusty avenue with around five other large houses, each with its own gate and guards. Pelham set off down the road at the same great pace and Effie jogged to keep up with him. It was still hot and calm, and the lovely silence still lay there underneath birdsong and the continuous sound of summer insects.

'Who lives in these houses?' she asked.

'The Keepers of Dragon's Green,' said Longfellow. 'Every single household does something incredibly important and utterly secret.'

'Like what?'

'Well, like guarding the Great Library.'

'But what do the other Keepers do?'

'If I told you, it wouldn't be a secret,' said Longfellow. 'In any case, I don't know. It's all part of the security of the place. The villagers have a choir, a cricket team, an annual flower show, tennis tournament, country fête and many other things, but no one ever talks about what they do. They all contribute to the high-level secrecy around the place, but beyond that . . . Aha.'

They had reached a small street on the edge of a large village green, with three square detached brick houses all in a row. One was covered in ivy, another in blue clematis and another in yellow roses. Then (rather bizarrely, Effie thought) there was a bus stop. She hadn't imagined that in the Otherworld there'd be much call for buses. But now she thought about it, surely even magical people needed to get around somehow?

'Here,' said Longfellow. 'Somewhere around here, perhaps . . .'

He mumbled something in what Effie was sure was Rosian. And then something she didn't understand at all. He turned around once, twice, three times, and touched the air in different places.

Then something began appearing slowly. It was an old-fashioned post office made of yellow brick. It had a thatched roof covered with pink flowers. Other pretty plants were growing all over its front. It fitted right into this street. It had a red sign that said POST OFFICE just above the door, and a postbox as part of its front wall. However, a large sign on the door said CLOSED.

Pelham Longfellow opened the door, which made a tinkle-tinkle sound, and Effie followed him in. The post office smelled dusty and old, although everything in it looked very clean and polished. The smell was a blend of paper, pencil shavings, the inside of cats' ears, white erasers, string and envelope glue. There was also a faint whiff of dunce's hats, which, as we already know, smell like mould and dead mice. Essentially, the place smelled a lot like the Tusitala School for the Gifted, Troubled and Strange.

'We're closed!' said a grumpy man from behind the wooden counter. 'I don't know what business you have summoning us when we are closed. It's an abomination, I tell you. I'll be writing to the village council and the Guild of Craftspeople in triplicate and . . .'

'Greetings and blessings,' said Longfellow.

'Greetings and blessings to you,' said the man. 'Although I repeat that we are closed. *Fermé. Shoot. Closen.* How many languages do you want? I was just settling down to my cocoa and my newspaper. Do you know what time it is? Curses on you. Oh, and blessings, too, of course. Double blessings and another curse. Oh, blast it.'

'She has come for her papers and her mark,' said Longfellow.

'Papers and mark?' said the man, wide-eyed. 'Well, why didn't you say? That's different. At least that's interesting. Worth being

253

summoned for. But . . .' He looked at Effie long and hard. 'Young, isn't she?'

'She's of age,' said Longfellow. 'Can you do it here? Or do I need a bigger post office? I can take her to a more significant town, I suppose, maybe Froghole or Old Wives' End, but I didn't want to go through the forest and across the plains in the dark. But of course if the complex paperwork is beyond you . . .'

The man sighed and then produced another strange combination of curses and blessings. Then he frowned and, still cursing and blessing, started pulling out pieces of paper and forms from different cubbyholes behind his counter.

'This one for the passport and that one for the portal tax and another one for the vaccinations and one in case she is, in fact, underage . . . and then the requisitions slip for the ink for the mark and one for the stencil and . . .'

Pelham Longfellow took the great pile of paper that the man produced and went off to sit at a little desk to fill it all in.

'You stay here and get the mark,' Longfellow said to Effie. 'It doesn't take long.'

'Does it hurt?' she asked, but Longfellow didn't answer.

'Sleeve,' said the post office clerk. 'Quickly, before we shut. Did I mention that we are supposed to be CLOSED?'

'Yes, and I'm so sorry for troubling you,' said Effie.

'A polite child,' he said. 'Well, that's something. Which reminds me. Are you of age?'

'Yes,' said Effie, not having any idea what this meant.

'Good. SLEEVE.'

'Oh, sorry.' Effie rolled up her right sleeve.

'Bring it closer, bring it closer. Aha,' said the clerk. 'Good.'

He mumbled away to himself as he first dabbed the area with a cotton wool ball with some sort of cold liquid on it. Effie wondered if this was going to be like getting a tattoo. Cait had a tattoo on her shoulder, but she had sworn she'd never get another one because it hurt so much. Effie bit her lip. Surely they'd use magic in a place like this, though, not . . .

'Ow!' she said, as a needle punctured her skin.

'That's your vaccinations. Not so bad, eh? Right . . .'

'Ow!' There was another needle now, but this one scratched rather than pierced. Effie wanted to cry out, but bit her lip again instead. She knew that this would be the mark that would enable her to travel freely between the worlds. It would make her a real traveller, like her grandfather must have been. She almost cried out several more times, but soon it was all over. When she looked down, she had a perfect letter M on her arm in a sort of faintly glowing, milky silver colour. It was the most beautiful thing she had ever seen.

'Thank you,' she said. 'And, er, blessings.'

'A nice polite child, at least. Well, you're welcome,' said the clerk. 'Now . . .' He coughed once, and then twice until Pelham Longfellow looked up. 'Did I mention that we are CLOSED?'

'Hold your horses,' said Longfellow. 'I'm almost there. I had no idea there were so many forms to fill in now. Last time I did this there was only one.'

'When the Guild puts its mind to something . . .' began the clerk. 'But there's no time for chit chat. Come on, quickly, quickly.'

Pelham hurriedly filled in the last of the papers and then brought them over for Effie to sign. While Effie signed them all, the post office clerk drummed his fingers dramatically on the desk in front of him. Then Pelham handed over the papers and the clerk stamped them without even looking at them, before laboriously filing each carbon copy in a different cubbyhole. Then he got out a small brown leather wallet and placed a folded-over piece of green paper inside it.

'That's your passport,' he said to Effie. 'And this,' he said, giving her a small laminated gold card, 'is your M-card for the other side.'

'Thank you,' said Effie.

'Well, you've no need to hang around,' he said. 'Especially as we are CLOSED.'

'Wait,' said Pelham Longfellow. 'Do you have something to put all this in? She doesn't have a bag with her.'

The clerk tut-tutted and moved slowly over to a cupboard which he opened to reveal a great stash of small velvet drawstring bags, leather satchels, briefcases and pouches. There was a soft brown bag with a brass clasp that looked like it would go crossways across Effie's body, leaving her hands free for other things. It looked sort of old and comfortable, like all her favourite things.

'Can I have that one?' she asked.

The clerk sighed and grunted and dropped a lot of other things getting the bag, but then it was Effie's. It felt as if it had belonged to her for ever.

'GOODBYE,' said the clerk pointedly, after Effie had stashed

256

all her things in the bag. She noticed that no money was exchanged, but thought it best to say nothing.

The door tinkle-tinkled again as they left, and then the whole post office disappeared.

'Where did it come from?' Effie asked Longfellow. 'The post office, I mean.'

'From your world,' he replied. 'Well, sort of. It's a liminal place. You've been to the bun shop, I think.'

'Yes, Mrs Bottle's Bun Shop.'

'Well, that's a liminal place that you can go through. A portal. Not that I recommend using portals, as I mentioned before. But now you have the mark and your papers you can travel wherever you like, of course.'

'And did we pay him with M-currency?'

'Hmm?' Longfellow seemed suddenly distracted.

'How did we pay? In Mrs Bottle's Bun Shop I paid for my bun with M-currency, although I didn't understand what it was at the time.'

'Oh no, no one pays for anything here,' said Longfellow. 'On the mainland you get lifeforce by giving things to other people, so everything is free. Now hang on, you'll need to concentrate for a minute.'

They were approaching a patch of dense forest.

'Before we go in,' said Longfellow, 'I must give you this.' He reached into his briefcase and drew out a small double-edged dagger with a bone handle.

'This is an athame.' He pronounced this *ath-ah-may*. 'It is not your true weapon, but you may borrow it until you get yours.

257

As a true hero you can use most slicing weapons, and it's the best I can do. There are creatures in the forest and on the plains beyond. The roots from some of the trees go as deep as the Underworld, which means that dark things can come out. It's not far to the portal, but we must take care.'

'Thanks,' said Effie, taking the athame. She had never held any sort of weapon before. It felt strange and heavy in her hands.

The forest was dark and dense, but the path through it was wide. As they went on, Effie began to feel properly frightened for the first time in her adventure so far. She remembered what Cosmo had said about what happens when you die in the Otherworld. If she died here, would she die truly, or would she have to be born again as a baby in the Realworld? Either way, she would forget all about her adventures, and her cousins and Cosmo, and the fact that her grandfather was out there somewhere on the plains – wherever that was. Would her death be painful? Probably. And what if there were creatures waiting to take her underground, to imprison her and . . .

Just as Effie thought that, something dark and scaly jumped up in front of her. It had thin, wiry arms and legs and very sharp-looking claws. It had indeed come from some sort of dark burrow underground. It hissed and shone its flame-red eyes at her and then flew into a tree. Then another came out, and one more.

'Oh no,' said Longfellow. 'Demons.'

'Demons?'

'They can't hurt you,' said Longfellow, 'as long as you don't engage with them. You need to kill them as soon as they come near you and keep on walking.'

Effie found she was shaking.

'But I've never killed anything before,' she said.

'If it helps at all, they're not real. Well, they are real, but they are not living beings in their own right. They're . . .'

Just then another dark, scaly creature leapt out and started darting around Pelham Longfellow. Longfellow reached for his weapon – a small silver pistol of the sort you'd find in a black and white film from the 1930s. He started trying to shoot the creature, but it simply dematerialised and then popped up somewhere else. It was hissing at him. The words weren't completely clear to Effie but she could pick up something about Clothilde and then the words, 'She doesn't love you; she never loved you.' Then another demon jumped out and started laughing at Longfellow's hair. Another one kept repeating the words, 'You killed your own father.'

Longfellow managed to hit one of them, but the others kept moving out of range. But suddenly Effie was more concerned about her own demons. Three of them popped up in front of her and all at once they seemed to be taunting her with the most painful things from her life. 'Come underground with me,' said one of them. 'Go on. You can live there for ever and cry about your grandfather and the fact that no one on earth loves you now he's gone. You may as well give in.'

'You have no true friends,' said another one.

'Everyone hates you,' said a third.

Longfellow hit another of his demons with a little pop of antique bullets. And then another. Now there was just one more for him to kill, and then perhaps he'd be able to help Effie. But his last demon was evading his bullets very easily.

Effie held the athame out in front of her. Longfellow had said not to engage with the demons, to just kill them, but they were actually making her quite angry, and when Effie was angry she always argued.

She looked at the first one. 'Why would I want to go anywhere with you?' she asked it. 'It's not logical. I'm not going to cry over my grandfather; I'm going to find him. And even if I don't find him, I am going to live out the destiny he planned for me. I will never, ever give in. And as for you,' she said to the second demon, 'you don't know anything. I do have true friends. I have Maximilian, and Lexy, and so you can say what you like, it won't make it real. And you?' she said to the third demon, 'I have never heard such utter rubbish in my entire life. If you're trying to upset me you'll have to try harder than that. You're ridiculous. Pathetic. And what's more, I think you have no power apart from these words. And as we all know, words cannot hurt anyone. You are powerless and insignificant.'

One by one, the demons disappeared.

'Bravo,' said Pelham Longfellow. 'Who taught you to do that?'

'To do what?'

He laughed, but quite admiringly. 'You're, what, eleven? You just faced your demons,' he said. 'I see what Griffin meant about you.'

But Effie didn't get a chance to ask him exactly what he meant, because suddenly they had reached the end of the forest and the beginning of the plains, and Longfellow was putting a finger to his lips.

'Shhh,' he said. 'We need to listen for beasts.'

'Beasts?'

He nodded. 'And these are real, not dark parts of you like the demons were. They will eat you if you try to argue with them. As long as it's quiet, we can run for it. The portal here comes out just by your school, I believe. It's the one Griffin used to use. I usually take the one on the other side of the village, which comes up in London, but I'll come with you today. But we'll split up as soon as we come out. I am mainly in London or Paris, but you can always get me with this.' He gave Effie a business card. Instead of a pager number it had three words on it. *Barre, Attempren, Fairnesse.* 'If you say those words, I will come to you as soon as I can. It does use up magic but I imagine that after facing your demons and completing the book you'll be pretty strong on lifeforce anyway.'

'Thank you,' said Effie.

'And don't forget that when you come out you must go straight home and destroy the book.'

Effie nodded. 'I know.'

Longfellow squeezed her hand. 'Ready?'

'Yes.'

'You see that weeping willow? After three, we're going to run for it. The beasts can't see you if you run fast enough. The portal is hidden by the tree's canopy. Just copy what I do and step through the curtain of leaves. One, two . . .'

29

O dile Underwood had tried very hard to keep magic from her son. For a start, she had called him Maximilian, which she had felt to be quite an unmagical name. She had also made sure they lived in the least magical place imaginable. A bungalow by the sea (but with no sea view). What could be less magical than that? Maybe a semi-detached on a new housing estate, but the bungalow had at least been cheap. Odile's sister Idony, an Adept druid healer, had not taken this approach, and look what had happened to her. She lived in an eco-treehouse in a sacred grove in the West Country. Her children were always muddy, sometimes ate worms, did not fit in at school, got bad grades, and social workers were always coming round and trying to re-house them.

Odile had not wanted that for her family, such as it was. And of course she had to keep the more interesting parts of her work at the hospital a secret. Kate, her daughter, was a success: blissfully unaware of magic, M-currency, liminals and the Otherworld. Kate's father – Odile's ex-husband – had nothing magical about him at all, which helped. Kate had grown up in the normal way and become an accountant in the New Town. She had a nice husband and baby and went on three holidays a year. She visited Odile sometimes on a Sunday afternoon and talked about her next holiday, or her last holiday, or what school her baby might go to when it grew up.

If only Odile Underwood hadn't fallen in love with that dark Master mage who had visited the hospital during that stormy spring twelve years ago. If only Maximilian hadn't had such magical genes. If only those genes weren't so . . . Weren't so . . . She didn't like to think about how her son's genes might turn out, given that her own family's genes had produced quite a lot of neutrals and the mage hadn't exactly been good. He had been fun, in a brutal kind of way, but not good. He had left her, of course, and run – or flown – back to whatever far edge of the Otherworld he had come from. He didn't even know about his son. But Odile's husband did. Once he knew she was pregnant, it hadn't taken long for him to put two and two together.

After the divorce, she bought the bungalow and prayed that Maximilian would keep out of trouble and grow up as ordinary as his sister. She bought him a computer and hoped that he would simply turn into the kind of normal nerdy boy who got good grades and liked playing old-fashioned videogames and looking at pictures of girls he would never, ever be able to meet. She thought he might make a good dentist one day.

But then she had allowed him to sit the entrance exam for the Tusitala School for the Gifted, Troubled and Strange, and that was where it had probably all gone wrong. Now Maximilian was friends with Griffin Truelove's granddaughter, who was bound to have awakened her powers after receiving the Ring of the True Hero that morning. The boy that had come earlier, Wolf, had obviously just epiphanised, too. Odile had liked him, had felt the goodness in him immediately.

But now Maximilian and his new friend had disappeared.

Odile wasn't stupid. She had sensed, from the minute Wolf had turned up, that her son was about to embark on his first magical adventure. Her efforts to stop him had failed. Well, that was life, she supposed. Now she would just have to try to help as best she could.

Like others in the Realworld, Odile gathered her M-currency slowly and diligently. A little prayer here, a candle there. It all added up. And she had enough that when she now opened her old magical box and pulled out her dusty crystal ball she was almost able, after rinsing the crystal ball in the pond in the garden (they did not have a clear spring, nor was there any moonlight), and then under the tap to get all the murky green bits off, to see where her son had gone.

He was in trouble, she could see that. She could hear it, too. There were several piercing screams and one word: 'spiders'. Maximilian hated spiders. She had to save him. But where, exactly, was he? The crystal ball showed dark rooms and cobblestones. Maybe the Old Town . . .

Odile got into her car – a small, unobtrusive, extremely unmagical hatchback – and started to drive towards the Old Town. But where was she going, and what was she looking for? She didn't know. All she could do was trust some combination of her sixth sense and mother's intuition. She drove past the hospital, with its lights all dimmed for the night, and past the Tusitala School for the Gifted, Troubled and Strange. There was the exotic pet shop. The antiquarian bookshop. The university grounds. But nothing was coming to her. She wasn't sensing anything.

Then she saw a young man lying passed out on the ground just near the turning to the Funtime Arcade. Most people ignore young men lying passed out on the ground because most people imagine that young men are going to be drunk or grumpy or unhappy or want to tell you their life story or – worse – that they are simply pretending to be unconscious so that they can attack you when you try to help them. But Odile Underwood was a healer and could not leave someone in trouble. She parked the car at the end of the cobbled street and went to see what was wrong with the young man.

'Uh,' Carl said, when she shook him. 'Uh . . .'

'What happened to you?' she asked.

'Some freak put some kind of spell on me . . .'

'Oh no!' said Odile. This was worse than she thought. Of course, she didn't realise that it was her son who was responsible for Carl's thumping headache and slight giddiness. She simply assumed that there was some other dark, dangerous magic in the area. And in fact she was right.

At this moment Leonard Levar, having returned from his unscheduled trip to the Underworld, was in his bookshop preparing for an unscheduled trip to the Otherworld. He was wondering where he should sell the spectacles. Would he get a better price for them on this side or the other? He was doing a bit of research on the dim web and also having a much needed cup of coffee and a ham roll. The boys were not going to trouble him any more. He had moved them into the smaller cave and released the spiders. He'd also put a minor cloaking spell on the whole arrangement, so that people would not hear them crying out. He could pay the pet shop owner, Madame Valentin, tomorrow. She had become quite used to Levar 'borrowing' her animals. And she always kept her mouth shut.

'Can you sit up?' Odile asked Carl.

She fumbled around in her handbag. She had some ibuprofen, some Rescue Remedy, a cough sweet and some homeopathic arnica. She gave all of these to Carl, knowing, as all Proficient healers do, that one of the great secrets of medicine is not what you give, but the spirit with which you give it. Most medicines simply do whatever the patient thinks they will do, after all. Carl didn't seem like the kind of person who would give his remedies much thought, so she simply murmured that what she was giving him would make him completely better, and that this small white pill was particularly potent and that he should only have one, or at the very most, two. The cough sweet, she told him, was so powerful it was illegal in fifteen different countries.

Carl sat up. 'Are you a nurse?'

'Yes,' said Odile. 'Nurse Underwood.'

'Underwood?' He had heard that name somewhere recently. Where, though? He shook his head. It didn't help. Where was he? What was he doing here?

Nurse Underwood was now asking Carl if he had seen her son. She was describing him: eleven years old, a little overweight, glasses. Hang on! Wasn't that the nerdy boy? But should he say anything about what had happened? Maybe she had some money to pay him. But . . . Carl's mind felt so feeble that it seemed simpler to just tell this kind woman the truth and hope that she might give him another one of those illegal sweets and help him to his car. His car! Yes, it was still there, down at the bottom of the hill. Slowly, Carl sat up. He explained that his brother had called him to come and help him and his friend rescue some books. And yes, the friend was quite fat and nerdy and . . .

Then Effie walked around the corner, still dressed in the jeans and boots she found in the dragon's underground castle, and still carrying the bag she had been given in the Otherworld. In it was her new passport and her M-card. It had all been real. She had emerged under a sycamore tree near the school playing field just moments after walking into the portal with Pelham Longfellow. Then, once he was sure she knew her way home, he had taken from his battered briefcase what looked like two thin sticks and a feather duster, but that turned out, when he put them together the right way and cast a small spell over them, to be a large broomstick.

'Still the most reliable form of transport,' he had said. 'Call me if you need me.' And then he was gone. Now Effie was on her way home with only one thought in her mind. She must destroy the book. *Dragon's Green*. The book that had given her the most important experiences of her life so far. Her favourite ever book. It pained her to think of it, but it had to be done. Just before he'd left, Longfellow had impressed on her the need to go straight home and get on with it. 'Otherwise,' he'd reminded her, 'time might change and you'll wake up tomorrow with no passport and no memory of your visit to the mainland.'

Which would, as they say, be a fate worse than death.

But now she was walking up this cobbled street and there in front of her . . .

'Effie Truelove?' said Odile Underwood.

Effie, thought Carl. This was the girl his brother and his nerdy friend were trying to help. Well, maybe now she was here, she could take care of her own books. But . . . Where were the books? Where was his brother and the nerdy boy? They had been here, he remembered that. Then they were gone. The bit in between was still rather hazy. While Carl was thinking all this very, very slowly, Odile was quickly telling Effie everything she knew: that Maximilian and Wolf had disappeared, believed to be trying to rescue some books of hers.

'My grandfather's books!' said Effie. 'Leonard Levar bought them. This is the side of his shop. Wolf and Maximilian must be in there somewhere.'

'Are they in there?' Odile asked Carl.

'Cave,' he said, nodding. 'Grille.'

Effie rushed over to the hole and looked in.

'They're in here,' she said. 'But . . . Oh no!'

'What?' said Odile.

'Maximilian?' called Effie.

It was quite dark in the cave, but in the dim candlelight Effie could see something of what the problem was. Or problems. The first thing she noticed was that Maximilian seemed to be clinging to an old light fitting in the centre of the uneven stone ceiling. This wasn't a problem in itself, exactly, but it meant that he couldn't help Wolf, who was lying prone on the floor below.

'Maximilian,' called Effie again. 'What happened to Wolf?'

'Spiders,' said Maximilian. 'Levar has shut us in with three Chilean six-eyed tarantulas. They're deadly, apparently, unlike normal tarantulas which are just hairy and horrible and only have two eyes and . . .'

'Did Wolf get bitten?'

'I'm not sure he did get bitten, but he's been unconscious for ages. Levar put a spell on both of us, but it didn't work so well on me.'

'OK. Let me think. Do you have the spectacles?'

'Levar took them. And I have no M-currency left. M-currency is . . .'

'I know what it is,' said Effie. 'We need to get you out. We need . . .'

'I can't hang on much longer,' said Maximilian.

'What about playing dead?' said Effie. 'They probably won't bite you if you leave them alone. Could you . . .?'

'What?' Maximilian was slowly turning purple with the effort of clinging on.

'I don't know.' Effie bit her lip. 'We'll get you out somehow. I just have to think . . .'

'Have you got Wolf's sword?' asked Maximilian.

'No. I could go and get it, though . . .'

'Go now,' said Maximilian. 'I think Wolf might be all right once he gets it. He can use it to kill the spiders, and Levar. Then we can work out how to escape.'

Effie moved away from the hole in the wall.

'What about the crystal?' said Odile quietly from somewhere

269

behind Effie. 'Your grandfather owned a Crystal of Healing, I believe, and—'

'I gave it to my friend before,' said Effie. 'She's a Neophyte healer and—'

'Right, well, we'd better get her and the crystal down here. You don't happen to know any true witches as well, do you?' Odile raised her eyebrows as Effie shook her head. 'All right. Do you have some way of getting hold of this healer? Have you got a pager?'

Effie shook her head again. 'No,' she said. But then she remembered the walkie-talkie radio. 'Actually . . . Yes. If I can get home I can radio her.'

'Good. And ask her if she knows a witch.'

Carl started staggering off towards his car. Effie and Odile ran down to Odile's hatchback and got in. Effie hurriedly gave Odile directions while trying to explain that she had a weapon that only Wolf could use, that might be of help to him if he had to fight his way out. Of course, he'd have to be healed first and . . . Her head was swimming with all this new information.

So Wolf was her friend after all. He'd been trying to help her. But what if he was dead? She could see what Levar had done. The boys – both troublemakers who had been on detention earlier that day – had broken into the storeroom at the back of his bookshop, and how could it be his fault if some spiders had escaped from the pet shop next door and bitten them? She could just see him getting away with this – not just taking her books, but murdering her friends, too.

Unless she could find a way to stop him.

270

30

E ffie let herself into her house as quietly as she could. She'd
seen from the clock in Nurse Underwood's car that she'd
been gone for just over an hour in Realworld time. If anyone
asked, she could say she just slipped out for . . . For what? What
does someone slip out for on a cold Monday evening, after they've
been told to go to bed without any supper?

Food. Of course. She could say she'd become desperate and gone
to the chip shop. She'd be in more trouble, but at least it was more
realistic than trying to explain where she'd actually been. Effie didn't
dare hope that she'd ever again know the kind version of her father
and Cait that she'd met at the beginning of *Dragon's Green*.

Mind you, how kind had those fictional parents been, really,
shipping her off just like that to the Princess School where she
would have had a 50 percent chance of being eaten by a dragon?
But it had been nice to have her father make her breakfast. Effie
would always remember that, even though it hadn't been real.

Luckily, the house was now in darkness. Everyone was in bed.

Orwell and Cait didn't like getting up in the night, so it was always Effie who gave baby Luna her bottle, rearranged her blanket, or picked up her favourite toy monster from the floor. Had Luna cried and alerted her parents to her sister's disappearance? It seemed not. When Effie got to her bedroom, she could see that Luna was sleeping soundly.

She got out the walkie-talkie and radioed Lexy as quietly as she could. Then she found Wolf's sword, and the other items that Dr Black had given her – including the strange stick her grandfather had called a 'wonde' – and put them in her new bag. She took another spoonful of her grandfather's damson jam. And then . . .

The book. *Dragon's Green*. She knew she was supposed to destroy it, but she didn't have time now, with one friend clinging on to a light fitting in a cave full of spiders and another lying perhaps dead on the floor. She had to just take what would help them and hurry. And the book would be safe here for a while longer, surely? She should hide it, though, just in case. But where? She thought for a moment, but couldn't come up with anything very good, except . . . Maybe . . .

After she had hidden the book as best she could, she threw the jar of damson jam in her bag and left as quickly as she had come in.

'Let's get Lexy,' said Effie to Odile as she got back in the car. 'She said she'd meet us on Black Pig Corner by the bus stop. It's just up here, and turn left.'

When they got there, Lexy wasn't alone. Another girl was standing there with her, wearing a long black coat and a slightly pointed woolly hat.

'You said you needed a witch,' said Lexy. 'So . . .'

'Hello,' said Raven, with a shy smile.

'You're a witch?' said Effie.

'Not a very powerful one,' said Raven. 'But I can try to help. I cycled here as fast as I could.'

As usual, no one had even noticed when Raven had left the house. Torben was still presumably in the process of serenading her mother, or possibly the publisher Skylurian Midzhar, and after a few drinks Laurel Wilde wouldn't have noticed if her daughter had boarded a rocket and gone to the moon.

Still, Raven wondered what her mother would say if she knew that her daughter was out right now, with her black nightdress on under her coat (well, it looked almost like an evening gown, and Raven hadn't had time to change), doing actual real magic with actual real friends? But of course Raven would never tell her mother about this. She just hoped some of her magic would work. She had brought her favourite wand – she'd spent her birthday money on it two years before – but it had never really felt that magical. Maybe that would change now.

They all got into the car and Odile sped off back towards the Old Town. But when they got to the bottom of the cobbled alleyway leading up to the bookshop, Odile made shooing, hurrying noises, but didn't get out herself.

'Aren't you going to come with us?' said Effie.

Odile shook her head. 'Neophytes get weak when their parents are in their vicinity,' she said. 'It drains their energy. And it's still forbidden for relatives to use magic on one another. Obviously if you weren't here I'd have to break all the rules, but thankfully you are here. Use the crystal,' she said to Lexy. 'You're a lucky girl, having that. And you,' she said to Raven. 'You're here because if you really are a witch, even a Neophyte, you should be able to talk to spiders. Just ask them if they wouldn't mind going back to the pet shop. If you are a true witch, they will do what you say.'

Raven gulped. 'OK. I'll try.'

'Try hard, dear. My son's life might depend on it.'

'But what do we do for poor Wolf?' said Effie.

'Lexy will know what to do,' said Odile. 'Good luck.'

And then she left.

The children gathered around the hole in the wall. Maximilian was still clinging to the old light fitting. Wolf was still lying on the ground.

'We need to give Maximilian the tonics somehow,' said Effie to Lexy. 'Have you got something to help Wolf?'

'Yes,' said Lexy. She had brought with her an embroidered bag, from which she now took a vial with a cork stopper. 'This is a tonic of resurrection. It will only help if he's not very seriously injured, though. If he's been bitten, then . . .' Lexy gulped. 'Then I'm not sure what we'll do.'

'OK, we'll get to that,' said Effie. 'What about these spiders? Raven?'

Raven's hands were shaking. This, of course, was the moment she had dreamed about for her whole life. Here she was, with the very people she hoped would become her true friends. And they needed her help. Raven didn't yet really understand how magical power worked. She didn't, for example, know that every time she fed the birds in her garden or filled their birdbath, and every time she lit a candle for a soul in need, and every time she saved up her pocket money and gave it to charity, and every time she meditated, that her M-currency went up a tiny bit.

But she sensed that whatever small amount of magical energy she had possessed earlier today had probably been used up on her friendship spell. Especially as the spell seemed – amazingly – to have worked. But what use was a friendship spell that got you friends who then needed you mainly for the magical skills that you didn't have any more?

Raven approached the hole in the wall and looked in. Yes, she could see one large spider scuttling across the floor. And she could sense two others. They were confused and afraid. Raven could feel that strongly. They were afraid of these large creatures – one hanging from the ceiling, waiting to pounce; the other playing dead – and they wanted to get out. The fact that she could sense all that. Did it mean . . .?

Raven had never really thought about her powers before. She had never stopped to think that her little communications with the robin in her garden, and her horse, and other creatures around the folly, were in any way properly magical. She'd had no idea that they meant she was a true witch. Now she realised that she could do something amazing; something others could not. But, of course, as soon as she became aware of it, the knack promptly left her. It's a well-known, but extremely annoying, downside to having any unusual abilities.

As soon as Raven thought, 'I am a true witch! Look – I can communicate with spiders!' the whole thing stopped happening and she was just a normal girl again. The spiders went silent. The world dulled and faded a little. Oh dear. And with all her new friends standing there with such high expectations of her. She knew she had to try to relax. To breathe. To stop trying so hard.

But LIVES WERE AT RISK! Oh no – that wasn't helping. If you want to relax you can't think about how many lives are at risk if you don't relax. You have to . . . What? Raven tried again to drop down into that zone of calm from which she had previously communicated with animals, but that was hard with Effie breathing so fast behind her, and Lexy letting out little yelps whenever the spider moved.

Raven needed her wand. Of course. That would help her focus. She reached into her coat pocket and drew it out. It was a thick black stick that was supposed to be a genuine hand-crafted piece of wood from a sacred tree. But she'd bought it from a mail-order catalogue she'd found in the wholefoods shop and couldn't be at all sure where it had really come from. One of Raven's spell books had suggested going into a forest and finding a tree yourself and using a sharp knife to slice off and then craft your own wand. But Raven couldn't bear to hurt a tree in this way.

'What's that?' Effie asked Raven, suddenly.

'This?' said Raven, holding out her wand. 'It's my wand.'

Wand. *Wonde*. Effie wondered whether . . .

'You could try this one if you like,' she said to Raven, pulling out of her bag the thin stick her grandfather had asked her to retrieve. 'I mean, only if you want to.'

But as soon as Raven saw the real wonde, which had been cut from a very mystical hazel tree several centuries before, and used for spells powerful beyond comprehension, the silly thing she had bought from the catalogue simply fell to the ground. The true wonde then jumped into her hands. It seemed to know that Raven was a true witch, and wanted to go to her, to feel her true witch's skin against its shiny ancient wood, to help her in whatever she wanted to achieve, which was, at this moment . . .

It's impossible to write out the language of spiders on the page. Spiders don't really have words made from letters in the way we do. But Raven was suddenly able to speak their language fluently. Before, when she was completely relaxed and alone, she could telepathically communicate in a basic way with animals – as all true witches can. But this was different. Now, with the extra lifeforce given to her by her communion with the wonde, and with the powers of the wonde itself, Raven could speak directly to the spiders in a way she had never before dreamed of.

She had already sensed the spiders' fear and confusion. Now she was able to talk to them about their life in the pet shop, and of the rough jerk of having their tank picked up by a man surrounded by the aura of very dark magic, and then being tipped out onto this cold floor and left with no food, no nest – nothing. Raven explained to them why this had happened and the spiders were very upset to hear that they were being used as some sort of 'weapon'.

There is no word in Spider – or indeed in any other animal language – for 'weapon', because animals don't have weapons.

The nearest that Raven could get was to explain that a human was trying to poison other humans by using the spiders – but even this was confusing because the spiders then thought that the other human wanted to eat these humans, and wondered why he couldn't poison them himself. But they certainly wanted no part of the evil one's plan.

'Can you come in and help us get out?' asked the biggest spider.

'No. The door is locked,' Raven said back. 'There is a human boy in there who will help you. He will pick you up and give you to me. But you must not bite him. Do you understand? He means you no harm. You will feel fear coming from him, but it is not a threat. It's just the way some humans are with spiders.'

The biggest spider spoke to the others. There was some argument from the smallest one, who said he had really had enough of being handled by humans anyway and just wanted to go back to his family in Chile. The biggest one said that once they were out they could negotiate with the witch about their return to the wild, and eventually the smallest one agreed.

'All right,' the biggest one said to Raven. 'We will gather together and wait.'

Then all three spiders made their way to the centre of the room and stood there, waiting patiently for Maximilian to . . .

'Arrrgh!' he cried. 'They're coming for me! KILL THEM! KILL THEM!'

'Maximilian,' Raven said. 'You have to get down carefully and pick the spiders up and give them to me. Be gentle. I think they want to travel together but you can give them to me one by one if you'd prefer, as long as you're quick about it. They have all agreed not to bite you.'

Maximilian, who had been quite purple from the effort of holding on to the light fixture, now went completely white.

'No,' he said. 'Anything but that. Please. I'm terrified of spiders. Phobic. Please. Someone just has to kill them.'

Raven sighed. 'What if they thought the same about you?' she said.

'You have to do this,' said Effie. 'Be brave. Trust Raven. She's a true witch. She's spoken to the spiders and they have agreed not to hurt you.'

'What if they lied?'

'Creatures from nature don't lie,' said Raven. 'They can't.'

'Why not?'

Raven rolled her eyes. 'Please, Maximilian. Don't make me explain. Just trust me. Put your hand near to one of them and wait for him to climb on. Then gently bring your hand up to me here and I'll take him from you.'

'If it doesn't work, I do have some tonic that cures spider bites,' said Lexy cheerfully. 'So you don't need to worry.'

This *was* a lie. But it worked on Maximilian. Well, almost. Sort of. He still needed to summon all the bravery he had in order to drop from the light fixture and land on the ground next to the spiders. He tried to think himself back into his experience – which had been real, he was sure of it, and not a dream – in the Underworld. He had been brave there. He just had to take the same approach here. He had to pretend the spiders were as unthreatening as coffee creams.

279

There they were. Big, hairy, bright orange and black, with those six little beady eyes that . . . Actually, when Maximilian looked into the eyes of the biggest one he almost thought he saw hope. Then his fear nearly overtook him and he had the urge to just stamp on them. To kill, kill, kill. But if he did that, then his friends would probably never speak to him again. And he'd never get his spectacles back. And the way that the spider was looking at him was . . . Well, its little hairy face was full of peace and trust. You couldn't kill something that looked at you like that, even if it was a deadly spider.

Maximilian breathed as deeply as he could, and put out his hand.

31

O nce the third spider had been delivered safely to Raven, Maximilian had almost begun to enjoy the sensation of the soft furry legs on his skin. For the second time today, he felt a bit like he'd just been on a very frightening and strange fairground ride and survived. He wanted to do it again. All of it. He wanted to eat lambs' kidneys and hold poisonous spiders and reach into people's minds and . . .

Raven gently put one spider on her right shoulder, and another on her left shoulder. The smallest one asked if he could make a temporary nest in her hair. To help him out, Raven swept up her thick, black curls into a loose bun and the spider crawled inside. When the other two spiders saw what he was doing they decided to join him, and so Raven ended up with three tarantulas in a nest inside her hair. For many girls this would not exactly be a dream come true. But Raven was not like most other girls. She felt honoured that the spiders wanted to live in her hair.

Now Maximilian was able to go and help Wolf. Lexy passed

him two different tonics and a dark yellow balm that smelled of lemon and vanilla. Maximilian followed her instructions to first rub the balm gently into Wolf's temples and then help him to drink the liquids as he started to come round. After five minutes of this, Wolf was able to sit up. Effie then passed the Sword of Orphennyus to Maximilian, so that he could give it to Wolf at the right moment.

'When Levar comes . . .' she started to say.

But Leonard Levar had no intention of going back into the cave until every living creature in it was dead. He hadn't decided quite what he'd do then. Probably call the authorities and express regret that these hooligans who had broken into his storeroom had not been able to get out – and what a shame about the spiders. Although would the police see it as something of a coincidence that both the boys and the spiders had decided to explore this empty storeroom at exactly the same time?

If only Levar still possessed the M-currency he'd had just a week before, he could have made the police believe anything. But of course he'd used it all up in his attack on Griffin Truelove. Never mind. At least now that he had this unexpected boon, these spectacles, he could increase his power a little.

Effie was the first one to see Leonard Levar leaving the shop. He turned the dark corner and headed straight down the hill towards the children. He had some kind of walking stick in his hand. Had he seen them? No. He looked quite distracted. Effie put her finger to her lips and got Raven and Lexy to duck into the shadows. Raven could not yet cast an invisibility spell, even with her new wonde, but she found she could now enhance the power of the shadows.

282

The children tried to breathe as quietly as they could as Levar walked towards them. Without seeing them, he turned left down the cobbled alleyway towards the Funtime Arcade. He was wearing a long grey overcoat, and Effie could just see the red case of the Spectacles of Knowledge poking out of his pocket. Her grandfather's spectacles! Levar was not going to get away with this. Once he was out of earshot, she told Raven and Lexy to stay and help the boys get out. And then Effie went after him.

The Funtime Arcade, to a normal person, was a tatty old establishment on the verge of dereliction with a cheap bar and a few antique fruit machines and pool tables. It was dingy and unappealing. But to Effie, newly epiphanised, the place looked rather different. The words FUNTIME ARCADE were now written in a bright pink neon scrawl across the faded grey stone of the old building. Underneath the scrawl was a blinking neon yellow arrow, and the words 'Mainlanders and travellers please go through the back door'. But there was no back door. Or was there? Suddenly, running alongside the arcade was a thin stone passageway that Effie had never seen before. She hurried down it, finding no trace of Levar. Around to the right and there, indeed, was a back door. It was dark wood with a big brass knocker.

Effie knocked, and waited. She was just about to knock again when the door opened and a huge man – almost a giant – peered down at her. He scanned her with a plastic box like the one Octavia Bottle had used. Satisfied that Effie had enough M-currency to enter, the huge man grunted and stepped aside to reveal a dark but cosy-looking bar lit with white candle-lamps of the sort Effie had last seen in Truelove House. Given how quiet it always was around the cobbled streets of the Old Town, Effie was surprised to see how lively it was inside the back half of the Funtime Arcade. But she soon realised that this was because many of its patrons must have come from the Otherworld.

At one table was an old bespectacled man, deep in conversation with a very wise-looking woman. They both had long, glossy white hair. He had a beard in a slightly different shade of white from his hair, and she had a cat that was almost exactly the same colour, curled up around her neck. Both of them wore several rings with different-coloured gemstones, and next to each of them was a polished wooden staff. He wore flowing white robes, and she wore a loose white dress with a red shawl over the top.

Another table had younger people at it, all studying large maps that were laid out in front of them. One of the men was wearing a cape lined with yellow silk; one woman wore an evening gown and had a violin case propped up next to her; the second woman was wearing a turquoise silk jumpsuit and diamond earrings; and the remaining man was dressed like a long-ago explorer, with a safari hat and a large pair of binoculars around his neck.

The air was warm, moist, and heady with scents of both worlds mixed together. Clustered around the bar were Realworld women who smelled of rare colognes from London and Paris and young Otherworld warriors who smelled of sweat, sword-grease and danger. There was a live band playing on a small, dark stage. The music was not like anything Effie had ever heard before. A harp mingled with a piano and a wooden xylophone while a red-haired woman sang deep, haunting lyrics over the top, all about love and loss and long journeys through forests and over mountains.

But where was Levar? If this was a portal, then had he gone through to the Otherworld? If so, how had he done it, and where? There were two doors off the bar area. Which to choose?

'Are you lost, young traveller?' said a man with a white beard.

'Um . . . Which way to the mainland?' said Effie.

'Through the arcade,' said the man, pointing vaguely. 'But don't stop and play on any of the machines.'

'OK. Thanks.'

The man pointed again at the far door. At least, Effie thought sure that was the one he meant. She hesitated.

'You can follow me if you like,' he said. 'I'm off to the mainland, too.'

Effie followed the man to the far side of the bar where there was a wooden door leading into a dark corridor. This led to a long room with games machines on either side. Many of these were being played by boys and girls not much older than Effie, but there were some adults, too. Every person here had very long hair and faded old clothes. Each player was completely absorbed in what he or she was doing. From every machine came a faint metallic tinkle of old-fashioned videogame music. Effie could hear electric harps, flutes, bells, and also the woeful sounds of digital things dying on the screens.

The man shook his head sadly. 'Some young adventurers from the mainland get lost or take a wrong turn and end up in here, trying to get to the island, which they have heard is full of riches. Of course, mainlanders can't wander onto the island just like that; they discover that as soon as they get here. And so, when they find the machines, with their perfect depictions of the

285

adventures they should have been having, they become hypno-
tised. Some of them stand there until their lifeforce runs out,
just hitting buttons, thinking they are rescuing a maiden from
a dragon but really doing nothing at all. You can't get their
attention once they are hooked.'

Effie followed the man through the long room and out the
other side into a dark, whispery area with what seemed to be a
boxing ring on one side of it and a number of booths on the
other. At the end of the line of booths was a door with a sign
saying OTHERWORLD. There was a queue, which Effie and
the bearded man now joined. Where was Levar? Effie couldn't
see him in the queue. He must have gone through to the
Otherworld already.

'These are the currency booths,' said the man to Effie. 'Use
these ones, if you have to, not the ones on the other side. Unless
you're selling a boon, of course. Not that you would sell a boon.'

'Why not?'

'People only sell boons when they are very desperate. You
must already know that winning a boon is a great honour. No
one sells one willingly.'

'What if someone has stolen a boon?' Effie asked. 'Then what
would they do with it?'

The man peered at her from beneath very bushy eyebrows.

'*You* haven't stolen . . .?'

'No,' Effie said quickly. 'No. But my friend has had one stolen
from him.'

'Ah. And you are trailing the thief, like a true hero would.'

'How do you know . . .?'

'You wear the ring.'

'Oh.'

'They'll offer you money for your ring, and for any other boons or weapons you have. Never take it.'

'All right. Thank you. My name's Effie, by the way.'

'Euphemia Truelove. Yes, I thought it was you. I'm Festus Grimm. At your service. Nicer than I sound, I promise, although I wouldn't trust anyone you meet here, including me. I knew your grandfather. I was so sorry to hear what happened to him.'

'Are you from the mainland?' Effie asked the man.

'No. I'm like you. A traveller. I was born in the Realworld, but I live between both worlds. By *kharakter* I am a healer, and I had many adventures myself before I decided to work in the Edgelands.'

'The Edgelands?'

'The only places in the Otherworld where there is money. You don't just get travellers like us here, coming and going. Lots of people are simply stuck here. They can get desperate. I try to help young people who have lost their way get back on their true paths and complete the adventures they set out on.'

The queue for entering the Otherworld moved forwards. Now they were right by the booths. Inside each one was a man or a woman who was calling out exchange rates. You could exchange pounds for krubles, krubles for francs, krubles for roubles and all sorts of other currencies Effie hadn't even heard of.

'Krubles for M-tech,' said one red-faced man. 'Any old M-tech.'

'Krubles for any cash,' said a woman in a blue-curtained booth.

287

'Krubles for dragon's gold,' said the red-faced man. As Effie walked past the booth he sniffed the air. 'Dragon's gold for M-tech,' he said, dropping his voice slightly. 'Dragon's gold for your boons, young lady.'

'No, thanks,' said Effie.

'*Much* dragon's gold for your very rare boon, miss,' he said, leaning forwards.

'She said no,' said Festus.

They moved on a few paces.

'Thanks,' said Effie. 'What's dragon's gold?'

'It's the only material currency you can swap for M-currency. People who get desperate sell their boons for dragon's gold, and then convert it to boost their lifeforce. You can only do the conversion to M-currency in here, or in a couple of other currency stations. People sell their boons in the market on the other side, because the prices are better there, but then come back in here to do the conversion. What on earth have you got in there?' Festus said, looking at her bag. 'I mean, your ring will be valuable enough, but he wasn't even looking at that.'

'Just . . .' Effie remembered what he'd said about not trusting even him. 'Nothing, really. He must have made a mistake.'

He smiled. 'Oh well. Good luck.' They had reached the front of the queue and it was now his turn to go through the portal.

'Thank you,' said Effie. 'Goodbye.'

'Farewell,' he said. And then, after exchanging a few words with the border guard, he was gone.

32

When Effie reached the door to the Otherworld she had to show the mark on her arm, her passport and M-card to the border guard there. While Effie was doing this, a woman scanned her with a machine like the one the giant on the door had used.

'M-currency is 12,340,' she said to a man behind her, who wrote down the figures with a quill pen. 'There is no other currency or money on her. There are several boons here. Would you like a price for them, love?'

'I don't want to sell them,' said Effie.

'Most people like to know their value, though, dear.'

'OK.'

'Right, I'm picking up one Ring of the True Hero. Very rare. Five hundred pieces of dragon's gold, roughly, you could sell that for. And at the current exchange rate you'd get one hundred thousand M-currency for that much dragon's gold. One Athame of Stealth. Less rare, but still pricey. One hundred pieces of dragon's gold for that, which you could trade for twenty thousand M-currency. And . . . Blimey. Look, Bill – look at what she's got in here. I'm picking up a cloaked boon worth five blooming million pieces of dragon's gold. You couldn't sell that here, love. We'd not have enough to buy it from you.'

'I'm not selling anything anyway,' said Effie.

A cloaked boon? That must be the calling card. The one that meant Effie could go to Dragon's Green whenever she wanted. Effie hugged her bag more closely to her. Was the calling card even safe in there? What if someone took it from her? It sounded as if it would definitely be worth someone's while.

Effie swallowed. She'd just have to be very, very careful. And she must remember to ask Pelham Longfellow for advice when she next saw him. Except . . . She remembered that he'd already told her never to go into the Otherworld by any means other than the calling card. And now here she was and . . . The door opened. It was too late. Effie was now in the Otherworld, completely alone.

Well, she would have been alone, were it not for the fact that she'd come out into a colourful and bustling market. It was daytime in the Otherworld, and bright sunshine fell on everything. There were numerous goblins selling fruits – some of which Effie had never seen before – on polished platters. All of the fruits looked juicy and luscious and she was very tempted to try something, even though her intuition told her that these fruits were dangerous in some way. Luckily she had no money, although several goblins rather bizarrely offered her fruit in return for a lock of her hair.

There were lots of stalls selling all kinds of things. One stall sold panama hats with bright blue phoenix feathers. Another sold Otherworld herbal blends and teas that you could take back to the Realworld with you. There was also a rare-book stall whose volumes were usually of great interest to Realworld collectors like Leonard Levar – although there was no sign of him there today. There were also were several stalls trading in boons. One had many different wooden staffs and broomsticks for sale, along with some brightly-coloured swords and a magic carpet that had seen better days. Effie saw a wonde like the one she'd given Raven on sale for two hundred pieces of dragon's gold.

'Dragon's gold for your boons, miss,' hissed a trader as Effie walked past.

She held her bag tightly and walked on.

'Lock of hair for a suck on our fruits, miss,' said a drooling goblin.

On the edge of the market was a food stall with two vast cauldrons, one bubbling with a bright yellow soup and another with something called mermaid stew. Effie gulped. Surely not real mermaids . . .? But then she saw a smaller sign explaining that mermaid stew was made from seaweed, samphire, brown shrimp, seashell paste and emerald pepper sauce.

Where was Levar? Had he already sold the Spectacles of Knowledge? Festus Grimm had said something about selling boons out here, rather than in the Funtime Arcade. Was that what Levar was doing? And would there be time to stop him?

Then it hit her. Effie suddenly realised that Leonard Levar did this all the time. Of course he did. In a flash she realised that she now understood everything – the reason why he was a book dealer, and why he'd wanted all her grandfather's rare last editions so much he was prepared to murder someone to get them. He'd known that he would never be able to get hold of them while Griffin was alive, so he'd killed him.

The reason was now clear. Those books were so rare that each one was the very last copy in the world. And so when Levar read one, all he would have to do was destroy it afterwards to ensure he was its Last Reader. Effie knew now that the Last Reader of any book receives one or more boons – just as Effie had been given the calling card when she'd finished *Dragon's Green*. And since you could sell boons for dragon's gold and then convert that to lifeforce, or M-currency . . . In some cases, quite a *lot* of M-currency . . .

That was what Clothilde and Rollo had been talking about. The Diberi clearly consumed books in order to make themselves powerful. They were Book Eaters, willing to convert knowledge into power and then use it to further their ultimate cause – whatever that was.

So now, presumably, Levar was going to top up his M-currency by selling the Spectacles of Knowledge, a boon he had come to possess without even having to read a book or complete an adventure. Well, they were not his to sell. He had to be stopped.

Where was he? Effie looked back the way she had come. The market was spread out before her, jumbled and confused as if each stall were a toy that had been laid out on a rug that had been shaken a little. Effie could not see which way to go, even to get back to the Funtime Arcade. Her heart beat faster.

She turned left and walked down a thin row of dimly lit booths, out of the light and heat of the sun. Many of these were housed in tents made from thick pattered fabrics. Effie peered into one of them and saw that it opened out into a complex network of chambers all lined with silk and beautiful old carpets. Everything smelled of orange peel, cinnamon, cloves and all sorts of exotic, unfamiliar spices. In one chamber there were black velvet chaise-longues with people lying on them drinking from ebony teacups or smoking silver pipes. Another chamber was entirely full of small harps. One contained only a golden hare.

Before she realised she had even entered the tent, Effie found she was quite lost in this network of chambers and antechambers, a sort of market within the market. Everything here was interesting to look at. There were candied fruits, music boxes, live snakes, precious stones and a whole stall selling items made out of dragon's blood. You could also, in one tiny chamber, buy a necklace made from frozen dragon's tears, which would, apparently, protect you from fire. Here, it seemed, was where you bought and sold much more exclusive boons and treasures than the ones outside. Many of these were so valuable that they were displayed in locked glass cabinets. In one cabinet, Effie saw a sword with a turquoise-blue blade and a polished wooden handle. In another was a beautiful silver bow with several feather-tipped arrows. Each was on sale for five hundred pieces of dragon's gold.

Then, suddenly, Effie got a glimpse of Leonard Levar. He was taking the spectacles out of his pocket and talking to a man at a wooden counter beyond a red curtain. She crept silently towards Levar, who kept talking to the trader, presumably explaining what he thought the spectacles were worth. The trader didn't seem to quite agree. He wrote down a figure on a piece of paper and showed it to Levar, who laughed dismissively and tore up the paper. The trader wrung his hands and now seemed to be offering Levar tea from a silver pot. Levar shook his head and pointed at the spectacles again.

'Give those back,' said Effie, pulling aside the curtain.

Both men looked at her. Levar's expression was similar to one you might see on a celebrity whose ugliest, smelliest fan had broken through security and was now trying to engage them in a conversation about how much their music had gone downhill since their first album. Levar looked at Effie like this for a few seconds longer and then went back to talking to the trader.

Effie took another step closer.

'I said, give those back,' she said. 'They're not yours. You stole them from my friend.' She looked at the trader. 'If he is trying to sell these spectacles to you, I should let you know that they are not his to sell.'

'Shoo, please,' said the trader. 'You are interrupting us.'

'Yes, can you remove this . . . this *thing* from your shop?' asked Levar.

'I'll leave when I have my spectacles back,' said Effie. 'They belonged to my grandfather, Griffin Truelove, who you attempted to kill last week. You're not going to get away with that, and you're not going to get away with taking his books and you're certainly not going to get away with stealing his spectacles.'

The more Effie spoke, the angrier she became. The Ring of the True Hero burned hot on her thumb. She pulled the athame from its holder and pointed it at Levar. She wished her hand would stop shaking. She willed it to stop shaking. It almost did.

'Give the spectacles back,' said Effie again.

Leonard Levar at least now paid Effie proper attention. He looked her up and down with contempt, but there was a small amount of respect mixed in with his hatred and annoyance. Not that Effie cared what he thought of her. He was a murderer. A book thief. An odious little man who was determined to keep knowledge from others in order that he could turn it into magical fuel for his own selfish use. He was . . .

'Well,' said Levar. 'I see you've decided to join us.'

He ignored the athame and pulled up Effie's sleeve, letting his cold, thin fingers brush her arm.

'Yes, here it is. Your little mark. So you found your way in, did you? How did you do that? No – don't answer. You are a ridiculous brat and I am a scholar of over three hundred years' standing. So I will tell you how you got in. You read the five hundredth book. Of course, I knew that Truelove would do something like that. He never was that bright, your grandfather. I could always sense what he was going to do next. I targeted him deliberately, knowing that he was the weak link who would make it easy for me to infiltrate Truelove House and the Great Library. Oh – *good* – your expression tells me you've been there. Ha! I am right. And I see you're as stupid as he was. So you read a book that took you there and then I suppose they told you to come back and destroy the book. To make certain you are its Last Reader. Because you know what being a Last Reader means, don't you? Have you destroyed the book yet? Oh – your innocent little stricken expression tells me you haven't. How very remiss of you.'

'I have,' lied Effie. 'I burned it.'

Levar let out another cruel laugh. 'Well, then you really have joined us,' he said. 'The ancient eaters of books. The Diberi. You think you're against us, but the only problem with your pathetic grandfather's stupid plan was that it means that you are forever tainted with the dark magic of the Book Eater.'

'What do you mean?' said Effie.

'The reason your lot hate the Diberi is because we use books to get power. We consume last editions and destroy them and reap the rewards. And now it seems you have done precisely the same thing. So I ask you . . .' Levar now pushed his face into Effie's, and his cold breath smelled like old fireplaces and dead birds. 'How, precisely, are you different from me?'

'I am not a thief and I am not a murderer,' said Effie.

'You will be in a moment,' said Levar, looking down at the athame.

'Give back what is mine,' said Effie. 'That's all I ask.'

'You talk quite rough for such a pretty little maiden,' said Levar. 'But you don't know anything. I'd give you five minutes with one of those goblins out there. You wouldn't last more than thirty seconds with me.'

'Well, then, what's stopping you?' said Effie. 'Here I am.'

Levar looked away briefly. The trader took a step backwards.

'I see. You have no power left,' said Effie. 'You used it all up on my grandfather. So now I've come to avenge him and there's nothing you can do about it.'

Effie had never spoken to an adult like this before. But the more she said, the less nervous she felt. Especially as Levar was not saying anything back.

'You're the one who is pathetic,' she went on. 'And stupid. You've made a big mistake. You thought no one would challenge you when he was gone. But you were wrong.'

Levar suddenly recognised the immense power in the child before him. And she had no fear left. Nothing he could use against her. Well, almost nothing. Was she about to strike? Suddenly, he wasn't sure.

'Get away from me,' said Levar. To the trader, he said, 'Call security.'

Effie took a step closer to Levar. 'Give me the spectacles,' she said.

Levar raised his wooden staff. 'I will fight you,' he said. 'And if that doesn't work, I know how to really hurt you. Where have you hidden the book, little maid? Oh, but you haven't even hidden it, have you? You didn't realise you'd have to. It's probably lying there on your little maiden's bed in your little maiden's house in— '

'No!' said Effie. She raised the athame.

But all of a sudden he'd flung the spectacles on the ground and was fleeing out of the chamber and into the next one. Effie picked up the spectacles, thrust them in her bag and set off following him as fast as she could. What he'd said about the book . . . Surely he wouldn't . . .

But she knew he would. He would now be on his way to find *Dragon's Green*, and as soon as he opened it Effie would no longer be its Last Reader. What would happen then? Everything she now was, and everything she now had, would be gone. She had to stop him.

33

'What do we do now?' said Lexy. The spiders were safe in Raven's hair, and the boys were out of danger, but it didn't look as if Levar was going to unlock the door any time soon. He'd hurried off towards the Funtime Arcade with Effie chasing after him. Lexy gulped. She hoped Effie would be all right. But now there was the problem of how to get the boys out of their prison.

Maximilian tried the wooden door one more time, but it was no use.

'What about the sword?' said Wolf. 'I could try that?'

'What sword?' said Raven.

Wolf coughed a bit and got to his feet. He looked a little unsteady.

'This one,' he said. 'Max?'

He had decided, while he was lying on the ground close to death, that one thing he would never do again (if he lived) was say the whole word 'Maximilian' when 'Max' would do fine.

Maximilian passed Wolf the letter opener, and the girls watched in amazement as it grew to become the Sword of Orphennyus.

'Wow,' said Raven.

Wolf walked over to the door and swung the sword at it – but it just bounced off the solid wood. Wolf suddenly had the strong feeling that this sword wasn't supposed to cut or physically damage things at all. But then he shook the thought away. What else would a sword be for? But then why wasn't it working?

'Ow,' he said, rubbing his wrist.

'Oh no,' said Maximilian. 'We have to get out!' He kicked the door a couple of times, but this just hurt his foot.

'We have to help Effie,' said Wolf. 'That guy is pure evil. What happened to Carl and his lock-picking kit?'

'Carl? What does he look like?' said Raven.

Wolf described his brother in the most flattering terms he could manage.

'Blond. A bit stupid-looking. Um . . .'

'There's a blond guy asleep in a car down there,' said Raven. 'Lexy, have you got something to wake him up?'

Effie had lost sight of Leonard Levar, but it didn't matter. She knew exactly where he was going. He was going back to the Funtime Arcade and into the Realworld and to Effie's house to get *Dragon's Green*. Effie had to stop him. The only trouble was that she didn't quite know how to get back to the Funtime Arcade.

Light was fading now, and the goblins were putting away their fruits. But each time Effie walked past one of them she was hissed at, and every goblin who saw her reached out his sharp little hands and tried to pinch or poke her.

'Don't want to suck our fruits, miss?' said one. 'Are you sure?'

'Look,' said Effie. 'Just stop it. How do I get out of here?'

'Ooh, ooh, the maid spoke,' said the goblin. 'Give her a fruit, give her a fruit.'

'I don't want your fruit. I . . . Never mind.'

But now, as she tried to find the portal, she found herself surrounded by goblins. She had to try to look over the tops of their heads to see which way she should go, but some of them were quite tall and . . .

'Oh, please go away,' she said.

'Make us, pretty maid,' said one of them.

Effie's silver ring grew hot. She sensed it making her stronger. And suddenly she found that she was able to pick up this annoying goblin, turn him upside down and simply drop him.

'Ooh, ooh, me next, me next,' said another goblin. He reached out a bony clawed hand and Effie threw him, karate-style, over her shoulder and onto the ground behind her. Before she knew it she was fending off another goblin, and then another. They seemed almost to be enjoying it. But she was winning. None of them came back to try to attack her again. And the more of them that came towards her, the more of them she simply threw this way and that. She sensed they meant no real harm, so she didn't get out the athame. When the last one had been flung aside she strode onwards, hoping she hadn't lost too much time.

'Well, you're just as brave as they said you would be,' came a voice.

'Festus,' said Effie. 'How do I get out of here?'

'The portal is in the lamp shop over there,' he said, doffing his hat at her. He must have been shopping today, Effie thought – it was one of the feathered panama hats that she had seen earlier.

'Thank you!'

Effie hurried on through the door of a vast bazaar-like emporium filled with old-fashioned lamps and strange glass bottles. There was a small area off to the right where a man in a bright blue turban was serving tea from a large gold samovar. Just by the counter was a door with a sign saying, simply, ISLAND.

Effie showed her mark and papers to a guard, and then she was through the door and walking down a corridor that somehow turned into the alleyway next to the Funtime Arcade. As soon as she was out, she started to run. And as she turned right towards the antiquarian bookshop, she was just in time to see Leonard Levar hurrying away as Wolf stood there with his sword, seemingly unable to do anything.

'What happened?' Effie asked.

'I just couldn't . . .' began Wolf.

Effie thrust the spectacles back at Maximilian. 'Here,' she said.

'Oh my God,' said Maximilian. 'How did you . . .?'

'He said you robbed him at knifepoint,' said Lexy. 'He said—'

'He said he was going to call the police,' said Raven. 'But I

301

think he was just bluffing. But then he said all this stuff about knife crime and . . .'

Wolf was shaking his head. 'I don't know what's wrong with me,' he said. 'I knew he was lying. I knew he'd already shut us in a cave with three live tarantulas. I still couldn't actually . . .'

'Don't worry about that now,' said Effie. 'But if we don't stop him soon, I think time might change and you might end up back in the cave with the tarantulas.'

In fact, Effie didn't know what would happen if Levar got the book and prevented her from being the Last Reader of *Dragon's Green*. Shouldn't time already have changed? Hadn't Cosmo said that time was wise? But there was no sense in standing around thinking.

'We need to get to my house before Levar does,' she said. 'We'd better run for it.'

But when they got to the next corner, Carl was there waiting for them in his car.

'Got any more of that fizzy pink water?' he asked Lexy.

'If you can get us to Effie's house before Leonard Levar gets there,' she replied, 'you can have all the fizzy pink water you want.'

The children all piled into Carl's car, and he sped away.

'Go as quick as you can,' said Wolf. 'We've got to stop this guy.'

Effie gave directions and tried to explain what was now happening, while Maximilian used the spectacles to try to work out what was wrong with Wolf's sword, although he suspected the problem was with Wolf himself. Maximilian seemed to have generated quite a large amount of M-currency from somewhere, enough to enable him to use the spectacles for a very long time. Raven slowly chanted a simple spell for slowing down Leonard Levar, and Lexy added a crushed moonberry to a tonic for Effie's recovery in case she had to fight him.

Soon they were going past the old village green, next to the abandoned pub by the bus stop. And there, skulking in the shadows, creeping along almost invisibly, his ancient body jerking like a fragile zombie, was Leonard Levar.

'There!' said Effie, spotting him. 'Stop the car.'

Effie, Wolf, Raven and Lexy all got out.

'I'll carry on to your house with Carl,' said Maximilian. 'I'll deal with the book. It needs to be destroyed completely, presumably?'

'How do you know . . .?' Effie began. 'Oh, never mind. Thank you. Here's my key. My house is number thirty-five.'

'I know.'

'The book's . . .' Suddenly Effie didn't want to say where the book was in front of Carl. Just in case. 'It's . . .' She searched her mind quickly for something she could use for a clue that only Maximilian would know. 'It's being guarded by the thing that Cronus likes to eat.'

Maximilian nodded. 'OK. And here's Wolf's sword.'

'Thank you.' Effie took it. 'You're a true friend.'

Maximilian sighed. 'I wish I always had been. Good luck.'

Effie didn't have time to wonder what on earth Maximilian meant. She ran towards Levar. Wolf did the same. Lexy and Raven were still working their magic, so they followed more slowly.

Effie threw Wolf's sword for him to catch and it immediately crackled and hissed as it grew to full size.

'Stop,' Effie said to Levar, running in front of him.

'Oh, you again,' he said, turning around. There was Wolf. 'And I see you've brought the boy coward with you.'

'I am not a coward,' said Wolf, raising his sword.

'Be careful with that,' said Levar. 'You might hurt yourself. These boons, you never know exactly what they will do. Now, if you'll excuse me, I just need to . . .'

Levar started trying to run across the green. He was about as fast as any unfit 350-year-old was likely to be, but he seemed determined not to let this stop him as he staggered on towards the old boarded-up inn. He managed about ten steps. Then he tripped and fell to the ground.

'Muggers!' he cried weakly. 'Thieves! Hooligans!' He seemed to be trying to reach in his pocket for something. 'Help!' he called. 'Someone save me from these vicious young thugs!'

In a moment, Effie and Wolf were standing over him. Lexy and Raven had almost caught up with them. Wolf raised his sword. Effie had the athame ready. But neither of them felt quite right about striking such a feeble old man who was already on the ground. Who should do it first? Wolf felt that Effie ought to, really. It had been her grandfather after all, and . . . Effie felt that Wolf's sword was bigger, and also that it was probably his turn to do something brave.

While they hesitated, Leonard Levar finally got out of his pocket the thing he was looking for. It was a pinkish-whitish seashell.

'Blast you!' he cried, tossing it to the ground in front of Effie and Wolf.

When it landed it acted like quite a different sort of shell and exploded with a loud crack. Both children fell to the ground. Then everything began to shake, slowly at first and then more violently. It was like the worldquake all over again. The earth beneath the children moved this way and that, becoming loose and precarious until – whoosh – it started to blow up all around them like a sandstorm. Or, more accurately, an earthstorm.

Anyone who has been in one knows that there are few things more horrible than an earthstorm. Soon, the air was full of everything that had been shaken from the ground: worms, gnarled roots, mice, caterpillars, slugs, maggots, ants' nests, the bones of long-dead animals and other strange things that lurk between this world and the one below. All of these were momentarily suspended in the air while the soil they had been in separated itself first into little clumps, and then into tiny pieces, all the time flying higher and higher. Then everything began swirling around and around, as if the whole world were being stirred by some uncanny force.

Wolf got up slowly. What was happening? The air smelled like damp sheds and old socks as the earth's innards circled around him. Insects and spiders, dead and alive, were gathering in his hair. Larger things were creeping up his sleeves and inside his socks. Wolf felt tiny sharp feet crawling up and down his back and his chest. He felt the soft wetness of worms trying to get into his ears and up his nose. Something had started gnawing on his elbow. Small skeletons of all sorts were reassembling and running at him before then exploding back into fragments again. In front of him now dangled a root that looked a bit like a boiled head. And another one that looked a lot like his uncle.

It had become darker and darker. Wolf was now completely alone in an expanding cloud of dust and dried mud and dead skin and creepers and tendrils and every underground horror you can imagine. And then something like an earthstorm started happening in Wolf's own soul.

Suddenly all his deepest and most painful memories were being unearthed, and flickering scenes from his life were forming around him. Wolf's father was hitting his mother and then she was leaving for ever, and then his father was doing it all over again with someone else and then *he* was leaving for ever. Then there was a blur, and Wolf's uncle was creeping up behind him, and then Wolf was beaten and left cold, afraid and hungry, and then locked in a cupboard, and then he was standing there, as he always did, while his so-called friends cornered one of the 'gifted' children, emptied the unlucky child's schoolbag into the river and then laughed.

While Wolf staggered around, lost in this world of darkness, shame and fear, with centipedes trying to get in his eyes and beetles wriggling down his neck, Effie was still lying on the ground not responding to anything. Bits of earth were now falling on her from the sky. The earthstorm was getting bigger.

'This is so unfair!' Lexy shouted at Levar. 'They could have killed you just then, but they felt sorry for you.'

But Levar didn't respond. While Lexy shook bits of soil from her hair and gave Effie a tonic, he staggered away towards the old inn. What did he want there?

306

'I'll go after him,' said Raven.

'What will you do?' said Lexy.

'I don't know. Try to stop him somehow. You need to break the earthstorm spell. It's earth magic, so you should be able to stop it with water or fire. Air will make it worse.'

But there was no water anywhere close by. And Lexy had no matches or any other way of starting a fire. Perhaps Raven could do some kind of spell? But she had gone.

'HELP!' shouted Wolf. 'Make this stop. Please.'

Lexy tried to think of some way to help him. Of course! She had a tonic left. It was intended to increase M-currency, but, like all tonics, it was mainly water. She pulled the little cork out of the vial and hurled it towards Wolf. She could hardly see him now in the dense cloud of dank earth and creatures. After a moment, there was a large belch of dead autumn leaves and black beetles. And then . . . The earthstorm was expanding. All of a sudden it looked as if it might engulf Lexy and Effie. Lexy cursed herself. How stupid. There had been M-currency in that tonic. She'd just fed more magic to the storm.

Water. Fire. There was no water. There was no fire.

A fat pink worm started to crawl up Lexy's arm. The storm was getting closer to her, and also to Effie, who was still passed out on the ground and could do nothing to defend herself. The only way to stop it getting worse would be . . . Water. Fire. Where could they . . .?

Water. *Tears*. If only . . .

'Wolf,' called Lexy. 'Wolf!'

From inside the storm, Wolf could hear someone calling his

name very faintly. He was reliving a particularly painful memory from his past, in which he'd won a goldfish at a fair. He'd carried it home carefully in its fragile plastic bag, only for his uncle to rip open the bag and flush the fish down the toilet. Wolf had felt . . . Had felt . . .

'Cry,' said a voice somewhere just outside his head. 'You have to cry.'

What? Wolf had never cried in his whole life. Well, except probably when he was a baby. He was a boy, wasn't he? And you couldn't cry around someone like Wolf's uncle. Or Wolf's friends. Occasionally he had considered crying on his own, but somehow the tears had never come. Instead he had focused on being tough. After all, if you have never cried, you don't know what is going to happen when you do cry. What if you never stopped? Or what if it became a habit? And then what if someone saw you?

'Cry,' said the voice again. 'Only your tears will stop the earthstorm. You have to try to . . .'

The images swirled around Wolf's head one more time. His mother. His father. His uncle. And also, faintly, a small girl, leaving the house at the same time as Wolf's mother. His *sister*? Wolf had almost forgotten he'd ever had a sister. Why had his mother taken her and not him? Was she still alive? Why hadn't he tried to find her? Coach Bruce had always said Wolf was weak. He *was* weak. He was pathetic, and weak, and he'd forgotten his sister and now couldn't even protect his friends when he had the chance. He'd been given this amazing sword and he couldn't even use it.

He was a complete and total loser.

Then he felt something in his left eye. A single tear. It rolled out slowly. When it came into contact with the worm that was trying to crawl up his nostril, the creature immediately vanished. It was working. Another tear came. And then another. Then Wolf put his head in his hands and finally let all the years of pain come out. He sobbed and sobbed, and, as he did, the earth came down from the sky and everything slowly fell back into its right place.

34

By the time Raven caught up with Leonard Levar, he had almost reached the old boarded-up inn. Its white painted exterior was now grey, and Raven could see that the words THE BLACK PIG had faded from black to almost the same grey. It was a grim and depressing place. Except . . .

As Raven approached the pub, it began to seem strangely beautiful. Was it because it was so old? It had the air of an ancient church or abbey. In the air Raven could smell something like incense and dried flowers. Where was it coming from? Leonard Levar hadn't looked behind him for a while, so intent was he on whatever it was he was doing. And Raven could see him quite clearly as he pressed his hands to the white brick wall of the pub and stood there shaking slightly and smiling.

What was he doing? Whatever it was, Raven suddenly wanted to do it, too. The incense, the dried flowers . . . She realised that she wasn't *smelling* these things exactly. She was sensing them, but with something beyond her normal five senses. It wasn't what people call a 'sixth sense', which, as everyone knows, is when you can tell there is a ghost in a room, or when you know what your friend is just about to say. The seventh sense is closer to smell than anything else, but it is still very different. It is when you detect the magic in things. It's when you know that something is full to the brim with M-currency, or lifeforce.

Stored-up lifeforce usually feels cool and peaceful, like a slab of marble or a timeworn stone wall. It usually smells faintly of sandalwood and roses and peat-smoke and the backs of mirrors. It also smells, although that is still not the right word, of pink lilies and beeswax. It is, in fact, very similar to the sensory experience of being in a very old and atmospheric church (which is where you can always find a small amount of lifeforce, should you ever need it).

Of course, people are always popping into churches to borrow a bit of lifeforce, left over from the residue of prayer, but no one had been near this pub for over fifty years. Raven's senses were almost overcome by the heady stench of raw magic trapped in the walls, in the wood, in the very smallest atoms of this building. And so, like Levar, she reached out and . . .

The sensation of touching a building imbued with so much lifeforce can be so strong it can knock people unconscious, if they are receptive to it. As a newly epiphanised witch, Raven was extremely receptive to it. And the lifeforce from the old inn was mainly light and life-giving and free, so when it realised that she wanted it, it immediately stopped flowing into Leonard Levar and started flowing into Raven Wilde instead.

In an instant, Raven realised what Levar had been doing. He'd been trying to top up his M-currency by taking it from this untapped source. All the years of joy and comfort this pub had provided to its patrons meant that there had been quite a bit spilled here and there and it had all added up, and . . .

'WHAT DO YOU THINK YOU ARE DOING?'

Leonard Levar hobbled towards Raven, his eyes black with anger. Raven ignored him. She had never felt as much pleasure and happiness as she was experiencing now, as the huge current of lifeforce flowed into her. For the few more seconds it continued, she had a curious sensation of knowing everything important about life, and love, and especially being a witch, and . . . Then she blacked out.

Maximilian let himself silently into Effie's house. It was not difficult to find her bedroom. There was a baby there asleep in a cot, with a toy monster lying on the floor. Maximilian had never had a younger brother or sister. He picked up the monster and put it gently back in the cot. Then he got on with the task in hand.

Where was the book? There weren't many hiding places in here. What was it Effie had said? Something about what Cronus liked to eat. *Cronuts*, thought Maximilian. Those deep-fried flaky doughnuts they used to sell at that stall in the Old Town. Did Cronus eat Cronuts, or something else entirely? While he thought about it, Maximilian searched in and under Effie's small bed, just in case. Then he opened a wooden chest at the far end of the room. Perhaps the book was here? There were certainly all sorts of other interesting things in the box, including a black book full of a foreign language written in a blue ink that Maximilian felt inexplicably drawn to. But no *Dragon's Green*.

Cronus. Wasn't he the Greek god who ate his own children? In fact, his own *babies*.

Maximilian went back over to Luna's cot. So Effie had been quite clever. Any intruder would have to risk waking the baby to find the book. So how did you avoid waking up a baby? Maximilian had no idea how you even moved one. What if it leaked? And, especially, what if it cried? He asked the spectacles, which helpfully suggested a lavender diffuser, lullabies in a variety of languages, an infant painkiller that caused drowsiness, a cough mixture that did the same, a pink teething ring, a strange concoction made from chamomile and lettuce, and then, finally, an ancient sleep spell. But Maximilian was not a witch or a high-level scholar, and so could not say spells. And according to the spectacles, this one did not work that well anyway.

Maximilian was a scholar, which meant he knew things. And, if Leonard Levar was to be believed, he was also a mage, which meant . . . What did it mean? He asked the spectacles what a mage could do to put a baby deeply to sleep. *Kill it?* suggested the spectacles. *Without killing it, you idiot*, replied Maximilian. The spectacles seemed to go into a huff for a few seconds. Then they just seemed confused. Maximilian found it hard to under-stand what they were trying to tell him. Still, he looked at Luna and thought about dreams and lullabies and moonlight and a comfortable hollow deep in a dark, dark wood, where . . .

Then he picked her up. He had never held a baby before. She was surprisingly heavy. He realised that with his mind he had pushed her into a faraway land of deep sleep – nourishing, rather than dangerous, although with a high probability of peculiar dreams. She didn't stir. Maximilian found a way of holding her with one arm, and with the other he searched her cot. Under her mattress there was a sort of hollow. And there was *Dragon's Green*. Maximilian took the book, and put Luna gently back in her cot. He tucked her in and put her toy monster where she could reach it.

Dragon's Green. Well. Maximilian's hand shook as he ran it over the pale green cloth cover. Of course, anyone who found this book could simply open it and read it and . . . Then what would happen?

Reading the book would not just create a wrench in time, but would mean that the new reader would gain entry to the Otherworld, with its adventures, mysteries and boons. Well, as long as they remembered to destroy the book promptly afterwards.

For a moment, Maximilian was tempted. All he had ever wanted in life was to go to the Otherworld, to find out everything he could about magic and mystery and how life really worked. Of course, that was before he had discovered the Underworld, which seemed rather more interesting.

Now something made him hesitate.

If he destroyed the book then he would, for once in his life at least, have been a true friend. He would be able to save Effie – not only from having her recent adventures wiped out, but also from having to become a Book Eater, a Diberi. Effie herself wouldn't have read the book and then destroyed it, as the Diberi do. She would have read the book but then found that it had been destroyed by someone else. It wasn't perfect, but it did technically mean she couldn't be called a Diberi.

Maximilian took from his pocket two folded sheets of paper, smoothed them out and read them one last time. They made so much more sense now, after everything that had happened. Should he leave them here for her? Could he maybe say he found them in the back of the book? No. He had to tell the truth. Effie deserved that. She had helped save him from the six-eyed tarantulas. And she was the first person who had ever really trusted him.

He put the pieces of paper back in his pocket. Hid the book under his jacket. Skulked to the dark, small kitchen to find a box of matches. Then he let himself out of the house and, in a dark alleyway around the corner, in an old metal bin that a local hooligan had once stolen from his school, Maximilian burned the last edition of *Dragon's Green*. Darkness flickered in him as he did this – burning books has never been something associated with goodness after all – but from this darkness would come light. He was almost certain of that.

Wolf, freed from the earthstorm, ran across the grass and found Leonard Levar cursing and desperately mumbling some sort of incantation, with his hands pressed against the wall of the old derelict pub, the Black Pig. Whatever he was trying to do did not seem to be working. Raven was lying on the ground, unconscious.

'What have you done to her?' Wolf shouted, raising his sword.

'The coward speaks,' said Levar. 'You couldn't strike me before, timid child, and you can't strike me now. Although I wouldn't bother striking me on her account anyway. She's . . .'

At that moment, Raven blinked and sat up. She had never felt so powerful in her entire life. Of course, she couldn't attack Leonard Levar. Witches cannot attack. But she could, with a flick of her wonde, cure Wolf of all the injuries he'd sustained during the earthstorm. What else could she do? Aha. She could lift herself off the ground just a little – not exactly flying, but something similar – and arrive just next to Effie on the other side of the green. With Raven's huge increase in M-currency, and Lexy's skill at administering tonics, they soon had Effie sitting up.

Leonard Levar was hobbling away from the Black Pig. So he couldn't get a bit of extra M-currency from the derelict old heap. Fine. It was now in the witch. Who cared? All he needed to do was find *Dragon's Green*, wipe out what the Truelove girl had done, get the boon that enabled him to find the Great Library, and then he could come back just as powerful as he had been before . . . and take some pleasure in killing these children. The boys could simply have their throats cut. But the girl hero he would kill slowly. And as for the witch who had stolen his lifeforce . . .

'Oh, yes I can,' said Wolf. Something about seeing Effie still lying on the ground had made him able to raise his gleaming Sword of Orphennyus and bring it down, now, hard, right through the centre of Leonard Levar's frail body.

'Arrrgh!' screamed Levar, falling to his knees on the grass.

Of course, he was not physically injured. Not exactly. Wolf had correctly realised that his sword did not cut or pierce. However, this blow had wiped out almost all of Levar's remaining M-currency. And since it was really only M-currency keeping him alive in both worlds, this hurt.

'No!' Levar shouted. 'Leave me alone. What did I ever do to you? I'll pay you. Hmm? How about that? I have millions of pounds and billions of krubles. Put down that sword now and come back to my shop with me. I'll make you rich, boy. You don't need to hang around with these stupid children any more.'

Wolf looked across the grass at Effie. She was slowly getting up. Lexy seemed to be giving her jam from a jar. The earthstorm had tinged the darkness with streaks of pale flame and russet. The odd earthworm still hung suspended in the air and there were autumn leaves floating slowly back down to the ground.

The girls were now hurrying over to help. Wolf raised his sword again.

'My friends are worth more than all the money in the world,' he said. 'So . . .'

Leonard Levar put up his hand. He used almost all his remaining M-currency to trap a small nerve in Wolf's spine, which made him freeze completely. Then Levar reached into his inside pocket and drew out a business card.

'Skylurian Midzhar,' he said, desperately, with almost the last tiny bit of his M-currency. 'Help your fellow Diberi. Now!'

Magical business cards are by far the most efficient form of communication in the modern world. If you possess one, you can call on its owner at any time of the day or night and they must come to you instantly. If they are far away, they must use magic to get to you. Skylurian Midzhar was, however, at that moment only three streets away in a taxi on her way home from a rather tiresome dinner party thrown by her publishing company's most successful author. Should she simply ask the driver to change course? Could one arrive to save one's evil co-conspirator in a minicab? Perhaps not.

Skylurian had drunk a lot of champagne, followed by an unexpectedly delightful Chablis and a dessert wine given to her by a poet. She was a little tipsy. No matter. She took out her ivory wonde and made herself sober. Removed the small soup stain from her black dress. Made her heels three inches higher. Smote the cab driver. And . . .

Suddenly, above Levar and the children, came a flash of something that could have been lightning, had it not been bright blue. The sky rumbled more deeply than it would ever do with normal thunder. The ground shook again for a few seconds. Leonard Levar might have lost almost all his lifeforce and been reduced to a trembling wreck on some unkempt village green, but Skylurian Midzhar was more powerful, beautiful and devastating than ever. She had so much lifeforce she barely knew what to do with it any more. And she knew the importance of making an entrance.

Perhaps a bit too much blue smoke? But when it cleared . . .

'Oh my God,' said Raven, coughing and trying to rub the smoke from her eyes. She could detect extremely dark magic in this fellow witch who had just arrived. Not just dark magic, but something beyond that. Something not just evil, but deeply, horribly evil. And there was something else, too. When the blue smoke had cleared a little, Raven realised she recognised this witch. She was that woman from the dinner party. The woman responsible for commissioning and then inexplicably pulping her mother's books. The owner of Matchstick Press.

35

While Leonard Levar coughed and blinked his eyes – that infernal woman really had created a lot of smoke – Raven unfroze Wolf, who fell to the ground and started trying to rub the painful spot on his back where the magic had entered. Raven and Lexy started work on curing him immediately, with Raven trebling the power in all Lexy's tonics with just a small flick of her wonde.

'What is going on here?' said Skylurian Midzhar, once she was sure everyone could see her in all her shimmering glory. 'Leonard?'

'Help me,' he said. 'These children . . . These brutes . . .'

Effie looked at Levar. 'You killed my grandfather,' she said to him. 'And you tried to kill my friends, and then me. I don't care who you've called to help you. I should have done this a lot earlier.'

She drew back the athame, ready to plunge it into his heart.

Skylurian Midzhar watched this with interest. She slowed the girl slightly with a spell, although of course spells don't work that well on someone wearing the Ring of the True Hero. Skylurian knew that true heroes were not to be messed with. Well, not much anyway. And this one looked as if she had potential for . . .

'Leonard?' she said. 'It looks as if I am a little too late. Is there anything I should know?'

Of course, there was a lot he could have told her. It was now too late to save *Dragon's Green*, but he could have explained where to find the other 499 books, in order that she could put them towards their great mission after his demise. But evil is not known for being helpful. Leonard Levar actually didn't give a stuff about what happened to Skylurian Midzhar and the Matchstick Press and all her other stupid sham companies, or the other Diberi, after he was gone. Skylurian had crossed him at their last meeting, after all. And even though he'd called her for help now, she was barely doing anything. He hoped she would suffer when the time came for her to . . .

The girl was raising the athame. It was almost too late. Except . . .

'Of course,' Levar said, in a tone that made Effie hesitate. 'I know where your mother is. I know where she went on the night of the worldquake, and I know where she is now. If you agreed to work with me, then I'm sure it would be possible for me to . . .'

Effie didn't move for a few moments.

'I don't know why he even bothered to call me,' said Skylurian Midzhar to Raven. 'If you possess information about someone's missing mother, and they are just about to kill you, then it is *always* possible to negotiate with them and . . .'

'You don't know anything about my mother,' said Effie. 'You're lying. I should have done this earlier, before you hurt my friends.'

And then Effie pierced Leonard Levar's heart, or what was left of his heart, with her athame. No actual blood was spilled. But the dagger did take away the very last of Levar's lifeforce. Once all his M-currency was gone, Leonard Levar became a mortal man again. Since mortal men do not live for three hundred and fifty years, once Realworld nature returned everything to normal Levar's body simply crumbled into a tiny pile of dust. A tiny pile of dust topped with a tattered three-piece suit, a grey wool coat, a pair of grey underpants, a small jar of mustard, a silver spoon and an ornate brass key.

'That was for my grandfather,' said Effie quietly. 'And you know nothing about my mother. Nothing.'

Skylurian Midzhar looked around at the other children, taking each one of them in, including the black-haired witch to whom she had just spoken, and who looked familiar, but whom she could not place. Her gaze returned to the strongest one. The traveller. The true hero. The one who had just killed Leonard Levar.

'Well,' she said. 'Who are you?'

'I am Euphemia Truelove,' said Effie. 'And if you had anything to do with my grandfather's death . . .' She raised her athame. Effie didn't want this accomplice of Levar's to see the key that was resting almost at the top of his remains. Better to distract her with the idea of another battle.

'I see. You're a little avenging angel. Interesting. Yet I sense you are almost, but not quite, one of us. Here's my card.' She strode over to Effie, with only magic stopping her high heels sinking into the grass, and presented her with a silver and blue business card.

'If you decide you want to join us more permanently,' she said, 'we could use someone with your power.' She looked around at Effie's friends. 'She'll let you down in the end,' she said to them. 'I'd watch out if I were you.'

And then, in another puff of blue smoke, she was gone.

Effie reached down and picked up the key. She was going to save her grandfather's books at long last. Even if that meant she never found out what had happened to her mother, it was what she had to do. She had to stop the Diberi from becoming any more powerful.

'Do you think she was serious?' said Lexy. 'When she asked Effie to join her?'

It was the following morning and the five friends were tired but exhilarated. They had met an hour before school began and Wolf had used his sports captain's key to let them into the tennis centre, where they'd made themselves as comfortable as they could in the dark cupboard among all the old tennis balls and bits of green fluff. Then they filled each other in on all the bits of the story they didn't know.

Maximilian told them all about burning the book in the alleyway, and Wolf explained all about trying to rescue Effie's books from Levar, and how he and Max had been trapped in the cave. Effie's story took the longest, and although she didn't tell them all the details of her visit to the Otherworld, they got the general idea.

After Maximilian had destroyed the book, Carl had taken him back to the old village green by the Black Pig. But Carl had taken one look at the scene there – the strange shades of red in the air, the worms still suspended above the ground, the weird swirling leaves, the powerful witch and so on – and decided to flee, leaving Maximilian with a very long walk home. This morning, Wolf had borrowed Maximilian's pager and was still trying to persuade his brother to come back this afternoon and help move the books. Otherwise, the children weren't sure how they were going to get them out of Levar's storeroom. They were safe, presumably, for the time being. But Effie wanted to move them as soon as possible.

'That Skylurian woman was just trying to mess with our collective spirit,' said Wolf. 'You get it in sports all the time. But we're stronger than that. We're a team.'

Lexy nodded solemnly. 'We're a good team,' she said.

When Wolf had arrived home late the previous night his uncle had been waiting for him, holding the thin birch cane that he'd used to beat Wolf since he was a small boy. Wolf had walked right up to his uncle, taken the cane from him and snapped it. 'If you ever lay a hand on me again . . .' Wolf had begun. But his uncle had looked so frightened that Wolf hadn't needed to continue. Wolf's uncle had even begun to stammer an apology and a promise to go to Alcoholics Anonymous meetings more often, but Wolf had just gone to his bedroom and quietly closed the door.

That morning he'd told his uncle that his early house clearance job had been cancelled, and his uncle had not even argued. He'd simply poured another cup of tea and nodded.

'It's significant that Skylurian Midzhar is a publisher,' said Effie. 'I'm just not sure how. But it's all to do with books, I can feel it. I'm sure she and others will still be trying to get to the Great Library in Dragon's Green.'

'I bet it's not the last we'll see of her,' agreed Raven. 'But we can defeat her if we have to, just like we defeated Leonard Levar.'

'She seemed a lot stronger than him, though,' said Effie. 'I wonder why she didn't try to hurt us last night. But we must investigate her. And I realised something about Miss Wright, as well.'

'Miss Wright?' said Lexy. 'Our old teacher?'

'You know she won that publishing competition and then disappeared? Well, three guesses who the publisher was.'

'Matchstick Press,' said Raven.

'Exactly.'

There was a lot more to talk about, but soon it was time for double English with Mrs Beathag Hide and none of the children wanted to be late. Even after facing and overcoming deep evil, none of them yet felt confident about dealing with Mrs Beathag Hide. And of course Maximilian, Effie and Wolf were going to be in severe trouble for escaping from detention. It seemed as if this had happened a lifetime ago, but really it had been only yesterday. Still, Maximilian knew he had to find a way to tell Effie his secret. He had to get everything off his chest.

As the others hurried towards the main school building, he

touched Effie's arm, got her to stop, and then handed her two folded pieces of paper.

'What's this?' she said.

'A copy of the codicil, and a letter your grandfather wrote you. I should have given them to you yesterday. I shouldn't really have them at all.' He looked down at his feet. 'I was going to pretend I found them in the book, but then I realised that true friends don't lie and . . .'

'And they do what instead?' Effie's tone was cool. 'How did you get these?'

'I stole them. From your grandfather's hospital room.'

As quickly as he could, Maximilian told Effie the story of how he'd been helping out at the hospital at the weekend – reading to elderly patients and getting them magazines from the shop and so on. He'd overheard a conversation between the surgeon, Dr Black, and his mother, Nurse Underwood. There was talk of magical boons, and of a complex and difficult operation that might succeed in getting Griffin Truelove's spirit into the Otherworld before his body died in this world. Maximilian was shocked – he'd had the most normal upbringing imaginable and now here, suddenly, was his mother talking to a magical surgeon! He heard about the boons and the codicil and everything. Because he had never seen a boon, and because he longed so desperately to have any connection at all with the world of magic, he'd snuck into Griffin's room.

Then, when Griffin was asleep, he'd looked at everything. He'd read the codicil, which was lying there on the table. He'd lifted up a sealed letter, addressed to Effie, in order that he could take a picture of the codicil underneath. But just after he'd pressed the button on his old phone to take the photograph, the door had opened. Maximilian had hidden behind a curtain, still holding the letter. Someone had come in and taken the codicil away. A man. Effie's father.

'He probably would have taken the letter as well if I hadn't been holding it,' said Maximilian. 'I know it's no excuse for what I've done. But I guess I did sort of save the documents for you. In a way. I printed the picture of the codicil and . . .'

'But why didn't you give them to me yesterday?' Effie said.

Maximilian shrugged and looked at the ground.

'I'm sorry,' he said. 'I thought if I pretended that the spectacles were telling me extra things that would help you, then you'd want to be my friend.'

'So the spectacles didn't show you that *Dragon's Green* was under the floorboards at all? You knew that from this letter? You read it, rather than just give it to me? How could you?'

'I'm so sorry.' Maximilian's eyes filled with tears, but he tried to blink them away. 'Once I'd lied the first time, I didn't know how to stop. I thought you'd hate me when I told you the truth. And now I have told you, you probably hate me anyway. But I thought it was important that you knew the whole truth.' Maximilian bit his lip. 'I really am sorry,' he said.

Effie didn't respond. They had to get to class. And she'd have to call Pelham Longfellow, of course, and . . . They were now very late as well. She walked away.

'Effie?' said Maximilian, following her. 'Please?'

But there was no time to say anything else, because they'd

327

arrived at their classroom. And there, staring at them through the glass section of the door, was Mrs Beathag Hide, her thin face drawn into the expression of someone who has just eaten fifteen lemons for breakfast and then read something distasteful in the newspaper.

Effie opened the door, wincing as it creaked.

'Euphemia Truelove. Well, well, how KIND of you to grace us with your presence for the second day in a row,' said Mrs Beathag Hide. 'And your tragic little friend, too. Well, the good news is that you can both have detention again today. Four o'clock. Same location as yesterday. Mr Reed has already agreed to join us. We will pick up where we left off, but with the added delights of the company of Miss Wilde and Miss Bottle, both of whom seem unable to stay awake this morning.'

It was true. Lexy and Raven had both fallen asleep with their unkempt hair all over their desks. At least Raven didn't have the spiders in her hair any more. They had agreed to spend their days in her garden, as long as they could sleep in her hair at night. They were nocturnal, but still on Chilean time, so everything had worked out all right.

Maximilian sighed and made for his desk. Effie started to walk towards hers.

'Oh, but you're not going anywhere,' said Mrs Beathag Hide, pointing at Effie with the wooden stick she always used to point at things on the blackboard, the thing that Effie suddenly realised looked very like a . . . like a . . .

'Headmaster's office,' said Mrs Beathag Hide. 'NOW.'

36

Effie walked to the headmaster's office feeling miserable. Yesterday had ended in such an exciting way. But after she had killed Leonard Levar, she had felt curiously empty. Yes, she had avenged her grandfather's death, but she hadn't rescued his books. She had the key to Leonard Levar's storeroom, but nowhere to put the books when she got them out. And what if Leonard Levar really *had* known something about her mother . . .? But he must have been lying. Even if he hadn't been, Effie would have had to do whatever he wanted in return for whatever information he claimed to have.

And what had Skylurian Midzhar meant about her almost being one of them? It was just like what Rollo had said in the garden, and what Leonard Levar had said in the market. Why was it wrong for the Diberi to use and destroy books for their power, but OK for Effie to do it? Of course, if it hadn't been for Maximilian, everything would have been much worse. As it was, she hadn't had to destroy the book herself at all, which had removed some of the cold taint of the Diberi that had been clinging to her like a wet mist ever since she had faced Levar in the market.

Maximilian, who was supposed to be her friend.

And he had acted like a true friend, hadn't he? More or less. Well, except for when he stole her letter and the codicil. Of course, this had actually turned out to be useful. But that wasn't how he'd meant it. He'd just wanted magical knowledge and hadn't cared who he had to hurt to get it.

Then again, if he hadn't taken the letter, Effie's father would have destroyed it and perhaps she never would have found *Dragon's Green*. But why had he read the letter? That was the thing she couldn't bear. Although he'd used what he'd learned to help her. Well, sort of. Oh! It was all so confusing.

Dearest Euphemia,

I did not mean to leave you so soon. I cannot write much. Find Truelove House. It is in a place very far away. If I don't come back for you immediately, you can get there yourself through the book, Dragon's Green, which is hidden under the desk. ONLY use this book if I do not come back for you, and if no one else comes for you from the Otherworld. Wait for at least a week. Your cousins will be waiting for you, and they will explain everything. Sadly, I cannot help you with the plot of the book. Nor can I tell you what must be done afterwards. Your cousins will tell you. Make sure this final task is done. Also, there is someone who wants my books. Save them from him, if you can. They are meant for you. But he is the one who tried to kill me, so be very careful.

Your destiny lies in Dragon's Green.

Goodbye, dearest child.

Your loving grandfather,

Griffin Truelove

When Effie reached the headmaster's office, she was surprised to hear laughter coming from inside the room. And a voice she was sure she recognised.

'Greetings and blessings,' said Pelham Longfellow, when Effie entered the wood-panelled room. 'Well, it's good to see that you attend the most appropriate school in the area. I hear you even passed the magical part of the entrance exam.'

The Tusitala School for the Gifted, Troubled and Strange had a number of places for gifted children and a number of places for troubled children. No one officially knew which children were which, although most people assumed, often incorrectly, that the ones with bruises and footballs were the troubled ones, and the ones with glasses and cellos were the gifted ones.

The magical places, for the 'strange', were only a rumour – mainly because magic didn't officially exist – but the school did have a very odd sixth form run by a man called Quinn, who made all his pupils wear silk robes, so anything was possible. Some parents, worried that their children might not be clever enough to qualify for a gifted place, encouraged them to pretend to be extremely troubled instead. Who knew what the parents would have done had they believed in the places for the strange.

The elderly headmaster nodded at Effie. 'It's time for my morning coffee,' he said. 'I'll take it in the staff room for a change. I believe this young solicitor has something important to discuss with you.'

The headmaster left, and closed the door behind him.

'You have found the copy of the codicil, I believe?' said Longfellow.

'How do you know that?'

'You called me. It will have happened automatically once you got the codicil. And I can smell it. A good lawyer can always smell a codicil. Well, better let me have a look at it.'

Effie got out the piece of paper Maximilian had given her and handed it to Pelham Longfellow.

'It's a copy,' she said. 'The original . . .'

'Yes, yes, I know,' said Longfellow, taking out a magnifying glass. 'That's fine. Right, let's have a look. Oh, I see. Quite straightforward. It simply says that if anything were to happen to your grandfather in this world before you come of age that you should be given access to Truelove House at Dragon's Green – although you've done that yourself already – and that each year you should be tested to see if you qualify for your ultimate boon and your special mainland role as a Keeper of the Great Library. Interesting. Right. Well, we'll do the test now.'

'A test?'

'That's right. OK.' Pelham Longfellow pulled a file from his briefcase. Inside the file were several sheets of yellow lined paper and one large piece of white parchment. 'The first question . . . You might want to sit down. There are several questions.'

Effie sat down. A test? She needed a few hours' sleep, not a test! But she found she was also shivering with excitement. Her ultimate boon? And becoming a Keeper of the Great Library? Even though she didn't completely understand what these things were, she felt she had never wanted anything as much in her life as she now wanted to pass this test.

'Right. Ready? First question. What's a dragon's favourite food?'

'That's easy. Princess.'

'Good. Next question. Oh. This is harder. What do goblins sell?'

'Fruit.'

'OK, we won't worry about how you know that, given that you were not supposed to go into the Otherworld by yourself. I wonder what was in Griffin's mind when he set these particular questions. Hmm. Anyway. What is a "wonde"?'

'It's a magical stick used by true witches.'

'Correct! Ah.' Longfellow's brow furrowed. 'Here's a trickier one. How much lifeforce can you buy with three pieces of dragon's gold? Oh, Griffin. These are too hard! Any idea? I can always come back next year if you . . .'

'In M-currency, it's six hundred,' said Effie. 'Although I get the impression these numbers don't mean as much on the mainland.'

'Good grief. Yes! Correct! Now . . . Translate the following Rosian phrase into English . . .'

And so the questions went on. Before Effie knew it, she had answered twenty more questions about all kinds of aspects of the Otherworld.

'Last question,' said Longfellow, eventually. 'Oh dear.' He coughed. 'Right. You are to imagine a Realworld room with three lightbulbs in it. Outside the room are three electric switches. You may only enter the room once, and you may only have one switch on when you enter the room. How can you work out which switch operates which light?' Longfellow scratched his head. 'Good heavens, Griffin,' he said. 'This is impossible. This is . . . Oh dear.'

'It's all right. I know the answer,' said Effie, after a long pause. 'You do?'

'Yes. I think I do.' Effie remembered her grandfather's last words to her. *The answer is heat.* She'd thought about this a lot since he'd said it, and although it had puzzled her a great deal, it suddenly made sense. Her grandfather was giving her a clue to help her pass this test as soon as possible so that she could take her rightful place in the family as a Keeper of the Great Library.

Effie thought for a moment longer and then gave her answer.

'I would turn on the first switch for a few minutes and then turn it off again. This would make one of the lightbulbs very hot. I would then put the second switch on and enter the room. The hot lightbulb belongs to the first switch, the one that's on belongs to the second, and the one that's off but cold belongs to the third.'

Pelham Longfellow clapped. 'Bravo,' he said. 'You've passed.'

'I have?'

'You have. Next time you're on the mainland, we'll go to the post office for your Keeper's mark. But in the meantime, here is your ultimate boon.'

334

Longfellow reached into his bag and took out a tiny silver box, which he gave to Effie.

'Be careful,' he said. 'When you touch the actual . . .'

Effie opened the box carefully. Inside was a very pale gold chain that looked, like so many magical things, polished and shiny but also very, very old. On the chain was a miniature sword with a wide, sharp blade. Effie took out the necklace and held it in front of her. The little sword flashed in the weak autumn sunlight. Pelham Longfellow got up and walked over to help Effie put it on. Once it was around her neck she touched the little golden sword and . . . Nothing happened. Effie looked at Longfellow.

'You need a magic word,' he said. 'It can be anything you like. Choose carefully and say it now as you are touching the sword for the first time. Then, whenever you want the sword, all you have to do is touch it and say . . .'

'Truelove,' said Effie. 'That's my magic word. *Truelove*,' she said again.

Bang! There was a crack and hiss in the air, and . . . It was just like what happened when Wolf touched the Sword of Orphennyus. Well, almost. In Wolf's case, something that was small became big. In Effie's case, something that didn't exist in this world suddenly appeared as if it had been beamed down from somewhere full of light, hope and beauty. In her hands now was a large gleaming sword made partly of mountain gold and partly from light itself. Holding it, she felt like she could go anywhere and do anything. She felt invincible.

'It's the Sword of Light,' said Pelham Longfellow. 'It's been in the Truelove family for hundreds and hundreds of years. Only a true hero can use it. I don't know when they last had a true hero born into the family – most of them are scholars, clerics, philosophers and composers. You're quite special, you know. Anyway, you'll find that no one will ever be able to take this necklace from you. Well, unless they kill you first.'

'Goodness,' said Effie. 'Why is the sword so *light*?'

'Because it's the Sword of Light, of course. And mountain gold isn't heavy anyway. It's your true weapon. I know you'll do only good with it. When you want it to become a necklace again you just have to sort of think it small and it will happen.'

Effie tried this. To her astonishment it worked.

'Thank you,' said Effie. 'Thank you for everything.'

'Is that the time?' Longfellow looked at his watch. 'I'm supposed to be in Paris in five minutes. So . . .'

Effie couldn't help herself. She rushed towards Pelham Longfellow and hugged him.

'Will I see you again soon?' she asked.

He nodded. 'At Truelove House. We'll have tea on the lawn. I think I'm going there this weekend. Although . . . You won't yet know how to calculate time from one world to the other. But I think you have a friend who can help you there.' He looked at his watch again. 'Anyway, I'd better be . . .'

'Oh!' Effie suddenly remembered. 'Your dagger. The athame.'

'Ah,' said Longfellow. 'Yes. The Athame of Stealth. I think you may know someone who can use that. Is he called Maximilian? I hear he tried to go to the Underworld on his own, which means he is potentially quite a powerful mage. He could help you a great deal.'

336

And then he screwed his broomstick together, opened the window and flew away.

The rest of the day passed in a haze. Double English went uncharacteristically quickly and then there was lunch, followed by outdoor games in the damp early afternoon mizzle. Effie remembered to take off her ring this time before doing sports in the Realworld. She now had a suspicion that the ring used up energy in order to boost her strength. This seemed perfectly proper if you happened to be fighting a dark mage, but was perhaps not so necessary for netball.

At break time Lexy gave her a sweet, herby green tonic which made the rest of the afternoon pass pleasantly and quickly. During double maths Maximilian kept trying to get her attention, but she ignored him. She was still thinking.

And then it was time for detention. At four o'clock Effie and her friends assembled outside the caretaker's cupboard and waited for Mrs Beathag Hide. When she appeared she was carrying a cream-coloured envelope in her long thin fingers.

'As you know,' she said to the children, 'I am not one for emotion. So I am going to give you this and leave. You may use it whenever you like. The cleaner comes to lock everything up at six o'clock, but I believe you already know the alternative way out. Good evening.'

She gave the envelope to Effie and walked away.

'What did she mean?' said Wolf.

When Effie opened the envelope she found a large key inside.

'Does she want us to lock ourselves in?' said Maximilian. 'Or . . .?'

'I think it's for this door,' said Effie. She tried it. The door opened.

The day before, this cupboard, which was really a small room with no windows, had contained nothing but a table, a sink, a couple of chairs, a stool and an old ladder. Now it also contained two large sturdy bookshelves. And on them were Effie's grandfather's books.

'What . . .?' said Effie. 'I don't understand how . . .'

But it didn't matter. The children went through the door and into their new library. As well as the books, someone had thought to bring in an old kettle and five mugs. There was a tin of tea and a jar of cocoa and a box of biscuits. There was even a little vase of flowers on the old paint-spattered table.

Each of the five friends now sensed properly how much their lives had irrevocably changed in the last two days. Raven had become a true witch, Lexy had become a true healer and Wolf had become a true warrior. Effie had become a true hero and a traveller between worlds. And now she was a Keeper, too. Each one of them felt extremely proud and happy. And now they had their own special place where they could meet and plan and read great tales of adventure and . . .

But Maximilian didn't feel any of these things at all. He felt like an outsider, a pathetic loser who had always dreamed of a

338

life of magic but who had blown it. He had the spectacles in their case ready to give back to Effie. And then that would be it. Back to his sad little bungalow, with his mother pretending there was no magic in the world, with no friends, to spend night after night on the dim web looking for hope and meaning but finding nothing. Without the spectacles, he wouldn't even be able to find solace in knowledge. But it was what he deserved for deceiving his first real friend.

After everyone had drunk hot chocolate and had several biscuits it seemed that it was time to leave. Lexy couldn't wait to tell her aunt about everything that had happened to her, and Raven was determined to go and find out whatever she could about Skylurian Midzhar from her mother. Wolf had rugby practice. And so Effie was left alone with Maximilian. He knew there was no chance of getting her to change her mind, so, after he had helped to rinse out the mugs, he got ready to go as well.

'Thank you for everything,' he said, holding out the spectacles to Effie. 'I was honoured to be your friend and I am so sorry I let you down.'

Effie touched the tiny gold sword around her neck. She thought again that if it hadn't been for Maximilian she would never have had a copy of the codicil at all. And he shouldn't have read her letter – of course he shouldn't – but that was just what he was like. He was curious, desperate for knowledge and . . .

'It's OK,' she said. 'But I think you'd better keep those if you're going to help us find out about Skylurian Midzhar.'

'Really? But . . .'

'And if you're going to hang out with us and get into more trouble with dark mages with deadly spiders and everything,' Effie said, 'it might help if you have this.'

She took out the Athame of Stealth and handed it to him.

'I think you might need it,' she said. 'Especially if you plan to go to the Underworld again.'

'Thank you,' he said. 'How did you know . . .?' He felt the weight of the athame in his hand. It was a complex and powerful weapon that he sensed could be used by both light and dark forces. Although Maximilian felt compelled to explore the darkness of the Underworld again, he decided he would only go there if it meant helping his friends.

The lock clicked quietly as Effie turned the key in the door, and she and Maximilian walked out of the Tusitala School for the Gifted, Troubled and Strange into the rain and gloom together, knowing that their adventures were only just beginning.

Acknowledgements

I could not have written this book without the love and support of my partner, Rod Edmond, whose enjoyment of early drafts of this book gave me great hope. My brothers Sam Ashurst and Hari Ashurst-Venn, and my sister-in-law Nia Johnston, were also incredibly encouraging during the writing process and read my first draft with a love and enthusiasm that one can usually only dream of. My mother, Francesca Ashurst, and my step-father Couze Venn, have also given me a huge amount of love and support. I am extremely lucky to have a family who are genuinely entertained and moved by the stories I create. Thank you to all of them. And a warm welcome to baby Ivy.

I also want to thank my other wonderful first readers. Molly Harman, one of the dedicatees of this book, and at the time a very perceptive ten-year-old, read a very early draft with such excitement that I became determined to make this the very best book I had ever written. Molly also asked an important question that helped me to understand Maximilian more deeply, for which

I am most grateful. Alice Bates also read the book with great enthusiasm and insight and gave me many encouraging words. She also unearthed a minor (OK, major) plot glitch that no one else had seen. Many thanks to her. My great friend Vybarr Cregan-Reid live-texted me his responses to the book as he was reading it, which meant I was going around grinning for days. I can't thank him enough for his friendship and healthy competition over the years.

Other people who made life easier or more pleasant in unfathomable (or even fathomable) ways while I was writing include David Flusfeder, Amy Sackville, Abdulrazak Gurnah, David Herd, Stuart Bennett, Daisy Harman, Eliza Harman, Max Harman, Ed Hoare, Jo Harman, Claire Forbes-Winslow, Charlotte Webb, Emma Lee, Marion Edmond, Lyndy McIntyre, Sue Swift, Pat Lucas, Roger Baker (a wonderful Master healer), Stuart Kelly (who showed me the rooms of the Speculative Society just when I most needed to see them) and Sasha de Buyl-Pisco, who put together the most beautiful event for my last adult book, complete with Victorian glasshouse and candlelight, and whose eyes lit up in just the right way when I admitted, after a few glasses of wine, that I was now writing a children's fantasy novel. Thank you too to all my other friends and family members not listed here, and also to all my fantastic colleagues in the School of English at the University of Kent.

I don't know how to begin to thank Francis Bickmore – my wonderful editor, dear friend and partner in crime for almost ten years now. What adventures we have had together! I hope there will be many more to come. The inimitable Jamie Byng took the book out into the world and found other people who loved it, for which I am very grateful. His brilliantly enthusiastic response to this novel meant a great deal to me. Many thanks to all my other friends and collaborators at Canongate, including the wonderful Jenny Todd, Andrea Joyce, Rafi Romaya, Anna Frame, Vicki Rutherford, Lorraine McCann and Becca Nice. Thanks too to all my other new and old publishers around the world. Geoff Morley and Mary Pender at UTA – thank you for believing in this book. I know it is safe in your hands. Finally, I would like to thank my agent and dear friend David Miller for his unwavering commitment to beauty, integrity and style. May he rest in peace.

Note: When Maximilian goes to the edge of the Underworld, his encounters include quotations from James Joyce, Katherine Mansfield and Mikhail Bulgakov. The book Maximilian's mother reads each year is *The Master and Margarita*, one of my very favourite novels.

FIND YOUR KHARAKTER

Are you secretly hiding the power of a Mage?
Perhaps you have the strategical ability
and strength of a Warrior?
Or do you have the bravery and knowledge of a Hero?

Find out by taking the Kharakter quiz . . .

worldquake.co.uk

WORLDQUAKE BOOK TWO:

~THE~
CHOSEN ONES

COMING SOON